The
of Woven Streets

Emmi Itäranta was born in Tampere, Finland, where she also grew up. She holds an MA in Drama from the University of Tampere and an MA in Creative Writing from the University of Kent, UK, where she began writing her award-winning debut novel *Teemestarin kirja* (*The Tea Master's Book*) under the title *Memory of Water*. Itäranta wrote the full text in both Finnish and English. In 2011, *Teemestarin kirja* won the Sci-fi and Fantasy Literary Contest organised by the Finnish publishing house Teos, and in the following years *Memory of Water* was nominated for the Philip K. Dick Award, the 2014 James Tiptree, Jr Award, the Compton Crook Award, Golden Tentacle Award and Arthur C. Clarke Award. Itäranta's professional background includes stints as a columnist, theatre critic, dramaturge, scriptwriter and press officer. She lives in Canterbury, UK, and has recently entered the strange world of writing full time. She can be found on Twitter @emmi_elina

www.emmiitaranta.com

Also by Emmi Itäranta

Memory of Water

The City
of
Woven Streets

Emmi Itäranta

HARPER
Voyager

Harper *Voyager*
An imprint of HarperCollins *Publishers*
1 London Bridge Street
London SE1 9GF

www.harpercollins.co.uk

A Paperback Original 2016
1

A catalogue record for this book
is available from the British Library

ISBN: 978-0-00-753606-1

This novel is entirely a work of fiction.
The names, characters and incidents portrayed in it are
the work of the author's imagination. Any resemblance to
actual persons, living or dead, events or localities is
entirely coincidental.

Typeset in Sabon LT Std by Palimpsest Book Production Ltd,
Falkirk, Stirlingshire

Printed and bound in Great Britain by
Clays Ltd, St Ives plc

MIX
Paper from
responsible sources
FSC www.fsc.org   FSC C007454

FSC™ is a non-profit international organisation established to promote
the responsible management of the world's forests. Products carrying the
FSC label are independently certified to assure consumers that they come
from forests that are managed to meet the social, economic and
ecological needs of present and future generations,
and other controlled sources.

Find out more about HarperCollins and the environment at
www.harpercollins.co.uk/green

CHAPTER ONE

I still dream of the island.

I sometimes approach it across water, but more often through air, like a bird, with a great wind under my wings. The shores rise rain-coloured on the horizon of sleep, and in their quiet circle the buildings: the houses grown along the canals, the workshops of inkmasters, the low-ceilinged taverns. The House of Words looks inward behind its high walls. Threads knotted into mazes run in all directions from the House of Webs, and air gondolas are suspended on their cables, dead weights above the streets.

At the centre of the island stands the Tower, smooth and blind. A sun of stone glows grey light at the pinnacle, spreading its sharp ray-fingers. Fires like fish-scales flicker in the windows. Sea is all around, and the air will carry me no longer. I head towards the Tower.

As I draw closer, the lights in the windows fade, and I understand they were never more than a reflection. The Tower is empty and uninhabited, the whole island a mere hull, ready to be crushed like a seashell driven to sand and carved hollow by time.

1

I also understand something else.

The air I am floating in is no air at all, but water, the landscape before me the seabed, deep as memory and long-buried things.

Yet I breathe, effortlessly. And I live.

Amber would sometimes wash ashore on the island; it was collected and shipped across the sea. As a child I once watched a jewel-smith polish it on the edge of the market square. It was like magic, one of the stories where ancient mages span yarn from mere mist or gave animals a human tongue. A sweet smell arose from the amber, the smith dipped the whetstone in water every once in a while, and in his hands the murky surface turned smooth and glass-clear. He handed the orange-yellow lump to me, and inside I saw an insect frozen in place, a mayfly smaller than the nail of my little finger. Its each limb, wing and antenna was so easy to imagine in movement that I believed it was still alive, ready to whirr and fly, when the hard shell would be broken.

Later I learned that creatures captured in amber cannot be freed. They are images of the past, fallen outside of time, and it is their only existence. When I turn the past before my eyes, I think of the mayfly. I think of the translucent brightness guarding it and distorting it. Its wings will not vibrate, it will never turn its antennae. Yet, when light pierces the stone from a new angle, the mayfly seems to morph into another. And in the posture stalled long ago is already written what will come later.

Likewise, this present already grows in my past that first night, when I see her.

She is lying on the smooth stones, face down, and it takes me a moment to understand she is not dead.

*　　*　　*

2

There is blood. Not everywhere, but a lot of it. She is still, like those who have stopped breathing are still. A red, glistening pool is spreading under her head; the ends of her hair are swimming in it. I see a rust-coloured streak on the hem of her dress and imagine the rest: a sticky trail running down the front of the garment, as warm as her mouth at first, before the air cools it down. The thought of the pain behind the blood twists my gut. I push it away, to where I am used to enclosing everything I cannot show.

There are not many of us yet. When the others move to make space for me, their glow-glass spheres tilt and hover in the dusk, and the pale light catches on the creases of their palms, on the coral amulets around their necks. Above the hands their faces are frightened or curious, I cannot tell which. Perhaps both. They are all younger than me, mostly first- and second-year weavers. I think of soft-bodied sea creatures, of how they slip away when something bigger comes too close.

'Has anyone gone to find Alva?' I ask.

No one says anything. I search among the faces, trying to find just one I can name, and fail. I kneel next to the girl on the ground and take her hand. It is soaked in blood, and so is mine, now. I do not mind; there will be time to wash it later. I see blood every month. Not only mine, but that of others, too. When hundreds of women live in the same house, someone is always bleeding. We do not get childbirths here, not often anyway, but we see enough of other varieties of bloodshed.

The girl's skin feels cold, her arm limp and heavy. I know I should not touch her until the healer comes.

'Go and find Alva,' I say.

They shift, a restless cluster of silence. No one takes a step to go.

3

Unexpectedly the girl moves under my hand. She turns over, raises her face and spits blood and strange-shaped sounds from her mouth. Bright red drops fall across my jacket. They make a pattern, like blood coral ornaments on a rich man's cloak.

'Go,' I order. 'Now!'

A second-year weaver turns and runs towards the other side of the square confined by stone buildings. The moments are slow, the whispers a surging sea around us. The wrist within my fingers is sinewy and narrow. More pale-blue spheres of light float through the dark towards us from the direction of dormitories and cells, more hands and faces behind them. A few weavers stop to fill their glow-glasses from the algae pool in the middle of the square; its shimmering surface vibrates and grows smooth again. Everyone must be awake by now. Eventually I see a woman in white approach across the square. She is carrying a stretcher under her arm. A tall figure I recognize as Weaver is walking at her heels. Light spills on the stones, catches in the folds of nightdresses and hair and limbs. Alva and Weaver order everyone to give way. When there is enough space, they place the stretcher down.

'I think you can let go of her hand,' Alva says.

I do. I get to my feet, withdraw into the crowd standing around us and watch as Alva and Weaver lift the girl onto the stretcher and begin to carry her towards the sick bay.

Somewhere, the bells of the city begin to toll sea-rise.

Some flooded nights I watch the city below from the hill. I follow the waters that rise high and wild, swell across courtyards, push aside chairs and tables stacked up in a futile attempt to make frail, treacherous bridges. But the sea never reaches the House of Webs. Weavers turn over when the bells toll and do not grant it much thought.

This night is different. Sleep is thin in the house, because strange blood is drying on the stones of the square. Sand flows slow in hourglasses. Coughs, footsteps and words exchanged in secret fade away little by little. I see the girl before me every time I close my eyes. Although I know the attacker must be far away, every shadow on the walls is darker than usual.

I pull the last dormitory door of the night-watch round closed behind me. My brother tells me I should get more sleep, but being awake has its advantages. The corridors of the house are long, and someone must walk them all night, look into every dormitory, listen behind the door of each cell. Those are the Council's orders, and therefore also Weaver's. It is not a precaution against those coming from outside the House of Webs. We have all heard the drinking songs about wet weaver wenches circulating in the taverns and on the streets, but those are just words. In order to get into the house, you would have to climb the steepest hill on the island and find your way through the maze of wall-webs undetected, and you would risk serious sanctions in doing so. No: the night-watch is to keep an eye on those who already live within the walls.

The luminous ribbons of the glow-glass pipes throw cold sparks along the corridors, revealing the unevenness of the worn stone. The current in the canals is strong; it drives the swift movement in the pipes, and in fast water the algae wakes to shine bright. A draught blows past me, as if a door is opened somewhere, but I do not see anyone. I could return to my cell. I could sleep. Or stay awake in the fading shine of the glow-glass, wait for the morning.

I turn in the other direction and step outside.

I like the air gondola port because you cannot see the Tower from there: its tall, dark figure is concealed behind the wall and the buildings of the House of Webs. Here I can imagine for a moment that I am beyond the reach of the Council's gaze. I like the port best at this hour, when the cables have not yet started creaking. The vessels are still, their weight hanging mid-air, or resting at the dock, or floating in the water of the canals. The gate cracks open without a sound. The wrought iron is cold against my skin, and the humidity gathered on its surface clings to my palms. The cable of the air route dives into the precipice, which begins at the rock landing of the port, and the city opens below. I walk along the landing close to the brink. It is steep as a broken bridge. Far below, the sharp edges of Halfway Canal cut through the guts of the island, outlining waters that always run dark, even in brightest summer light.

The sky has begun to fade into the colours of smoke and roses. The first light already clings to the rooftops and windows, to the glint of the Glass Grove a distance away. The flood has finally ceased to rise, and down in the city the water rests on streets and squares. Its surface is smooth and unbroken in the calm closeness of dawn: a strange mirror, like a dark sheet of glass enclosing a shadow double of the city.

My eyes are heavy and stung. I could catch an hour of sleep before the morning gong if I returned to my cell now. It is a short enough time. It would be safe enough.

I stay where I am.

The gate creaks behind me. I turn to look.

'The gate should be locked,' Weaver says.

'It was open when I came.'

'I was not reprimanding you,' she says. 'What happened there?'

6

She points towards the strip of sea on the horizon, north of the Glass Grove. I had not realized, because it is something you do not notice.

'The air highway,' I say.

The north side of the island is dominated by air gondola routes: light vessels travelling an intricate network in all directions and on many levels, cables crisscrossing between the trading harbours in the west and the inkmasters' workshops in the northwest. But the skyline of the city above the rooftops has changed.

'The largest cables are down,' Weaver says. 'There must have been an accident.'

'The flood?'

'Maybe.'

The floods do not usually damage the air routes. But if one of the supporting poles has fallen, it could affect the whole network.

'I expect we will get word when the watergraph starts working again,' Weaver says. She turns her face towards me. It is the colour of dark wood. 'But that is not why I was looking for you.' She pauses. 'Alva would like to see us both.'

'Alva?' The request surprises me. 'Did she say why?'

'She believes we should go and meet the patient together. She has something to show us.'

The thought of seeing the girl again is a cold stone within me.

'I had hoped to get some sleep before breakfast,' I say.

Weaver's gaze is deep in the growing daylight, full of thoughts.

'Come,' she says.

When the house-elder says so in the House of Webs, you obey.

* * *

The first thing I sense is the surge of heat through the door. Then, a cluster of scents. In the House of Webs, the sick bay is the only place apart from the kitchen where live fire is allowed. Even laundry is washed in cold water most of the time. Alva stands by the stove, feeding wood into the spark-spitting metal maw. A steaming pot of water sits on the stove, and next to it another one with an inch of dark-brown liquid in it. I inhale, recognize liquorice and lavender, hops and passion-flower. The rest blurs into a blend of unfamiliar scents. On the table, next to scales, mortars and bags of herbs, I notice a neatly laid-out row of needles cooling down on a polished metal tray.

Alva closes the hatch of the stove and wipes her hands carefully with a steaming towel.

'We'll need a gondola,' she says. 'We cannot keep her here.'

'I will send for a gondola to take her to the Hospital Quarters as soon as I can,' Weaver says. 'The watergraph pipes are too badly flooded.'

'Again?' Alva picks up a glass jar from the tall shelf that fills the space behind the table. I see dozens of teardrop-shaped wings stirring, hair-thin legs moving, and something round and black and bright. Eyes stare directly at me.

'There is nothing we can do but wait,' Weaver responds.

Alva turns towards us with the jar in her hand.

'She's awake,' she says. 'But she can't talk.'

'Why not?' I ask.

'It's best if you see her now,' Alva says. 'She'll need a new singing medusa in any case.'

Alva walks across the room to the medusa tank. It sits on robust legs of stone, as wide as the wall: a smooth, oblong pool of glass rounded on the edges, covered by a lid with a slim opening at one end. The singing medusas float through the water without hurry, their translucent swimming bells pale green and blue, weightless in their water-space. Alva unscrews the lid of the jar and holds the jar upside down over the opening. Wings and limbs and eyes move, first behind the glass and then briefly in the air, as she shakes the jar.

The medusas reach their thin tentacles towards the insects raining into the water, close their round, murky bells around the black-green gleam of the beetles and flies. Alva lets the last sticky-limbed insect fall into the tank. Then she dips the glass jar in, collecting some water into it. She picks up a small hoop net from a hook on the wall and pushes it into the tank. The bloom of medusas opens and pulls away, their tentacles wavering like broken threads in a breeze, but Alva has already caught one. It is small and slippery and blue-green, and it seems to shrivel, to lose its colour and grace as soon as it is out of water.

Alva slips the medusa into the glass jar, where it opens again like a flower, but now constrained, without joy. As we watch, it begins to open and close, open and close, and in an echo of its movements, the bloom in the tank begins to do the same. A low, faint humming vibrates in the water, refracts from the glass walls, grows towards the ceiling until it seems to ring through our bones.

Alva hangs the hoop net back on the wall hook. The water dripping from it draws a dark trail on the wall towards the floor. She parts the curtains covering a wide doorway into the back room and steps through. Weaver and I follow. Slowly the singing recedes behind us and fades into a silence as dense as mourning, or farewells left unspoken.

There are only six beds in the room, and despite the faint lighting I can see that five of them are empty. In the furthermost bed by the back wall lays a narrow, motionless figure. She is covered by a rough blanket, but I can discern her form under it: long limbs, softness sheltering angular bones. The warmth from the iron stove spreads across the skin of my neck.

Our shadows fall deep and shapeless, interlacing where the fragile halos of the glow-glasses overlap, hemming in the bed we are approaching. There is no light on the back wall. Thick curtains cover the window.

Dimmed glow-glass globes hang on the walls. Weaver picks one, shakes it and places it on the girl's bedside table. A blue-tinted light wakes up within the sphere. Slowly it expands and falls on the girl's face. I notice there is also an empty cup on the table.

The girl is approximately my age, between twenty and twenty-five. There are still dry, rust-brown tangles in her red hair, but the garment she is wearing is clean. Or so I think at first, until I notice the burst of tiny speckles on the front. As if someone had tried to paint an impression of faraway stars on it, the sparkling Web of Worlds that holds the skies together.

She struggles to sit up on the mattress. Her eyes are grey and full of shadows in the glow-glass light, and her skin is very pale. Her lips are squeezed together so tightly it makes her face look older, shrivelled upon itself. I realize Alva has made her drink a calming herbal brew. Yet behind its artificial languor the girl is tense and all edge, like a dagger drowned in murky water, ready to cut the first skin that will brush it.

'In order to help you,' Weaver says, 'we need to know who you are.'

The girl nods slowly.

'She is not island-born,' Alva says.

The lines on Weaver's face seem to sharpen. She looks at Alva.

'Why didn't you tell me earlier?'

'I wanted to show you,' Alva says. 'May I?'

The girl's eyes close and open again. The question seems to sink in letter by letter. Eventually, she moves her head slowly up and down. I do not know if this is because nodding hurts, or because she is too dazed to make faster movements.

Alva directs the girl to rotate her upper body slightly, face turned away from us. She gathers the girl's hair gently in her hand and lifts it. The skin of the neck is bare: there is no trace of ink where the sun-shaped tattoo marking everyone born on the island should be. I glance at Weaver, catch a glimpse of the shadows on her brow. There are not many people on the island who were born elsewhere. Seamen and merchants come and go, but most islanders avoid mingling with them.

'May I see your arms?' Weaver asks.

Alva lets go of the girl's hair and the girl turns her face back towards us, her movements still underwater-slow. She nods again.

'I already checked,' Alva said. 'She must have moved to the island when she was very young.'

Weaver pulls up the sleeves of the girl's garment. One of the arms is bare. Not from the Houses of Crafts, then. The other has a row of short, black lines on it, like wounds on the pale skin. Weaver counts them.

'Twenty-one,' she says. That is two less than I have.

Weaver lets go of the girl's arms. The girl leans back into her pillows in a half-sitting posture.

11

'Were you born on the continent?' Weaver asks her. The girl nods.

'Are your parents from the island?'

Now she hesitates. Weaver sighs. A mixed marriage, perhaps. They are rare, but not impossible. Or perhaps she does not know her parents. But foundlings have their own mark in place of the birth tattoo, and she does not have one.

'Never mind,' Weaver says. 'We can talk about that later. I brought pen and paper.' She pulls a slim notebook from her pocket. The covers are well-worn, stained leather, and the pages are yellowed on the edges. She places the book on the girl's lap and a pen on top of it. 'If you know how to read,' Weaver says, 'please, write down your name.'

The girl stares at the blank page. We wait. After a long moment, she shakes her head, slowly and painfully.

None of us is surprised. Word-skill is only taught in the House of Words, and women are not allowed there. Most women on the island are illiterate.

'Whereabouts in the city are you from?' Weaver tries. 'Can you draw that for us?'

The girl's face changes slowly like shadows on a wall. Eventually she draws an elongated lump that bears a vague resemblance to a fish.

'The island?' Weaver asks.

The girl nods. Her hand shakes a little, as if the pen is too heavy between her fingers. She marks a cross in the northwest corner of the lump.

'The Ink Quarters?' Weaver says. I have only been there a couple of times. I remember narrow streets thick with pungent smells, canals where water ran strange-coloured, and tall, vast buildings with darkened windows you could not see through. Gondolas carrying blood coral in large cages to be ground in the ink factories, and red-dye transported from the factories to the harbours in big glass bottles.

The girl nods again.

'Are you able to tell us anything about the person who attacked you?' Weaver asks.

The girl lifts two fingers.

'Do you mean there were two of them?'

The girl begins to nod, but pain cuts across her face and stops the movement short.

Weaver looks like she is about to say something else, but a few red drops fall onto the page from between the girl's lips. A narrow trickle of blood follows. Alva's face is taut. She pushes Weaver and me to the side. The glass jar in her hand is still holding the medusa, which lies motionless, like a plucked petal.

'Open,' Alva orders.

I only realize now why the girl cannot talk. I only catch a brief glance at her mouth, but that is enough. Where the tongue should be, there is only a dark, marred mass of muscle, still a bleeding, open wound. I have to turn away for a moment. Alva holds a towel under the girl's chin, fishes the medusa out from the glass jar and slides it into the girl's mouth. Relief spreads on the girl's face.

'She is in a lot of pain,' Alva says. 'She must rest. But there is one more thing.'

She places the jar on the night table and picks up the glow-glass. She turns to look at me.

'Are you certain you don't know her?'

The question makes no sense. I look at the girl again, just to be certain, although I do not need to. She has closed her eyes and her breathing is turning even. Her muscles twitch slightly. She does not open her eyes.

'Of course I'm certain,' I say.

Weaver stares at Alva, then at me, then at Alva again. 'Why do you ask such a thing?' she says.

Alva steps right next to the girl. She does not react when Alva takes her hand and gently coaxes open the fingers closed in a loose fist.

'Because of this,' Alva says and turns the palm upwards. The light from the glow-glass falls on it. Bright marks begin to glow on the skin, the letters forming a word I recognize immediately.

Eliana.

My name.

14

CHAPTER TWO

The girl's hand is narrow in the grip of Alva's fingers, the angles of her bones sharp around the dent of her palm. I am aware of Alva's and Weaver's attention, a tense net around me. But I have done this countless times before. I turn the perception inside out, as if I am focusing my eyes on something close by and letting the background soften into a haze where all boundaries are unclear. I look at the letters as if they are mere contours and colours in a landscape, akin to cracks in the walls of houses, or the black and green algae growing in the canals.

I turn to look at Weaver, taking care not to let my face reveal a thing.

'What does it say?' I ask.

Weaver does not answer immediately. Her gaze perseveres in the dusk, but I do not shiver under it.

'Has your brother not taught you anything?' she asks.

'He never thought it necessary,' I respond.

Weaver is still looking at me when Alva says, 'Eliana, someone tattooed your name on this girl's palm in invisible ink.'

15

I let my face and body react as they should. They adjust to the situation. I know what Weaver reads on them: surprise, confusion, just the right amount of alarm.

'I don't know her,' I say. 'I've never seen her before.'

'Eliana is not a common name,' Weaver says.

It is true. I am the only one in the House of Webs, although there must be others on the island.

'Maybe it's her name,' I suggest. 'Have you asked?'

Alva sighs.

'Of course I did. And no, it's not her name. Or so she claims, at least.'

'Quite a coincidence,' Weaver says. She turns to Alva. 'This is no ordinary tattoo.'

'No,' Alva says.

She covers the glow-glass with a towel, reaches for the window and parts the curtain slightly. The early-morning light floats into the room, settles on the girl's skin. The letters turn invisible. Her palm looks no different than mine; only a few lines and callouses are discernible on it.

'Interesting,' Weaver says. 'I have not seen one of those before.'

'Neither have I,' Alva says.

She lets the curtain fall back to cover the window and removes the towel from the top of the glow-glass. My gaze turns towards the letters as their outlines slowly grow visible. They run across the narrow lines on the girl's palm, towards the fingers closed around my name, as if to keep it safe. Alva places the girl's hand back on the blanket.

'We must let her sleep.' Alva's voice is firm.

Weaver turns to face me.

'You may return to your room,' she says. 'I will let the City Guard know about this as soon as the watergraph is working again.'

16

I bow my head slightly in acknowledgement of the order.

'And keep me up to date about her condition,' Weaver says to Alva.

The girl's eyes crack open and close again. Her breathing flows calm and even. The pain seems to be gone for now, and the bleeding has stopped. Very gently Alva coaxes the girl's mouth open, holds the towel and the glass jar against her skin and pulls the medusa out. Its lifeless weight drops into the jar, where the bright-red blood tendrils begin to spread through the water cradling its dead body.

Alva picks up the cup from the night table. We turn to go.

After the warmth of the sick bay, the morning is cold around us. Weaver stops a few footsteps ahead of me.

'I don't expect you in the Halls of Weaving until this afternoon,' she says.

I am grateful that she remembers. It is nearly time for the morning gong. I bow. Weaver nods at me and continues towards the building where the Halls of Weaving are located. I suspect she sleeps even less than I do. The incoming day is unfolding on the horizon, and for a moment I am alone under the sky of the house.

The cell is cool and silent. The thick curtain lets in a thread-slender rectangle of light around the edges of the window. I turn the key in the lock and shake the glow-glass on the table. As the water inside the globe moves and wakes up the algae, the shine begins to grow. In the dim light I examine my skin from head to toe more carefully than usual. The back is always the most difficult; there is no mirror. I find nothing apart from the perpetual callouses on my fingertips and soles. I look for clean clothes to wear and fold the dirty ones into a pile I will carry into the laundry room later. I can sense the faint scent of Alva's brew on them: herbs that bring sleep and rest. Perhaps I should have asked Alva to mix me a similar potion. She would have said no at first, but then done it anyway.

I sit on the bed until the morning gong begins to echo in the stone walls and vibrate on the webs.

I walk together with the weavers who are on unravelling duty and on their way to work in the web-maze today. It is said on the island that the district of the House of Webs is mapless, a shapeshifter: careless travellers never find their way out if they wander too deep. Yet the weavers know the way. The three solid buildings of the house are surrounded by a zone where the streets and buildings are formed only by woven webs hung between stone pillars, seemingly arbitrary narrow alleys and dead ends. It is here that strangers will lose their way, and sometimes weavers too, when they have not yet learned how the routes are shaped and transformed. Here, walls are unravelled as soon as they are completed and woven anew somewhere else when they have ceased to be. Everything follows a predetermined order, yet you must hold the exact keys to it in order to perceive it.

As I draw further from the heart of the House of Webs, stone fences grow onto the landscape almost unnoticeably. The city no longer flits and filters light everywhere, but takes a more solid shape. Amidst the soft view of yarn frayed on the edges rise stairways covered in dark algae, walls eaten by humidity and whole houses with no woven parts. Eventually all of the maze is left behind: a city of stone where the work of weavers does not belong swallows the walker. The canals flow brown in the chasms among

18

the buildings, and gondolas rise and fall between water and air. None of the other weavers come to the city with me.

The banks of Halfway Canal are still burst and rippling. The pavements have been claimed by water, and I have to climb up steps cut on the outer wall of a tall building to one of the rope bridges that are lowered from rooftops during floods. The bridge wobbles under my footsteps. There is a small crowd standing at the far end, waiting for their turn to cross. Below, people are wading in water, some of them in high-leg oiled leather boots, others barefoot. They are all scooping up something limp and leaf-like, placing armfuls of it in half-drowned wheelbarrows and small boats and large baskets. At first I think it is just seaweed, not the web-thin algae used in glow-glasses, but a leafy variety that grows deeper. Floods often throw large amounts of it across the island.

The bridge comes to an end and I begin to climb towards the next one. I have to cross a high rooftop, and there I stop. Usually this would cause pushing and shoving and protests, a rush that tries everyone's patience. But today there are others beside me who have stopped on the roof to stare at the sea and the rising tide that is slowly swallowing the shores.

At first it looks as if the waves are bubbling, or growing soft scales, translucent and circular. Their surfaces turn coarser, their density different. When the first wave carrying the dead weight crashes onto the rocks, I am not certain. When the second one does, I could not be wrong if I wanted to, and I understand the people with their baskets and boats, the scooping movements of their hands.

The sea is carrying dead singing medusas to the island, throwing them to the shores and driving them into the canals. Their bodies lie quiet and lifeless, only cradled by the movement of the water. There are thousands, tens of thousands of them, each one as alone as the others, each one as unable to sing ever again.

I think of the medusas in Alva's tank, of their soft rippling. I wonder if they know, if they sing their farewells to the lost ones.

I climb down the other side of the rooftop and fit my steps to the unsteady planks of the next rope bridge.

The rooftops are crowded and the flooding streets too, as always on the Ink-marking days. The sound of a seashell horn soars above the rooftops from the Tower, inviting city-dwellers to gather. A steady stream of people moves towards the museum. I choose a circuitous route I know to be more quiet. On the way I must cross a square bordered by porticos on each side. The ground is a little higher here, the stones humid only from fog and drizzle. A small group of black-clad people is gathered in the square. There are maybe five or six of them. They stand there as a dark and silent front, like rain on the horizon. I recognize the mourning garb immediately. Many families of Dreamers hide their shame, but some wish to remember those they have lost.

As I am crossing the square, one of them detaches herself from the group and walks towards me. I turn my gaze downwards, trying to ignore her. She walks past me, so close it is more a push than a brush. She drops something to the ground. I hear a faint clink and before I know it, I have stepped on the item without even looking.

A guard is there in an instant. I had not noticed him. Neither had the woman, probably taking a bigger risk than she had intended. But he has seen the sea-green coat of the House of Webs on me, he has seen the woman's black garb. He will have drawn his own conclusions. The guard grabs the woman by the arm, his fingers hard and tight.

'You're not going anywhere,' he tells her. Then he turns to me. 'Did she bother you in any way? Try to give you anything, say anything inappropriate?'

I stare at the woman. Her face is expressionless, mask-like. If I say yes, she will be in trouble. Perhaps all of them will be, the group standing behind me, wordless and unmoving. Their eyes are on us. If I say no and the guard notices the item she dropped, I may be in trouble, whether I am from the House of Webs or not. I can feel a flat surface through the thin sole of my shoe. The item is small enough to be hidden from sight until I move. I do not even know what it is.

'No,' I say. 'She did nothing. I wasn't looking where I was going and walked into her.' I direct my next words at the woman. 'It was entirely my fault. I apologize.'

The woman nods. If she is surprised, she hides it well.

The guard relaxes his grip on the woman's arm.

'Be more careful next time,' he tells her. 'Your kind have no business bothering folk from the Houses of Crafts.' The woman does not move. 'On your way then,' the guard orders.

The woman begins to walk towards the group, slowly at first, then accelerating her steps. The guard looks after her.

'If you ask me, her sort should be thrown into the House of the Tainted along with their family members,' he says. 'Who knows if they are clean, either.' He glances at me. 'Good day to you, Miss Weaver.'

I nod at the guard. He nods back, then turns away. I wait until he is close to the other side of the square, taking his post in the shadows between the pillars.

21

I tug at the string that ties a small leather pouch to my belt. The pouch falls. The coins inside clink against each other. I deliberately avoid glancing in the direction of the guard. If he is looking at me, he will simply see me pick up my coin pouch which I had tied in place carelessly. He will not see me move my foot and take the item from under my shoe. I have time to feel cold metal in my fingers before I slip it into the pouch with the coins. The guard will find me clumsy. He will find me unsuspicious.

The group in mourning on the edge of the square will see something else, but they will not tell. Not if I do not.

The Museum of Pure Sleep has always reminded me of a sea monster, the kind described in children's tales. The statues standing on its roof rise tentacle-like against the sky, ready to reach and grab and pull down into the abyss anything that comes their way. The round windows gleam orange and blue, and sometimes shadows close to cover them like eyelids, to let the sleep in. But never the dreams.

I plunge into the stream of people. The steps are slippery and wide under my feet, their edges rounded and worn hollow by the weight of all who have climbed them. The throng is already suffocating me. I sense the warmth and movements of human bodies forced too close together, their smells and impatience. Before me, I see other museum visitors disappear into a portico. The columns in front of the entrance shine pale as teeth against the dark stone-skin of the building.

I walk into the monster's mouth.

It is always dim at first. I join one of the four long queues. They all trickle towards checkpoints where men in uniforms guard the gates. The light only begins beyond the iron bars dropping down vertically from the tall ceiling. There, I can see a group of visitors that has stopped on the landing halfway up the coral-red staircase. The skylight casts brightness upon them, separating them from us.

My eyes focus on the bars again. They look like the weft of an enormous wall-web. I imagine a giant hand passing a warp through them.

When my turn finally comes, I show the guard my birth tattoo. A cold draught brushes the hair of my neck. Although I checked my skin this morning, my breath runs tight as I pull up my sleeves and wait. Every year I fear that the guard will find more on my skin than the lines tattooed on my arm. Yet he counts the tattoos with the customary bored expression on his face and nods. He checks the house-tattoo on my other arm, finds my name on a list and draws a mark next to it. He opens the gate to let me through and closes it again before beginning to examine the next citizen. Two new groups are already gathering around the guides at the bottom of the staircase. I join the group appointed for me.

Blood coral, amber and tapestries woven from dyed yarn glow around us, making the light pouring from the skylight grow and burst into flames. We wait until the previous group has disappeared into a room at the top of the stairs. The guide asks us to follow. We all know where to go.

We walk across the entrance hall and climb halfway up the staircase, where we stop. The guide begins to talk and gestures towards the large mural on the wall above the top landing. Our gazes are turned to it, but I might as well be looking through a window, not noticing the uneven-ness of its surface or the stains left on it by weather. I have seen the mural too many times. Even as a child I did not like it. The tall Tower in the middle frightened me, as did the eight masked figures standing in front of it. I told my mother they were ghosts. She placed a hand over my mouth and ordered me to be quiet. I still remember the looks the guide and the other visitors gave me.

It was only later that I understood how afraid my mother was then. My words could easily have been interpreted as an indication that it was common in my family to speak of the Council in blasphemous tones. But the image had come of its own volition and had not originated from my parents' conversations. With their black cloaks and featureless, blood-coloured masks, the mural-Council looked like an image of death in my child's eyes.

The guide's story about how the Council ended the Reverie Revolution, purged the island of Dreamers and restored peace and prosperity to our city is the same every year. I know parts of it by heart. *And thus dream-plague was banished from our midst, with those spreading it sent to colonies or enclosed within walls where their disease could be contained. Night-maeres ceased to roam free and fled to the dark places they had come from, never to emerge again except for the cursed few who carried them within their blood.*

The group keeps their eyes fixed on the mural while the guide speaks. I take quick glances at the people around me. There is a young mother with two children. I wonder which one of them is here for the Ink-marking. I hope it is not one of the children; although if not today, they will have to endure the pain when their time comes. There is an old man in a grey waistcoat and brown jacket, with a powdery white stain on his dark trousers. A baker, perhaps. Another man is clearly from the Ink Quarters: his hands are tarnished with black and red dye. Several young women are among the group, wearing bonnets and dresses made from slightly finer fabric, and skilfully polished bone coral pendants. Daughters of merchants, I think.

I notice a man glancing down to the entrance hall over his shoulder, as if searching for something. He is not young any more, and there is nothing about his looks that gives away his craft. Grey trousers, a brown hooded jacket, worn boots. No stains on fingers. Hair tied neatly to the nape of the neck with a leather ribbon, his hands clasped behind his back. He returns his gaze to the mural. The sky above shifts, the light falling from the glass ceiling burns deeper and hits the man's hand mere steps away from me.

The hollow of his palm bears a strange, gondola-shaped scar. It is wider in the middle, narrowing towards the ends.

I raise my gaze before anyone sees me staring.

As we walk up the staircase and proceed to the next room, I notice the man looking around again with the same searching face. I also notice something else: he is careful about the way he does it. Before looking away, he pays close attention to the guide and only turns his gaze for the briefest moment when he believes he will not be seen.

A guard with a short spear stands beside one of the walls. His uniform carries the sun-emblem of the Council and the City Guard. The man's eyes stop on him, then return to the pictures on the walls the guide is talking about. These too are words I have heard before. *Once the island was a tangle of forest with wild beasts inhabiting it: a cruel and dangerous place where a man could easily be lost and never found again. But our ancestors brought their torches and swords to drive the beasts away, and with heroic courage and suffering great losses they laid the first foundations of the city we know today. From the cradle of the sea they harvested silkweed and blood coral, and they took their ships across wide waters and established the first trading routes, which you can see on these maps.*

We continue to walk through rooms filled with images of the past: weavers and scribes at work, the building of the Tower, codices spread on the square for the annual Word-incineration. I keep an eye on the man with the scarred palm. In each room he glances around as soon as he has entered, before turning his focus on the guide.

We reach the room I have always liked the least. Glow-glasses hanging from the ceiling light the windowless space. The guide points to a picture on the wall, showing the bodies of those dead from dream-plague being burned. But there are more than paintings here. Glass cases hold medical instruments made from coral, both bone white and blood red. Their points and blades are sharp, their jaws wide and hard. Thick, spread-open books lie next to them under the glass. The illustrations show skin lesions and bulbous growths where the limbs meet the torso, like darkness boiling under the skin.

The man with the scarred palm has stopped in front of a painting portraying a young woman. She is lying on a bed with her eyes closed, a hand fallen towards the floor over the edge of the bed. Her lips are cracked open in an anxious arc. A dark shadow sits upon her chest with hands reaching for the woman's neck: a night-maere visiting a Dreamer. The man pulls his hand out of his pocket and scratches his head.

That is when I see it. It is a mere glimpse, but I am certain that it is there.

A tattoo glows white on his palm, where the scar was. I do not have time to discern any details, but the shape is similar to the scar's: elongated, pointy at each end.

He pushes the hand back into his pocket.

The image rises within me like water: the injured girl's hand holding the letters of my name.

As in all the other rooms, there is a guard in here, too. When the guide urges us to move on, the guard steps closer to the group and speaks.

'You,' he says to the man. 'Halt.'

The man freezes. An alarmed expression appears on his face. He opens his mouth, but no sound comes out.

'You may continue,' the guard tells the guide. 'This man will join you after I have had a word with him.'

The guide gives a bow. We walk after him to the next room. I glance behind. The guard is speaking to the man in a low voice and quick words I cannot hear, his face less stern than I would have expected. They both notice me looking. The guard's lips stop moving. The room begins to fill with new visitors. I turn my head and follow the group.

No one speaks after we exit the final room and walk down the staircase. This is the way the tour is designed. First the monster swallows you, then it digests you and eventually you come out of the other end feeling filthy.

The exit hall resembles the entrance. We have to queue for the gates in the iron-bar wall again. Only here the queue is slower and stretches all the way outside. I look at the others who have come to receive their annual tattoos. Many of them have brought families and friends, and some of them will be throwing parties today. But even they must first come to the Ink-marking. No one on the island avoids that.

27

As I scan the space, I spot the man with a scar on his hand again. He has taken his place in another queue a little ahead of me. Dozens of glow-glass globes hanging from the ceiling paint the space blue. The man clasps his hands behind his back. His palm turns up. I expect to see his tattoo again.

It is not there.

The distance is long enough that I may not discern the scarring, but I am certain that I would see the glowing tattoo. He was not standing further away from me in the room where I first noticed it. But now his palm is bare, his skin without any markings.

I almost move to join the same queue with him, try to find a reason to talk to him. But the queue proceeds and people flow between us, a whole open sea, impossible to cross. I lose sight of him.

The exit opens to a square on the other side of which the Tower rises larger than I remember, a storm-grey column against a blue sky. The sun glistens dimly on its stone surface and the mist has dissipated on the streets. The queues trickle towards the checkpoints and the inkmasters' tables behind which they meld into the billowing crowd.

I look where I cannot help looking, none of us can.

The Dreamers stand in the middle of the square on a dais, four women and four men. None of them is young. One of the women wears an eyepatch and one of the men is missing a hand. They are barefoot and grey-clad, and the mark of the Tainted is clearly visible on each of their foreheads. A City Guard with a hand on spear-haft has taken a place at each corner of the dais, and at the foot of the dais an entire front of them stands in formation.

The queues reach and move. The autumn-dampened sun pours lukewarm light on faces. The prisoners stand silent, still, have been standing for hours. No one offers them water or food.

Eventually it is my turn to sit in front of an inkmaster. He wipes his tattoo needle and dips it in an ink jar. I pull my sleeve up to bare my arm above the dark lines.

The song of the seashell horn pauses. A wave passes through the crowd, another. It is finally time for what everyone has gathered to wait for. On the upper balcony of the Tower the wide doors open, and the Council steps out through them. Their coral masks glint in the sun like freshly shed blood against stone-coloured cloaks. The noise growing from the crowd resembles the whistling of the wind.

The inkmaster brings the needle onto my skin and begins to tap its handle with a stone in order to pierce the skin, drawing another mark right next to the crook of my arm. I look away and clench my hand into a fist. My eyes water from the pain. Weaving will hurt for a week at least, and the itch left by the needle where the ink has entered under the skin never quite goes away.

The ringing of the bell is crisp and sharp as the edges of the afternoon shadows.

I turn to look at the dais again. A man wearing a loose coat bearing the sun emblem leaves the foot of the Tower, approaches the dais with unrushed footsteps and climbs onto it. He holds an opaque glass bowl in which eight wooden sticks have been arranged. The man stops before the first Dreamer.

I have wondered many times which stick I would wish to draw from the bowl if I were to stand on the dais one day. I change my mind every year.

The Dreamer woman draws from the bowl a wooden stick approximately the length of her palm. I do not discern her expression clearly from this far away, but I notice she turns her head in order to see how the Dreamer next to her will choose. When the man carrying the bowl moves to stand before the third Dreamer, I see the first two holding wooden sticks of similar length in their hands. I cannot tell if their faces are disappointed or relieved.

I shiver. The inkmaster wipes the droplets of blood from my skin with a cloth that does not look very clean. I pull my sleeve back down to cover the twenty-four lines on my arm. I am officially one year older. My skin smarts when the fabric touches it. I get up and move into the crowd through the checkpoint gate.

The bowl-bearing man has proceeded to the second-to-last Dreamer. The other six are holding sticks of similar length in their hands. The breathing of the audience has quieted, and no one speaks. Somewhere, a child bursts into tears.

The Dreamer pushes his only hand into the bowl and slowly draws out one of the two wooden sticks. It is twice as long as the others. A howl-like scream rises from the audience and people begin to clap and stomp, when the man lifts the stick high in the air for everyone to see. Something resembling a smile visits his face, wide and stiff as if it were painted on. For form's sake the last Dreamer draws the remaining short stick.

The bowl-bearing man turns to the audience.

'In their great fairness the Council have pardoned this Dreamer,' he says. 'He is free to walk the world and leave the island at dawn. In the name of the Council!'

'In the name of the Council!' the crowd yells in return. The words leave my lips too before I even know I have formed them.

'And now we shall together swear an oath of loyalty

to the Council, who in their wisdom pilot the island through all storms,' the bowl-bearer says.

The words of the oath begin to flow from me with the choir of voices. *They who raised the Tower with their own hands and watch the city from atop of it, to them I am faithful.*

The Dreamer who drew the long stick is walked down from the dais and led away from sight behind the museum. The guards guide the seven other Dreamers into a cage on wheels, which they begin to transport towards the large black gondola of the House of the Tainted. The oath pours past me like water.

They who feed us and clothe us and make us strong, to them I am faithful.

The wheels of the cage clatter on the stones of the square.

They who drove sickness away from the island and purged our sleep forever, to them I am faithful.

One of the Dreamers in the cage throws herself against the bars, the old woman with an eyepatch.

'Lies!' she shouts. 'It's all lies!'

If the stones of the streets crumbled from under me and the canals escaped their confines, I would place my life in their hands and be faithful to them.

Two guards wrench the door of the cage open and tear the woman out.

'Lies!' she yells again. 'Ask yourselves why—'

One of the guards hits the woman so hard she goes quiet and begins to weep with pain. The guard ties a scarf to cover the woman's mouth. I see a red stain spreading on the scarf.

If the sea climbed over my doorstep, I would let their ships carry me to safety and I would be faithful to them.

31

The City Guards drag the woman into the crowd and I do not see her again. Somewhere another gondola is waiting, a narrower and more enclosed one, and aboard it is a cage covered with black fabric. I think of the woman inside it. I think of the longer stick that she might have drawn from the bowl, and of the man who did draw it: of the ship he will be taken to in the faint light of dawn that will carry him somewhere with a strange language and jobs different from those he is used to. I think of the man looking back towards the island from aboard the ship for the last time, knowing he can never return.

Above everything the Council stands quiet, does not raise a hand, does not move.

The oath comes to an end and my lips are still moving, but my voice has faded away.

CHAPTER THREE

I am seated on a hard, wooden chair in Weaver's study. It is the one she offers when she wants to scold someone in private. She has another one for visitors, a high-backed, cushioned chair she has upholstered again every few years; but that one is pushed into the far corner, and she is sitting on it herself.

Two City Guards are facing me across the long table. This room is usually brighter than any other in the house, the Halls of Weaving included. But today the lattice of the large window in the corner only filters dark grey and dim white. The fog rests thick and still in the furrows of the city below, and the glow-glass pipes emit but little light despite the fast flow of the water. The lack of light makes the guards' faces look hollow, as if they could be removed to reveal something else underneath. Or perhaps nothing at all.

'And you do not know this girl?' one of the guards asks for the third time.

The chill of the room wraps itself around me and strangles. The Council watches us from a large painting on the wall. I anchor my gaze on the tapestries hanging behind the guards, use them to build a wall between myself and the questions. In them, Our Lady of Weaving holds every thread in her multitude of hands, and waves and clouds and stars behind the clouds obey her will.

'No, I don't,' I answer. Again.

The guards look at each other. One of them introduced himself as Captain Biros, the other as Captain Lazaro. I am not entirely sure which one is which. They are about the same height, and they both have deep-set eyes and thick eyebrows, although one of them is more robust than the other.

Captain Biros, or perhaps Lazaro, nods. Captain Lazaro, or perhaps Biros, writes something in his notebook.

'And you were on night-watch the night she came to the house?'

'Yes, I was,' I say. Again.

'Are you certain you did not steal away to the city between your rounds without anyone noticing?'

This question is new.

'Of course,' I say. 'Besides, it would have been impossible. The air gondola would have been too noisy. By foot, it would have taken too long. And someone in the house would have raised alarm when they noticed movement in the web-maze in the middle of the night.'

'Yes, we have heard about the extraordinary system,' says Biros. Or maybe it is Lazaro. 'Of course, it would help our investigation if we knew how it works . . .'

'That is secret information.' The voice from the shadows belongs to Weaver. The words are quiet, yet they cut the air clear.

'Of course.' Biros closes his mouth. Lazaro scribbles in his notebook. Or perhaps it is the other way round.

34

Lazaro, if it is not Biros, lifts his eyes from the page he is filling. The sound of the pen is cut short.

'Did anyone raise alarm when the girl moved through the maze towards the house?' he asks.

'Eventually, yes,' Weaver says. 'But she made it all the way to the house before she was found. It was as if she knew the way. Yet she is not one of our weavers, Captain Lazaro.'

The guards glance at each other again. They probably arrived by air gondola. Visitors usually do. If they had walked through the maze, they would have needed a guide, and they know it.

'Biros,' Biros says. 'Interesting.'

'Fascinating,' Lazaro says. He turns to look at me. 'And you say you don't know this girl, and you have never seen her before, and you don't know why your name is tattooed on her?'

A draught passes through the room, waves knotted from threads move under the eyes of Our Lady of Weaving.

'I don't, and I haven't.'

'In invisible ink,' Biros says.

I think of the letters glowing on the girl's skin and of the scar-handed man in the Museum of Pure Sleep, of the tattoo that appeared and vanished.

'It means nothing to me,' I say. 'I didn't even know invisible tattoos existed.'

Biros and Lazaro wait. When I do not continue, Biros whispers something to Lazaro. Lazaro whispers something back. They speak in a low voice which blends their words into a soft hiss. I only discern one among them: *Dreamer*.

A cold current passes through me. Above them, Our Lady of Weaving reaches in all directions and not one strand comes loose from her grip.

Biros and Lazaro nod at each other and turn to me.

'Fascinating,' Biros says.

'Interesting,' Lazaro says. He closes his notebook and slips it into his pocket together with the pen.

'We will look into it,' Biros says.

'And we will let you know,' Lazaro says.

They get up. I get up too. They both take a quick bow at me. I bow my head slightly in return. Then they bow at Weaver, and in a few fast strides they are gone, the echoes of their footsteps vanished into the fabrics covering the walls. Twelve of Our Ladies of Weaving look from the tapestries far beyond this room and hour, and speechlessly their limbs spin new meshes for the Web of Worlds.

I turn to go, but Weaver's voice stops me.

'I wish to have a word with you as well,' she says. She closes the door. We stand in the shadows and watch each other across the distance of the room.

'If there is something you are not telling me, now would be a good moment to mend the situation,' she says. 'That way I might be able to help you.'

'There isn't.'

She regards me.

'You know I'm not unfair,' she remarks. 'I have trusted you with more than I have many others. It would make me sad to know that trust is not returned.'

It is true. She often lets me send water messages, showing me the symbol to insert in the watergraph without telling me what it means. She does not know that I have learned most symbols over the years. The skill is not much use, however, because she only ever asks me to send unimportant routine messages, such as vegetable or seafood orders to the market, or notes to let the merchants know how many antique silkweed tapestries the House of Webs will be auctioning off this year.

Weaver has also let me keep my cell to myself for a long time without questioning it. Most younger weavers have to share their cells with someone else, and the only reason I am on my own is because my cellmate left the house without warning a year ago. I suspect she was pregnant.

'I would tell you if there was anything,' I say.

Weaver smiles almost unnoticeably.

'Of course you would,' she says. 'Before you go back to work, could you take a message to Alva for me? Tell her I will send for a gondola to take our patient to the Hospital Quarters tomorrow. I know the sick bay is running out of space.'

I bow my head slightly. As I walk to the door, I half-expect Weaver to stop me again, but she does not. When I glance back, she is standing by the watergraph, waiting for me to go, so I do.

I find Alva placing a sample under the microscope. It is an expensive device. She has told me there are only three of them on the island. She glances up when I walk in. Two bright lanterns are burning on the table. The curtains between the sick room and the front room are closed. I hear coughing from the other side. I imagine the girl in her bed, her long limbs, the dampened pain on her face. The tattoo that is like an invitation written on her, one I cannot understand.

'The ointment is between the scale and the opened bag of camomile,' Alva says and turns a small, round mirror in her hand. 'It's been waiting for you for days.'

I pick up the glass jar from the table and push it into the pocket of my jacket.

'How did you know I needed it?'

'You come to ask for it every year after the Ink-marking,' Alva replies. 'Do these seem the same to you?' She points at two grey strips on top of the mirror. A scent of mud and seaweed rises from them. I look at them more closely and notice that they appear to be slices of medusa flesh.

'Exactly the same,' I say. 'Why?'

Alva places the mirror under the microscope lens and pulls one of the lanterns closer. She looks into the microscope and adjusts it by the wheel on the side.

'What about now?' she asks.

I walk around the table next to her and peer into the microscope. The view makes me think of trunks of strange trees, a pile of maggots or budding branches of unfamiliar sea plants.

'You're looking at the part of medusa skin that helps them feel and sense light. It also contains their medicinal properties, the cells that produce a pain-relieving chemical,' Alva says. 'There are samples from two medusas under the lens, not just one.'

The difference is clear. The tree-trunk and budding-branch patterns on the left look translucent, but on the right dark streaks show on them, as if they have been dipped in ink that is slowly dripping off.

'What is that?' I ask.

'I asked someone to bring me a dead medusa from the shore, the freshest they could find,' Alva says. 'That's the one on the right. The other one is from my tank.'

'I thought they all died of polyp fever.'

It has been a week since the flood. A few days after the first wave of dead medusas washed to the shores, the Council sent a water message around the city. The word spread quickly: polyp fever, a rare disease that was not harmful to humans but could become an epidemic. Unfortunate, because it would take years for the medusa population to recover. Ships had already been sent to collect healthy singing medusas from the open sea to be planted in the waters close to the island.

'That's what I thought,' Alva says. 'But then I began to wonder. Polyp fever doesn't usually strike during the cool season. According to lore, there have only been three epidemics on the island before, and they all took place in late summer.'

I remember the mute and still blooms of jellyfish that people are still collecting from the streets and shores, their stench that floats around the midden ships. I think of the humming of the medusas in denser-growing evenings, the silence spread across the shores, and the air feels heavier to breathe.

'What is it, then?'

'I don't know, but it is not polyp fever. Could be a different kind of disease.' She reaches for the side table and picks up two glass jars with water and a dead medusa in each. The animals are missing a slice of their bells. 'There's something else, too,' she says.

Alva walks across the room to the tank and pushes one of the jars against the glass wall. Inside the tank, a bloom of medusas begins to gather near the dead one, and a faint humming grows in the water. The medusas settle into the shape of a circle and the slow gauzes of their swimming-bells ripple behind the glass. Alva waits, pulls the first jar away and presses the other one against the tank. The singing medusas keep their formation for a moment, some of them even swimming closer in curiosity. Then the humming is cut short, and all goes quiet. A few seconds later the whole bloom bursts like a large soap bubble. The medusas scurry in all directions, far away to the other side of the tank.

'Have you ever seen them do that?' Alva asks.

'No.'

'Neither have I.' Alva turns and walks back to the table. Only after some time do the medusas return to their languid paths in the water-space.

'What are you going to do?' I ask.

'I don't know yet,' Alva says. 'I need to look into this further.'

I will soon be missed in the Halls of Weaving. You can stretch a temporary absence from work for a while, but you have to do it carefully.

'Weaver asked me to tell you that she wants to move the patient to the Hospital Quarters tomorrow,' I say. 'The . . . visitor.' My hand has moved to gesture at my mouth before I realize, and Alva needs no further specification. She nods.

'Good. I've already had to put spare mattresses to use. A severe cough is spreading in the house, and it seems to come with a dreadful rash.'

'Is it contagious?'

'Presumably,' she says. 'Do you want to come and say goodbye?'

I glance in the direction of the Halls of Weaving.

'I will take full responsibility if Weaver comes after you,' Alva says. 'Medical emergency.'

'Offer accepted,' I say, more out of temptation to stay away from weaving a little longer than anything else. Or so I tell myself.

Alva leaves the glass jars with dead medusas on the table and we head into the other room.

There is more light today, and sound, the kind created

when you put many people in a small space and tell them
to rest but they are in too much discomfort to do so. Two
spare mattresses have been wedged in the narrow gaps
between the beds. There are three younger weavers and
four older than myself in the sick bay. Two seem asleep,
but the rest are tossing and turning restlessly. Their
breathing is distorted and ragged, heavy with cough. Their
skin is covered in a rash that looks like they have been
dipped in red or purple ink. I smell the heavy scent of
burning herbs, and under it sweat and sickness.

The girl is awake. She is sitting at the back of the room,
propped up with pillows, and is putting together a puzzle.
Alva must have given it to her. She turns to look at us.
Alva puts a jar under the girl's chin and she opens her
mouth. A dead singing medusa drops into the jar.

'I'm afraid I cannot give you another one,' Alva says.
'I don't know when I will be able to get more, and I need
to keep a few in reserve.'

The girl nods.

'But I have good news,' Alva continues. 'We can finally
arrange your transfer. It wasn't possible earlier, because
there was an accident in the north.' I remember the flood
night: the empty sky, the missing cable. 'An important air
route crashed the night you came. Cleaning up has caused
so much work that the route has only just started operating
again.'

The girl looks like something is troubling her, but nods
again slowly. Her face begins to darken in a way I do not
understand.

'A gondola is coming to take you to the Hospital
Quarters tomorrow,' Alva continues. 'They have more
singing medusas. And if not, they'll have something else
to ease the pain.'

41

The girl's face continues to darken. She takes a deep breath and stares at Alva.

'What is it?' I ask.

She grasps my wrist. I start, but do not pull my hand away. Her fingers are warm and narrow, and their grip seems to reach deeper than the skin. I glance at Alva.

'Everything is fine,' I say to the girl. 'There will be more space in the Hospital Quarters. They will be able to take better care of you there and find your family.'

The girl holds my gaze with hers: grey as rain, or flood-waters in the light of dawn. A slow shiver travels through me, as if she is pulling an invisible string somewhere inside. The corners of her mouth tremble once, she draws breath again, and then lets go of me, turning her face towards the floor. She is very still, as if holding a deep tremor within.

'I just came to say goodbye,' I say.

The girl raises her gaze. She nods slowly.

'I hope you feel better soon.'

They are worn and hollow words, but I cannot find any others.

Before I turn to go, something moves in her eyes. A knot tightens inside me, but I choose to treat it as just another shadow. One more will make little difference.

I step into the hall where the others have already settled to work. I kneel in front of the statue of Our Lady of Weaving and the image of the Council. I touch my forehead to the floor. I get up, walk to my seat and pick up the shuttle. My fingers know the paths and cannot err, for they never change. Wall-webs must be strong enough to survive even heavy rainfalls and storm winds carrying across the sea. Yet they must also be easy enough to unravel, so the yarn can be used again. The hours slip through my fingers uneven, in slow knots.

This evening, after I have placed down my shuttle, taken my supper and returned to my chamber, sleep is deceptively easy to come. It puts me behind a door in a place that is the web-maze, and yet is not: the walls are gauze and yarn, but the door is a robust wooden door. It is ajar, and behind it opens a deep and dense darkness. On the other side there is a rustling sound, like someone breathing. I turn around. The web walls close to form a dead end before me. As I approach them I think I hear words swishing, and behind the walls I sense many solitudes interlaced with one another. But I know it is a dream, and my dream is mine to command. I will my body to be lighter than air. Wind blows through the crack in the door and over my skin, picks me up from the maze with lithe fingers and floats me towards the skies. The starry night sky pulls me up until I am wind and light, rips apart to reveal a universe where nothing withholds me.

Then I am back in my bed, the mattress hard under my back, breath struggling in my throat. My body is tired, as if I have spent all my strength on hard work. The walls of my cell are close.

I am not certain what has woken me.

There is no light yet around the edges of the curtains. The glow-glass draws a faint blue ring around itself. The house is frozen around the mutest heart of the night. If there are weavers walking and guarding the corridors, they are far away from my cell.

I realize I have forgotten my night-watch.

The glow-glass almost shatters to the floor when I reach out to shake it brighter. I catch it just before it slides over the edge of the table. I throw my blanket aside and pull a cloak from the foot of the bed to cover my nightgown. The sand sits still in the hourglass next to the door. I forgot to turn it before I went to bed. I push my feet into leather-soled shoes.

The door closes behind me more loudly than I intend.

Half-running, I pass a long row of quiet cell doors. When I turn the corner at the end of the corridor, I hear the sound.

It is a hardly discernible rift in the wall of silence, thinner than a line drawn with a needlepoint. A narrow moan is rising and falling along the ceiling vaults, in the chambers of stone that throw it back from their walls. I recognize it. My steps turn faster.

Past the washrooms I reach the first dormitory doorway. The sound fades. I peek in. All is quiet. A drowsy third-year weaver lifts her head and lets it fall back on the pillow. I do not see anything unusual in the next dormitory, either. But when I close the door, the sound begins again. This time I know where it is coming from.

In the first-year apprentices' dormitory everyone is awake by now. A flood of whispers and half-spoken words washes over me. At the far end of the room, where the youngest apprentices sleep, a group of girls is gathered around a bed, but not too close. Their ring leaves an empty space full of fear around the source of the sound, and they are all fiddling coral amulets between their fingers. A faint, anxious moan carries from the bed, circling the room like a starved ghost seeking a way out.

I hope to be wrong. I walk across the dormitory towards the bed.

When I see the girl from whose mouth the moan is rising, I know there is nothing I can do for her.

She is lying on her back, her body completely still and

her lips slightly parted. I remember her name: Mirea. She cannot be older than ten. Her breathing is strained, as if her throat is trying to close around it. But it is her eyes that really give her away. They are open, black holes. Her pupils have widened like dark water, washed away all colour, and there is nothing between their edges and the frightened whites. Because frightened she is, her whole face brimming with terror as she stares into the space above her that seems empty to everyone else. Yet I know what she sees. And I know the strange song of her low, bare moan: the kind people always sing when a night-maere is riding them. The sound marks the sleeper as soon as someone else hears it.

I seize my own coral amulet and speak her name softly. 'Mirea.'

A violent shudder runs through her, and then she grasps my arm. The grip is tight enough to bruise.

'Help me,' she says.

'Everything's fine, Mirea,' I tell her, although it is not.

'There was a shadow,' she says. 'It tried to strangle me.'

Her first time, then. She does not know yet what happened. Does not know how to keep the secret. Not that it would help now. The others stare at us. I see some girls whisper to each other. There is no easy way to do this.

'Have you heard of night-maere possession?' I ask.

Alarm stains Mirea's face. Of course she has. Everyone on the island has.

'It wasn't like that,' she says, but without certainty.

'I'm so sorry, Mirea,' I say. The rims of her eyes are turning red and her cheeks quiver once, twice. 'Everyone saw you. Your eyes were night-maere black. You carry the dream-plague.'

45

'My mother says night-maeres are invisible,' Mirea tries. Her voice cracks and fails. 'It was here. Someone else must have seen it.' A single tear rolls down her face.

The girls around us shift uncomfortably. Someone sniggers. Anger burns in my throat like white-hot glass.

'Only those who carry a night-maere can see them.' Weaver's tall figure has appeared in the doorway. Her words cross the room before she does.

I look at Mirea, who has begun to shake with sobs.

'I don't want to sleep in the same room with a Dreamer.' It is a blonde girl. Her face is smooth as polished white stone, and equally hard.

Weaver looks at her with an expression that betrays the slightest crack of impatience, and behind it, something buried far deeper. For a moment I think her words are going to be something else entirely, but then she just says, 'We will want to avoid contamination, of course.' She pulls a small notebook from her pocket, tears out a page and draws three symbols on it. 'Eliana, go and send this message immediately.' She hands the piece of paper to me.

Mirea is still crying. Her nose is dripping large, wet drops to the sheets, and the softness of her child-face is distorted with fear. The coral amulet hangs around her neck purposeless, incapable of keeping the night-maere away, a piece of dead seafloor. I see the blonde girl look at her in disgust. I nod and turn slowly to go. I have to stop myself from giving Mirea's hand a quick, encouraging squeeze. It would be a lie. She has nothing to feel encouraged about.

The door to Weaver's study opens without a sound. It is never locked. The glow-glasses shine faintly. Through the window in the corner I can see the ever-burning fires

46

of the Tower at a distance, like sharp eyes blinking in the face of darkness.

I missed my night-watch.

Perhaps there is nothing I could have done for Mirea. But if I had been walking the corridors and listening to the sounds of night-rest in the rooms, I might have heard her before anyone else. Quietly, without anyone knowing, I could have woken her up, and she could have hidden her illness – if not forever, at least until the next time. She might have lived through the dormitory years and even through sharing a cell without another visit from a night-maere, and no one would ever have known.

The watergraph stands tall and robust in the corner. The glass tank embedded in its stone body reflects my face dark and distorted when I step close. I select the lever that bears the emblem of the House of the Tainted. The metal creaks. The message-pipe leading there opens. In the faint light I can just barely see the index and the scale plate with its engraved symbols inside the tank. I do not need the paper Weaver gave me, because I recognized the symbols when she wrote them down. *Fetch a Dreamer from the House of Webs.* I turn the wheel on the side of the machine until the index points at the first symbol. The surface of the water rises in the tank as the index moves along the scale. In the tank of the watergraph in the House of the Tainted, the water level will change accordingly, showing the same engraved symbol.

When I have inserted all three symbols, I wait until a small bell chimes to signal that the message has been received at the other end of the pipe. Then I turn to go. I am nearly out of the door, when I stop. I listen. The corridors are night-silent and all I hear are the movements of my own body. There is no one else in the building.

I move behind Weaver's table. Slowly I coax the drawer open and stop to listen again. No light flickers to life and no footsteps brush the floors. The message-book is pushed to the back of the drawer, but like the door, the drawer is never locked. I pull the thick book out and place it in my lap. The pages are yellowed and brittle on the edges, and full of water message code, which no one in the house knows apart from Weaver – as far as she is aware.

She is not in the habit of writing down the dates, but she records moon phases with precision: how Our Lady of Weaving hides a silver coin in her palm behind the sky, reveals it little by little and hides it again. The last full moon was two days ago. I only need to find the circle marking it and count from there backwards towards the day the girl arrived at the house.

There are no entries for that day. Then I remember: the flood. The watergraph could not be used. I find three entries from two days later. The first one is a request to the trading harbours to buy more yarn. The second seems equally casual. *Herbs*, it reads. The third and final one is in the column for incoming messages. To be certain, I check the symbol against the translation sheet Weaver keeps placed between the final pages of the book.

Intrusion at the museum, the message says. The sender is the City Guard.

I remember the scar-handed man I saw at the Museum of Pure Sleep.

A stone-cold draught blows across my skin, too sudden and sharp to ignore. It is possible that I hear a soft creak of weary metal. I turn to look, and take a moment to see what I am looking at. In the corner of the room, a tapestry billows like a sail in wind. Behind it a dense and deep darkness cuts the wall.

There is a modest wooden door in the wall. I have always imagined it to be some kind of storage room, if I have ever even taken notice of it. Now I do.

The door was closed when I came to the room. I am certain of it.

I push Weaver's watergraph logbook back into the drawer.

This time I hear the creak of the hinges clearly. The door is swinging slowly in the draught. I walk closer. I listen closely, and for a moment I think I hear a rustling sound, as if someone is breathing in the darkness. But when I try to catch the sound again, it is gone.

Another breeze blows through the chink and across my skin, making every hair stand on end. The door slams shut, as if pushed by an invisible hand from the other side. I take a step back, then another, and as I walk towards the tall door of Weaver's study, I hear the quick beating of my heart against the bones of my chest, like an animal struggling to break free.

I do not slow down until the long, shadow-soaked corridor is halfway behind me and another landscape opens ahead, a world that is ready to crumble or change.

She dreams dark dreams of a place where longing settles in limbs and thickens into fog on window panes, where a hunger to run free and feel the salt of the sea on one's face makes the air bitter to breathe and fear crawls dense along the floors. The walls fall quiet into deep water, every door is held by a lock and branch-stiff lattices cover the windows. If you go close enough, you may hear words swishing, and behind the walls you may sense many solitudes interlaced with one another. Even closer you may sometimes catch screams, but perhaps they are of seagulls.

Those who carry marks on their faces and are confined within walls scratch the doors until their claws break, and under the weight of their dreams the city subsides and cracks, poles and foundation stones under houses shift out of joint and crumble, the edges of shores and canals corrode into the sea. But ink chains others also, flows under skins and in the veins of the island. It grows *slow wounds at the core of all life, hiding from sight what is meant to be seen.*

Hands reach for the threads of sleep and fall towards them, and they do not thwart the touch. Their stirring started long ago, elusive, adaptive, impossible to stop. The door into darkness is closed, the door into darkness is open, air flows and through it

CHAPTER FOUR

A gondola arrives for Mirea at dawn. We all hear the squeaking of the metal cables as the vessel approaches, hovers above the drop and climbs slowly to the port on top of the hill. I am not outside to see it, but the walls of the Halls of Weaving make every sound swell in my ears: the heavy footsteps, rarely heard in the house; the indistinct words of Weaver's voice; and, eventually, Mirea's weeping. I imagine two silent and dark figures taking her into the black gondola bearing the emblems of the City Guard, which will return down to the city across the void. Once its bottom touches water, the large hooks holding it to the airway will be detached. The vessel will float down the canal, turn to a waterway running towards the House of the Tainted and finally stop before the locked iron gate. I imagine Mirea: struggling and fighting, her body wriggling like a slippery fish at the bottom of the boat. Or quiet, submissive, her face closed.

None of us flinches, or slows down the work, or stops it.

Later, when the weather turns warmer, the folding doors of the Halls of Weaving are opened towards the square.

Many weavers carry their looms outside, under the canopy woven of web-yarn. If interior and exterior spaces can be separated from each other in the House of Webs, that is: here, rooms move often. The dormitories and cells remain. They are built in stone, because sleep must be confined within solid walls, it cannot be released to wander free. But around the stone buildings the rooms, walls and streets wax and vanish, nor are they supposed to stay. That is the will of Our Lady of Weaving.

Days are seldom warm this late in autumn. The sun draws soft shadows on the walls and casts them across the floors, falls through the half-woven wall-webs. Clouds break the edge of the light. The long rows of weavers reach from the room all the way to the square. Their hands pass the weft through the warps, building within the frames fabrics that are all alike. No exceptions are allowed. The only sounds in the hall are the rustling of clothes, the swishing of yarn and the breathing of dozens of women. The coarse sea-wool stings my fingers until their skin cracks, and my weave is not as smooth as I would like.

I pat the weft with a wooden weaving fork to make it a tighter fit with the rest of the web. The warp rises tall and bare ahead of me. On my left side Silvi, who came to the house three years after me, has already woven twice as much as I this morning. My weft twists into a tangle and leaves a large, protruding loop in the wall-web. I am so focused on tugging the knot free that it takes me a while to notice the low chatter that has grown in the hall, and the stopped movements. Silvi stares away from the square and folding doors, towards the arched stone doorway between the hall and the corridor.

The girl tattooed with invisible ink stands at the door of the hall. She has changed her white patient gown for a long, grey wool dress and tied her hair low in the nape of her neck. The skin around her mouth still looks slightly swollen and bruised, but she stands straight and without hesitation. Her gaze circles the hall and stops on me.

I place the shuttle down. The girl begins to walk towards me. I catch uncertain looks and tense postures from the corner of my eye. Outsiders are not allowed in the Halls of Weaving. Yet no one rises to stop her; neither do I. Outside clouds part, and the sky casts sudden light across the hall. A shining forest of halfway webs reaches in all directions. She walks to me, tilts her head and the corners of her mouth lift, just a little. I do not know what moves on my face, but something must do. She sits down on the narrow seat next to me, so close I smell the soap on her skin. For a few moments, neither of us moves. I breathe her in.

She places a hand on top of the shuttle resting in my lap. Her fingers brush it briefly before settling on the polished wooden surface. Its shape is a familiar fit against her touch. She looks at me, face close to mine, and tilts her head again. Her expression poses a question.

It is quiet enough to hear a hundred simultaneous breaths drawn in the hall. Only those chosen as apprentices are allowed to weave in the house. Anything else is forbidden. Everyone stares at us.

I nod.

The girl nods back. I feel her breath brush my neck. She picks up the shuttle and begins to pass it through the warp. Her movements are swift and sure. The yarn slides without clumping, and I see immediately that the resulting weave will be smooth and dense. When the wall-web is ready in its frame, it will show the place where the shuttle passed from my hands to hers: the lumpy, sometimes too tight and occasionally too loose texture turns even and made with skill.

I remain seated, although the seat is too narrow for both of us, and she is tightly pressed against me. There are footsteps at the door. Alva steps into the hall, her face red and her breathing heavy.

'I'm sorry,' she says. 'She disappeared while I was outside drawing water from the well. I will take her back immediately.'

I look at the girl's hands again, the endlessly intertwining strands sliding through her fingers.

'I don't think she wants to go back,' I say.

The gondola from the Hospital Quarters arrives that evening and takes away six rash-covered, violently coughing weavers. The girl is not among them. On the second day after I have handed my shuttle to the girl, she steps into the halls with Weaver. Together they set up a new loom in the corner and stretch the warp between the upper and lower beams. The girl carries a seat in front of the frame and sits down, places the shuttle, a skein of yarn and a weaving fork next to her, and begins to work. Weaver keeps an eye on the girl for a while, and when she leaves, no one says anything. We all take secret glances at the girl. Once she glances back at me. I can only see her face diagonally from the back, but the cheek turned towards me lifts as if she is smiling.

After supper I sit in my cell, detach the coin pouch from my waist and pour the coins in front of me on the bed. The House of Webs pays a small monthly salary and clothes its residents, because the servants of Our Lady of Weaving are expected to look tidy. But my socks have worn thin, and there will not be new ones on offer until spring. I begin to count the coins to see if I can afford to buy a pair of warm socks at the market for winter. My fingers brush something oblong. For a moment I am confused, but then I remember the metal object the dark-clad woman dropped at my feet on the day of the Ink-marking. I pick it up. It is a small key. I turn it in my fingers. Its teeth are simple, but one end is unusually shaped: it is tapering, like an eye, and in place of a pupil an eight-pointed sun shines at the centre, the emblem of the island and the Council.

There is a knock on the door. I drop the key back into the coin pouch, collect the coins from the bed in a hurry and tighten the mouth of the pouch. I get up to open the door. Weaver stands behind it with the girl who is carrying a pile of clean bed linen in her arms.

'Eliana,' Weaver says and places her hand on the girl's shoulder. 'She will stay in the house for the time being. At least until we find out where her home is.'

I glance at the bed linen and understand.

'Can we come in?' Weaver says. 'I have no doubt she would like to prepare her bed.'

'Can't she live in the sick bay?' I ask, and my voice sounds harsher than I had intended. The girl shifts her weight from one foot to the other. 'Or in one of the dormitories?'

'The sick bay has five new cases of rash, and we do not want more infections. After what she has been through, I trust you understand that she would prefer more privacy than a dormitory can offer.'

'I cannot sleep when there is someone else in the room,' I try.

Weaver looks at me from her heights, eyes black in the dark face.

'I thought you did not sleep anyway,' she says. 'She is your roommate for the time being. I will leave you to make closer acquaintance.'

I know the conversation is over. I move to the side and let the girl in. She places the bed linen on the night table next to the empty bed. The table is too small, and the sheets fall to the floor. She picks them up with hasty hands and begins to make the bed without looking at me. Weaver simply nods and leaves.

I do not know where to look. There is little to do in the cell in the evenings after work. My former roommate usually wanted to chat about seamen and jewellery sold in the market, or how many children each of us would have when we found husbands and left the house. I mostly responded with a few syllables, if at all. That never seemed to bother her.

The girl gets the linen in place and begins to take off her dress, which seems slightly too big for her. I look away and hear her slip under the blanket in her thin under-garment.

'It would be good for you to know that I sleep less than most others,' I say. 'I'm often on night-watch.' It seems like a sufficient explanation.

Her eyes are wide in the dusk, their colour metal-sharp.

'I didn't mean to be rude,' I say. 'I'm sorry. I just haven't shared a room with anyone for a long time.'

I close the curtains. The glow-glass globe on the night table dims slowly. I take off my jacket, change into my nightgown and lower myself to bed. I turn towards the wall.

I hear the sheets rustling and the bunk creaking under the girl. Apparently she too has turned her back on me. It feels as if I can sense the warmth of her body across the room. I close my eyes and fear falling asleep. From her breathing I can tell she is not sleeping, either.

As weeks pass, the girl and I try to get used to each other's presence in the small space that is now new to both of us: to her because she does not yet know it, and to me because the strange, shifting element of her limbs and hair and shape has been added to my former privacy. I begin to understand I am also responsible for introducing her to the ways of the house. She follows me into the wash-rooms in the morning and to the supper table, although she cannot eat normally yet. She bends her head down to the floor of the Halls of Weaving after me and goes to sleep when I do. I stay awake and watch her, but some nights exhaustion eventually drops me to sleep. When images begin to form behind my closed lids, she seems to chase them, too. The walls of sleep fall quiet into deep water, and she climbs on them before me. I follow her through low and tall doors to dream-rooms where branch-stiff lattices cover the windows. I seek her in dream-halls where black water rushes in the rifts of cracked floors and walls are fraying webs, because the threads run from their meshes and every-thing unravels. I want the floors to be unbroken and they close their cracks in front of my footsteps. I want the walls to be whole again and the yarn interweaves back into meshes, but it escapes my grasp and I cannot reach it, and each new wanting is without strength.

When I wake with a start in the light of night or dawn, I hear the girl's breathing on the other side of the cell.

I should perhaps know how to read these signs:

That morning, when I arrive at the Halls of Weaving with the girl at my heels, I see two City Guards enter Weaver's study.

My shadow has moved two palm-widths on the wall, when a weaver who is on messenger duty steps into the hall, bows her forehead to the floor, walks to the girl and says something to her in a low voice. They leave the hall together.

The air gondola cables screech under the weight of a vessel.

At lunch I keep a vacant seat next to mine, but she does not come.

No one touches her wall-web for the rest of the day.

I am on my way to the cell after supper, when Weaver stops me in the corridor.

'Come to my study,' she says. 'I must tell you something.'

The tapestries on the walls are dark and their patterns seem to move while you look away. I sit on the chair Weaver has offered me. This is not the Scolding Chair, but one of the better ones, with a high back and a smoother shape.

'Two City Guards came to the house today,' Weaver says. 'They were trying to track down someone who missed her Ink-marking recently.'

For some reason I think of the key, of the woman on the square. Of the guard who saw me. On the wall Our Lady of Weaving raises all her hands, inviting the sea to storm.

'I did not miss my visit,' I say.

'I know,' Weaver replies. 'But someone named Valeria Petros did.'

She pauses and watches me. I search my memory for the name and do not find it.

'Who's that?' I ask.

'Your roommate,' Weaver says. 'She confirmed it today when the City Guard spoke to her.'

I reach for the girl's thoughts, try to imagine what I would have done. She must have been too badly injured and heavily medicated to even know what day it was. She could have gone later, but how would she have explained what had happened without words? And whoever attacked her probably still walks the streets of the city, eyes perhaps ready to see, hands ready to capture and kill this time.

'Will Valeria Petros leave the house now?' I ask. The thought hits me deeper than I expect.

'She will stay,' Weaver says.

'Doesn't she want to return to her family?'

'I am certain she would like to,' Weaver says. 'Unfortunately it is not possible.' She pauses. 'You will remember that air gondola accident the night she arrived.'

I nod.

'Her parents were in the gondola that crashed. There were no survivors.'

A cold weight settles into my chest. I think of the cables in the sky, of their distance from the ground below, or water. When you fall from that high, it matters little what is underneath. An image from the week before arises in my mind: Valeria's darkening face when Alva mentioned the air route crash. She must have known her parents were travelling by gondola the night she was attacked. She must have wondered.

'Doesn't she have anyone else?' My voice is evened by years of practice, as if it belongs to another.

'She has an aunt, an inkmaster. I have sent her a message. But Valeria has indicated she prefers to stay here. And I do believe her skill is put to better use within these walls.'

I recall the night Valeria arrived at the house. I see the

pain curled on her face, the bloodstains on the stones of the square.

'Do you know who attacked her?'

Weaver shakes her head.

'I'm afraid the City Guard do not seem to have made progress on that front.'

She is quiet. The tapestries move, are still and move again. A cold draught travels across the room. I glance at the corner. The door is closed behind the glass frame of the watergraph. Weaver has pushed the hood back from her face. She does not do that often. Her face is dark and nearly smooth, although it cannot be young. Her short hair curls close to the curve of her head.

Weaver breaks the silence.

'There is one more thing.'

I wait.

'Valeria's parents have already been cremated. She didn't want a place for them in the burial ground. But as their daughter she must collect the ashes from the House of Fire. She will need someone to accompany her.'

'I will do it,' I say.

'Yes, you will,' Weaver says. 'You may go now.' She turns to the pile of papers on the table and picks up a pen. It begins to rustle on paper.

I walk to the door where I stop, because an unexpected thought takes shape in my mind. No one should have to travel beyond the Web of Worlds without thoughts and deeds to smooth the way. I cannot do much for the girl, but this I can.

'What were their names?'

The rustling stops. Weaver looks up from the papers. The pen hangs mid-air in her fingers, ready to be raised, ready to fall.

'Valeria's parents,' I specify. 'What were they called?'
'Mihaela and Jovanni Petros,' she says.
'Thank you,' I say and leave.

I knock on the door of the cell. No response. Quietly I open it. The curtains are closed, and the girl – Valeria, I fit her name in my mouth – has thrown a shawl over the glow-glass on her night table. She is curled under the blanket, a lump of darkness, like grief sealed in a throat. I listen to her breathing and am almost certain she is awake. But I do not say anything, in case I am wrong.

My bed makes a soft creak when I sit down on the edge, even though I try to do it slowly, without sound. Valeria does not move.

My hand wants to reach out to her, stroke the curve of the shoulder and her side, very softly, because words are too heavy right now. Instead I get undressed in the dark as quietly as I can and go to bed. I think of the broken cable, its end swaying in the wind, or perhaps cradled by water, and everything she will never tell her parents. Of how her hours have suddenly turned briefer and her days more brittle, because there is no longer anything between them and emptiness, and she is the next in line.

Valeria stays in the cell for days. I do not see her cry, but when I return from work in the evenings, her eyes are red and swollen. Sometimes she merely lies facing the wall. I bring her soup and bread, the hard crust of which I have scratched off. Sometimes she eats. Mostly she does not.

A week later I climb up a tangled path to a hill where cables do not squeak or webs divert walkers from the way.

Low wind-whipped bushes grow here and there among the stones, and stunted trees sticking from the thin soil like gnawed bones. Their yellowing leaves are dappled by bruise-like spots I do not remember seeing the year before. The day is bright, the wings of the white gulls sharp against the sky, but their cries are drowned by the distance. The hill is veiled in silence.

Far at sea I discern earth-coloured ships that do not bear the flags of trading vessels on their masts. Everyone on the island has seen them, but no one knows what they are for. They sail to a secluded harbour near the House of the Tainted, and people do not go there. Some say they have seen pale figures in the port who vanish from sight when they are spoken to. I turn my gaze away from the ships. This day does not need more ghosts.

Janos stands before the arching stone gate at the end of the path, waiting for me. We meet here on the last day of the week after every new moon. He clasps me into a wide hug. The gesture seems out of place, too loud and large, but I do not push him away.

Janos lets me go and looks at me.

'You have been missing sleep again, sister,' he says.

'So have you, brother,' I respond.

'Must run in the family,' he says. His smile is our mother's.

We both glance around. There are no others on the hill. Or if there are, they will be inside the Glass Grove. From there, they cannot hear us speak.

'I hear someone was taken from the House of Webs the other week.'

So he has heard. I should have expected it. News always finds its way to the House of Words. I wonder if they have already received word of a strange girl who collapsed on the stones and nowadays sleeps only a cell-width away from me.

'She was one of the youngest,' I say. 'She didn't have the privacy of the cell to protect her.'

Janos pushes his hands into the pockets of his blue scribe's cloak. His eyes look to the sky, then at me again. I see serious concern in them.

'Someone was also taken from the House of Words recently,' he says.

I do not remember Janos telling me about any Dreamers being discovered in the House of Words in years. Memories come without looking: our mother's night-maere-black eyes and her moan in a candle-lit room, our father's hand dropping to her forehead and stroking the evil spirit away. Torn breath in my throat and my mother's cool fingers on my face, her soothing voice, as I sought the shadow I had seen in the room mere moments earlier. Janos's face, a dark patch in the light of faint flames. My mother's words in the dusk: *never tell anyone.*

'No one knows,' I say.

'I do,' Janos replies.

'You would never tell.'

Janos's smile is our mother's, but his way of frowning is our father's.

'A speculation: one day I'm careless, spill ink over an important codex and spoil it,' he says. 'Or make a disrespectful mistake during the next Word-incineration, before the eyes of the whole island. Scribe gets angry with me and throws me out of the House of Words. The City Guard nabs me and tortures me for information.'

'You are never careless,' I say. 'And they don't do that.' Except to Dreamers, perhaps, I nearly add. But the truth is I do not know what the guards do in dusky rooms, behind closed walls. Nor what kind of orders the Council do or do not give them from the Tower, from the shelter of their masks.

'I could compose an essay on the probability of the event, if you want,' Janos says, raising an eyebrow.

'No doubt.' I shove him lightly. He rarely talks of his work, but I imagine the House of Words to be like the House of Webs: rows of scribes in the large Halls of Scribing bent over their desks, dozens of pens rustling on paper and filling the library of the house with copies of old codices, trading contracts, nautical charts, essays on learned subjects.

Our footsteps settle into a shared rhythm, and no one else carries the same childhood memories as the two of us. It makes the world a little less alien to us, and we both know it.

We walk through the gate side by side. The exterior of the arch is worn smooth by winds and rainfalls, but on the inside you can still discern faint traces of figures once carved on the gate. Their shape is not human, but older, stranger. I see more than two limbs, and something that might be a network of threads, or only toothmarks of weather and time in lichen-covered stone. Beyond the gate a path paved with flat, grey slabs crosses an open field of grass, and then, through a narrow opening, leads into the Glass Grove.

Here, light has an underwater quality, like sun sifting through the sea. It glimmers and dapples gold-green along the smooth arches of the glass walls, catches on the metal plates we pass and creates pillars of rays where dust speckles float without weight. This is how I imagine it would be to lie at the bottom of the sea, looking up at the surface and seeing the world above, but different, its shapes unfamiliar, softer, melting into each other, free from the forms assigned for them. Perhaps that is what those who built this place had in mind. Perhaps the rusty hooks in the ceiling above had fish hanging from them once upon a time, smooth and slippery and colourful, or singing medusas. The glassmasters still know how to make their tails swish without movement, how to capture the shape of swimming-bells mid-billow. But if they ever were here, they would have been stolen away long ago. Why leave something beautiful in a place where almost no one comes any more?

We stop before a plate with a waxing moon above waves engraved on it. For generations, only seafarers and fishermen came from our family. Janos and I are the first to be accepted into Houses of Crafts. I sweep aside a vine covering a small shelf under the metal plate. A leaf covered in bruised stains comes loose and floats onto the ground. Nothing is left of the heel of bread we brought last time. All the surrounding shelves are empty, but further away I see a cluster of wasps crawling over a rotting piece of fruit. Someone else still visits, then.

Janos pulls a simple earthenware cup from his pocket and detaches a wineskin from his belt, then pours a little bit of wine into the cup. He places the cup on the shelf, and we bow our heads to speak a quiet greeting to our parents. I think of my mother's arms, slender and fragile as winter branches, and eventually as grey. I can no longer remember her voice. Every time I visit, yet another piece of her has fallen away, and what remains is so deeply entwined with my own being that I can no longer tell them apart. I think of my father's eyes, losing their colour under the folds of his lids, fading away like the rest of him. The slow-growing disease they called it, first the neighbours and then the healers, when our parents finally sought them, each in turn. My mother was already gone when Janos was accepted to the House of Words; he was only ten. I was twelve, and had been rejected three times by the House of Weaving. I did not see my father again after they took me in two years later.

Goodbyes were said many times but always buried under other words, and in the end, they were never said at all. Thus we come here again and again, farewells weighing our steps. They are forever late and out of place: a moment gone by we did not recognize when it was within reach, and the ghost of which we will therefore never cease to carry.

But this is what the Glass Grove is for. No remains are kept here. Once the ashes leave the House of Fire, they are scattered into the sea. There is also another burial ground on the island, the place where most people go now. I have heard that there the dead are kept in dark glass coffins, and their features are clearly visible through the lids. The bodies are prepared in such a way that they look like a still image of life even decades later. Their families go to see them and talk to them, and in response they get a mute stare that looks unchanged yet entirely different.

I do not intend to go there. My ashes can be claimed by the sea, and if anyone remembers me once I have left the world, they can come here and whisper their farewells to the sky and trees and vines treading the glass walls.

'I would like to go to the forest for a moment,' I tell Janos.

He shrugs.

'I'll wait,' he says. 'If you don't mind.'

'Not at all.' I had been counting on it.

He makes a space for himself on the stone floor, leaning his back against the wall. I see him close his eyes from the watered-down sunlight coming through the ceiling.

The curve of the inner wall is steeper than the outer, its glass opaque and thick and murky. My mother once told me it was the oldest part of the Glass Grove, perhaps of the city. The treetops rise above it from the encircled forest inside, the only one on the island. The rusty iron gate croaks when I slip through the gap.

The stalks of the bright broadleaves and dark-drizzling conifers push towards the sky smooth and straight, and all is covered by a roof of intertwining branches. Ancient webs of stone are petrified between the trees. There is a tale in the city, one that all weavers know: it tells of the first people of the island, those who were already old before humans came. They taught our kind how to weave, and these webs are all that is left of them. I have walked here many times, touching them and memorizing their shapes. But of course I can never try to replicate them. There is only one way to weave wall-webs, and the patterns, knots and twists of these tapestries of stone are as strange as the creatures that weather has worn away from the gate of the Glass Grove: placed there to be remembered, yet now all but forgotten.

I dig out a piece of bread from my pocket, something I slipped in there at breakfast this morning. The newly dead need nourishment to make their trip to Our Lady of Weaving beyond the Web of Worlds. Valeria can weave, so a web of stone is as good a family crest as any other I can offer. I place the bread under it and kneel. With closed eyes I speak the names of Valeria's parents and wish them a safe journey, say the words that Valeria can never speak again.

A wind does not rise. A rain does not come. The dead stay dead, and do not respond.

When I get to my feet, sunlight scutters along the stone surface of the webs, and for a moment the air seems to burst in flames, ready to scorch the world and make it anew.

I breathe in. Clouds close the sun away again, and the ancient webs rest shadow-coloured like things that must remain unspoken. I follow my own steps back across snapping twigs and leaves turning into earth.

On the way to the city I tell Janos about Valeria. He listens, then speaks.

'An invisible tattoo?'

'Do you know something about them?'

He takes his time to think before saying, 'Maybe.'

'You have access to the census records, don't you?' I know they are kept in the House of Words.

Janos looks doubtful.

'The City Guard imagines I have something to do with Valeria because of the tattoo,' I continue. 'If you could find anything at all about her family . . .'

'It shouldn't be too difficult,' he says. 'But no promises.'

'No promises.'

We part near the edge of the web-maze, and he continues along Halfway Canal towards a closely-guarded gate that can only be accessed from water. The House of Words does not wish to offer a too-steady foothold to visitors. The low-burning evening sun catches on the webs as I climb up the hill through the paths that only the weavers know.

The door of my cell opens into an empty room. Both beds are neatly made, and the only thing revealing that there are two of us living here now is a half-made ribbon on a weaving tablet, neatly folded on the other bed. I run my finger along the ribbon. Its texture is like in Valeria's larger work: smooth, dense, skilfully shaped. Without openings you could see through. Behind the window, beyond the forest of webs, the soft lights of the city are slowly flickering to life. I shake the glow-glass awake and take the opportunity to examine my skin all over. It has turned more difficult since Valeria moved into the cell, because I am rarely alone. All I can find are the familiar birthmarks and callouses. I shiver as I get dressed; the room feels crammed and cold. I take to walking along the corridors of the house.

I like the Halls of Weaving best when there are no others there. The rooms that can get crowded, stuffy and sometimes noisy in the working hours feel spacious, fresh and silent. The unfinished works in their wooden frames sleep undisturbed. The Tapestry Room at the far end of the building is my favourite. No tapestries are woven in the house any more; Weaver chooses a few every year to be auctioned off, and their value sustains the house for another year. The old tapestries are made of silk yarn, now impossible to spin, because silkweed died from the seas centuries ago. Their colours are still unfaded, and when I wish to be alone, I often walk among their green trees and flame-coloured flowers and ice-blue waters. The red-dye of blood coral glows brightest of all in them.

On my way I pass the hall where my seat is, and something makes me stop.

There is movement in the darkness of the hall.

Most glow-glasses have gone to sleep and the foldable doors are closed. I wait for my eyes to adjust to the half-dark. Yet I am sure already before I see her clearly, because

I recognize the spot in the space of the room. I am always aware of it, the zone she occupies while working. Her hands move ceaselessly, anticipating the exact density of the yarn and unravelling the knots even before they are formed. She sees with her fingers. I can only see her backside, but it would not surprise me if her eyes were closed.

I take soundless steps towards her. She is so focused on her work that she does not notice my presence. I stop behind her, a short distance away.

'Valeria,' I say.

She gives a start and turns around. Her face is wrapped in shadows, but I see tears drying on her cheeks. I feel like an intruder and turn my eyes away, look at her work instead. I only realize now that it looks different from the usual wall-webs. There is a pattern forming, the start of something complex and new, although it is too early to tell what shape it is going to take.

'What are you weaving?' I ask.

Valeria frowns. Her face tenses. She whimpers, and her eyes well up again. From pain or grief or both, I do not know.

'You don't need to tell me,' I say.

I see her thinking about how to explain this without words. The empty space of silence grows around her like a shadow. When I imagine the agony every sound must create, I feel it as a disease-like prickling at the root of my own tongue. I wish to wind my voice into a skein and hand it to her, even if only for a brief moment, so she could shape from it the words she needs and tell me what there is to be told.

Valeria places the shuttle in her lap and rolls up her left sleeve, revealing the lines of the annual tattoos on her arm. She presses her palms together, lifts them to her cheek and tilts her head against the back of her hand like onto a pillow. She closes her eyes. She breathes deeply with her eyes closed.

'Something . . . to do with night-rest and sleep?' I ask.

Valeria opens her eyes and nods. She runs her finger along the annual tattoos and taps one of them in imitation of the movement of the tattoo needle. She forms a pillow with her hands again and pretends to sleep.

'And tattoos?' I say.

The sound of footsteps carries from the outside, but they do not approach. The water of the algae-pool splashes and its surface shatters. Someone is filling a glowglass. Valeria nods and repeats the series of movements. Tattoos, night-rest.

'The tattoos . . . help you sleep better?' I try. It does not sound sensible, but it is all I have to offer.

Valeria frowns, moves the shuttle next to her on the seat and gets up. She traces the surface of the web with her fingers. I understand she is drawing the invisible pattern that is not there yet. Her hands trace several long lines that run from the centre of the rectangular web radially towards the corners and edges. She draws a circle at the centre of the web, tapping at it emphatically several times. Finally she shapes an outline around everything that resembles a fish, or perhaps an eye.

I stare at the pattern in the air, in my own imagination. In her mind, where I cannot see.

'I'm sorry,' I say.

Valeria stares at me through the half-dark.

'I do want to understand,' I say.

Valeria's shoulders fall a little. I see her eyes tear up again. I see her fight it, and lose. She begins to cry, quietly, without loud sobs. I place my hand on her arm. The warmth of her skin hidden by the fabric flows into my fingers and deeper, settles into a glow inside me. I almost pull her into an embrace, but I know nothing about her, and I have no words that will help. We stand there, keeping a distance that does not seem quite short enough or quite long enough.

'I will try again,' I say eventually. 'And again, and again. Until I understand.'

Valeria offers me her hand. I shake it. It feels strangely formal, and yet binding at the same time, something I cannot turn back from. She holds my hand for longer than I expect. When she lets go, I do not have many words left.

'Are you staying here?' I manage to ask. 'You should get some sleep.'

Valeria sits down and picks up the shuttle.

'I won't tell anyone,' I promise. The words leave my mouth the same moment I understand there is no need for them. Weaving outside the working hours is not forbidden. It is just that no one ever does it. It would be considered unusual, but not punishable.

Yet Valeria nods, her face serious. I sense the words 'thank you' from her.

I cannot help looking behind me once before I walk out. To my surprise, she looks back.

The heavy weariness of the day pours into me, and I feel sleepier than in ages. The Tapestry Room no longer seems inviting. I return to the cell, close the curtains and lie down in the dark.

Sleep sinks me without warning.

The spell settles into my limbs slowly, before I see the creature approaching. When its dark, faceless form walks towards the bed, I am bound in place.

Its shape is not different from mine, its outline could be my own. It climbs astride me and seizes my wrists. Black waters rise in me, pushing the terror ahead of them, and I struggle against it, try to lift both my hands onto the creature's chest and shove it away. Only my eyes move, and every sound is crushed in my throat.

Behind the visitor's black edge flares an orange-crackling light, like a fire the heart of which I cannot see, only the halo emanating from the flames. The creature's silhouette is drawn sharp against it. Behind my door, on the night-empty corridors roams a cluster of whispers, as if all the weavers of the house are flocking outside my cell, ready to break in and see me in the embrace of the night-maere. Yet I know it is a fragment of the invisible world brought by the creature, a window it has opened for me alone. No one else would hear.

The night-maere's fingers are tight around my wrists. I already know all this: the way my breathing shrivels, troubled under the weight of the creature, how my chest tightens around my lungs, when the night-maere drags itself towards my face and sits down upon my heart. Its face that light never falls on approaches mine. Side by side with the susurrating background whispers another sound rises, low and slow-screeching like metal breaking under the sea.

My ear burns when the creature turns its head and its breath hits my skin. Hair brushes my cheek. The night-maere speaks to me, but I cannot distinguish its words, not one, and I do not understand what it is saying.

I try to scream, but the only sound that leaves my mouth is a narrow moan. Slowly it floats across the room, hits the wall and surrounds the other bed.

Valeria's hand is on my shoulder. The night-maere flees

the touch immediately. I am able to move again. I draw several heavy breaths.

'Light,' I manage to say. 'Wake up the light.'

Valeria shakes the glow-glass, and the globe begins to emit a soft shine. I know the night-maere is not in the room any more. It always leaves as soon as the chains give in and I can move again. Yet the terror never takes leave with it, but stays squirming slowly inside me after each visit, like a nest of snakes.

When I see the expression on Valeria's face, another fear takes its place.

Valeria has seen. She knows.

CHAPTER FIVE

Valeria stares at me. The blue-tinted shine of the glow-glass highlights the shape of her face, an unfamiliar landscape rising from the dark. I hear my own breathing, which fills the air between us, fills the room, fills the house and perhaps the city and the world, until there will be no one left who cannot hear it. I try to read in Valeria's expression, in her posture, what she intends to do. She sits frozen on the edge of my bed and does not move for a long while. Eventually something crosses her face; a decision, perhaps. She stands up. The mattress rustles as the seaweed filling is released from under her weight. She turns her back on me.

She will walk out of the door and get Weaver, I think. Even if I tried to run and made it as far as the city on the air gondola, the alarm would be raised everywhere by the time I stepped to hard ground from it. If I could reach the harbours and had something with which to buy myself a place on a trading ship, my tattoos would reveal me. No ship would let me on board, because merchants cannot afford to lose the favour of the Council. If I am not caught tonight, I will be found within a week, and from then on I will wear a mark upon my face and walk between one wall and the next, one lock and the next, one barred window and the next, and no one will know which other marks will appear on my skin, and which marks inside. I will never again breathe like free people, will not take another step that has not been confined with visible or invisible chains.

Valeria shifts, stops. I watch her back, tall and narrow, and her smooth shoulders. I wait.

She walks across the room to her own bed, sits down on the edge and looks at me. She raises two fingers to her lips as a sign of silence. My heart still beats blood into my veins, cold and hot at once. I do not know how to respond to Valeria. Her fingers fall to the blanket. She lifts it, lies down underneath and closes her eyes. I sit and wait. Sand flows in the hourglass on the wall. Its stream is black and blue and endless.

Much, much later I lie down again, but I do not turn my face away from Valeria or let the glow-glass fall asleep. Every time she moves, I start and my chest clenches.

The slow-growing light outlines the window. When the morning gong sounds, Valeria rises, makes her bed and gets dressed. She does not avoid my gaze, or seek it. Her movements are no different from those I have seen her make on other mornings while preparing to leave the cell.

We walk together to break our fast, and she does not turn towards the building where the Halls of Weaving lie, nor towards Weaver's study at its end.

My neck feels strained. I turn back to my wall-web and order myself not to look towards the corner of the hall until I have woven thirty new rows. If someone has noticed,

I hope they interpret it as concern for Valeria's wellbeing. This is her first day of work after she heard about her parents' death. Her face remains pale, her eyes red, but she is fully focused on work. She has only left the hall to go to lunch, where she sat next to me, and, once, to the lavatory. I saw through the windows how she crossed the square. She did not stay long. I try to estimate if she could have had time to go and see Weaver on the way back.

Silvi looks at me, but the look is bored, passing. It does not examine or cling. The weaver sitting on my right side gets up and straightens her loom, moves it a little towards the door, away from me. But she does not even glance in my direction.

On my way to supper I see Valeria among the group of weavers, but in the dining hall I lose her. After swallowing a few forkfuls of root vegetable stew I get up and leave to return to the cell. The chilled air of the room stands empty. I walk to the end of the Halls of Weaving where Weaver's study is. The door is slightly ajar. No one moves or speaks behind it. The glow-glasses on the corridor walls have dimmed down, but not yet fallen asleep.

I hear talk from the halls then, quiet words and long breaks in between.

I stand still, trying to pinpoint which hall the voice is coming from. When I begin to move, I take care to keep my footsteps as faint as possible. I recognize Weaver's voice.

'It is against all the rules.'

I do not hear a response. Something clatters to the floor. Perhaps a shuttle.

'Other weavers will notice soon, if they haven't already.'

Breath catches inside me, tries to hide in my throat.

I imagine the cell where I no longer live, the space

Valeria can fill alone from now on. Maybe she will move to my bed, claim my half of the closet. If I have left a mark of myself in the room, it will wear away quickly. I try to imagine the new cell in the other house, behind even higher walls. There is only darkness.

I hear Weaver again.

'Is someone out there?'

I have not been silent enough, after all.

'Come in,' Weaver calls.

I step into the hall, all muscles tight, my heart pounding.

'Eliana,' Weaver says. 'Shouldn't you be on night-watch?'

She stands in the corner of the hall. Next to her, Valeria sits in front of the loom. On the floor, at her feet, lies a shuttle from around which the yarn has unravelled slightly.

'Not tonight,' I reply.

Weaver raises her eyebrows but does not press the matter.

'I just told Valeria that her work is extraordinarily skilled,' she says, 'but that I cannot give her special permission to weave patterns that depart from a wall-web. Perhaps you could help her unravel the weave and create a new warp.'

Weaver's face is in shadow, and I cannot see her expression. Yet nothing in her voice suggests that she is not telling the truth or that she has something else to say to me.

'Of course,' I reply.

Weaver nods and approaches me. She walks past. At the door she stops for a moment and says, 'You are going to the House of Fire tomorrow, are you not?'

'Yes,' I say.

She nods again. Her tall back disappears around the corner and her footsteps draw further in the corridor.

Weaver has never failed to raise immediate alarm over a night-maere possession. She believes it is best to tell the truth right away, to cut the cord in one strike. I have seen it many times in the years I have spent in the house.

She does not know.

Valeria looks at me in the dusk. I pick up the shuttle from the floor and hand it to her. I study her face as she takes it. Her expression is focused, but not tense, and a short smile appears on it. I look at the result of her work. Weaver is right. It is carefully crafted and skilled. Even when they are half-finished, the patterns invite the gaze, draw a strange path you want to step on.

'Do you want me to help?' I ask.

Valeria's fingers squeeze around the shuttle. She shakes her head, cuts the yarn and begins to unravel the tapestry with slow movements.

'Are you certain?'

Valeria stops working and looks at me. I nod and leave. In the corner of the room the yarn runs in reverse, makes an emptiness where the patterns were growing.

The light shines dim in the cell. Our shadows are larger than ourselves. Valeria has returned to the room. She sits on the bed and stares at the grey surface of the wool blanket. I do not know what she sees. Another room, and there someone who is not me. Perhaps a pattern that is clear in her mind and does not exist for anyone else.

Finally I speak.

'Are you going to tell anyone?'

Valeria turns her face to me. She looks like she does not realize immediately what I am asking. Then she shakes her head.

'Why not?'

She stares at me, unmoving. I do not know what to think. I ask the question that has been bothering me since

I felt her hand shaking my shoulder, pulling me out of the night-maere possession.

'Aren't you afraid that you will catch it from me?'

Her gaze is direct, unfaltering, and filled with absolute certainty. She shakes her head again.

'Why not?' I say.

There it is once more, the unmoving stare through which I cannot see. She draws a deep breath, tries to form words, but they dissolve in her mouth. The sounds that emerge are unfamiliar to us both. I taste them as pain in my own mouth.

Yet I cannot be silent, because another question has been on my tongue for a long time, ever since Valeria came to the house. I keep my voice careful, stripping it of all demand.

'Why is my name tattooed on your palm?'

Valeria's expression grows more alert. She turns up her palm and opens her mouth, searches for the sound slowly and with care.

'Muh,' she says.

'Muh?' I repeat.

She shakes her head.

'Fuuh,' she says and finds the correct sound. 'Fatthh.'

'Fath,' I say. 'Is that it?'

Valeria concentrates.

'Myy. Fatthhh. Err.'

I think.

'Myy-fatthh-err. My father?' I look at her. 'Your father?'

Valeria nods. A quick unexpected smile changes her expression.

'Your father made your tattoo?'

Valeria nods again.

'Why?'

She sighs. I see tears in her eyes. I understand that forming just two words has taken enormous effort, and it is all she is capable of for now.

'It doesn't matter. Another time.'

Valeria closes her eyes and her expression closes too. We sit in the cell, and outside night scratches the walls. I do not get up. I do not walk across the narrow strip of floor separating the beds, and I do not sit down next to her. I do not place my hand on her skin, because I have no permission to do so. Somewhere within other walls people press against each other, and the air is a little lighter to breathe for them. But all we have is a wordless space and thoughts drowned in it, and no bridge across.

I spread a shawl over the glow-glass and turn to the wall. Later, after the last light of the globe has fallen asleep, I hear the small sounds Valeria makes whenever she does not want me to know she is crying.

We leave the house after breakfast. The mist rising from the canals swells past us on the paths of the web-maze and on the city streets. A red flag waves on many rooftops in the Hospital Quarters: no space for new patients. Valeria walks next to me narrow and tense as a tight-strung cord, closed within her own grief. I think of taking her hand in mine but dismiss the thought. When she takes the first wrong turn, I assume she either knows a shortcut I do not, or is disoriented. I say nothing. We can always return to our route in the next block.

When she takes the second one, I think she does not know the way.

'The House of Fire is in the other direction,' I say.

Valeria does not stop. She turns another corner, straying further from the route.

'Valeria,' I call, because she is a few steps ahead of me.

She stops and looks at me. Her mouth is tight, her gaze direct, and something cracks inside me when I see the grief behind it. She nods, just once, and continues to walk. I realize she is going somewhere else, whether I am going with her or not.

'I can't let you go alone,' I say. 'Weaver sent me to accompany you.'

She stops again and makes a gesture with her hand.

I think for a while. We could both get in trouble for this. She repeats the gesture: *follow me.*

Clouds drift further. Sunlight falls upon the mist. She stands as a sharp silhouette in its hazy wrap.

I follow.

Valeria leads me towards the north side of the island. We cross Halfway Canal and walk along the narrow streets. Smaller canals break the landscape, their flow slow and their edges stained from dead algae. The water is murky, and nothing seems to move under the surface. A strong, metallic reek rises from the canals, with a subtle undercurrent of rotting flesh underneath. Gondolas come and go with their cargo of blood coral and red-dye, and the sky is splintered by the high outlines of dye factories.

I no longer know where we are. She could be taking me anywhere. I could turn away, or I could give up all maps and trust that her path will carry me.

We stop in front of a large house. One of the fish-shaped drainpipes decorating the edge of the roof has split in two. Another is missing altogether. The balcony rail above the entrance is rusty. There is a niche in the outer wall with the pedestal of a statue in it, but the statue is missing. Valeria lifts the heavy iron knocker and knocks four times.

A woman whose bare arms are covered in images of tree branches with snakes gracefully curling around them opens the door. Her expression changes when she sees Valeria. She pulls her inside.

'You too,' she says to me. I cross the doorstep. She pushes the door shut. Her hand is quick, the screech of the key sharp in the lock. She looks at Valeria's face for a moment, during which the flames on the torches shiver and change the shapes of shadows, on the walls, on the floor, on all of our skins. Then she pulls Valeria into her arms.

She is a head shorter than Valeria. After a spasm-like embrace, she draws away and stares at her.

'What has happened to you?' Her face is like a fruit that wrinkles and dries before my eyes. 'I have been looking for you for weeks!'

Valeria points at her mouth and makes a sound. A tremor of pain on her forehead follows it.

'What is it?' the woman asks. 'Tell me.'

Valeria glances at me.

'She cannot,' I say.

The woman turns to stare at me in turn.

'I will throw you out this very moment,' she says, 'if you don't have a damned good explanation for what is going on. What happened to Valeria? Who are you?'

I tell her my name and craft.

'She was attacked. She sought refuge in the House of Webs,' I say. 'We are on our way to collect her parents' ashes. Who are you?'

As the question leaves my mouth, I realize I know the answer. The woman's face darkens. I glance at Valeria. Her eyes are red, but there are no tears in them. I want to step closer and touch her. I do not.

'Yes, the ashes,' she says. 'I thought that task had been left to me. My name is Irena Petros. Valeria is the daughter of my deceased brother, Jovanni.' She wipes her hand on her leather apron and offers it to me. I shake it. The sea-wool of her fingerless glove is coarse against my palm.

Irena turns back to Valeria and pulls her into a wordless embrace. They remain there for a long while. I hear Valeria sob, and I feel like an intruder in the room. This grief is strange to me, but they inhabit it together.

Eventually Irena detaches herself from the embrace. She looks at Valeria carefully and strokes her cheek.

'What have they done to you?' she asks quietly.

Valeria opens her mouth with reluctance. I have noticed she avoids doing it. I thought it was because of the pain. Now I realize she does not want people to see.

Cold horror appears on Irena's face when she understands.

'Monsters.' She drops the word like it is poison on her tongue. 'I should have believed Jovanni when he told me.'

I wait for an explanation, but Irena does not give one. She rests her hands on Valeria's shoulders, concern in her eyes.

'Are you in a lot of pain?' she asks.

Valeria shakes her head slowly.

'I thought our house-elder had already been in touch with you to let you know Valeria was alive and receiving medical care in the House of Webs,' I say.

'I haven't received any messages,' Irena says. 'I thought she too might have been killed in the accident, perhaps washed away by the floods. She should have come to me immediately after she was attacked.' She turns to Valeria. 'Why didn't you?'

'She has not been well,' I say. 'I think she was also

afraid to leave the house. That the attacker would pursue her again.'

Valeria looks at me and nods.

'Do you know who attacked her?' Irena asks.

'No.'

She looks contemplative.

'Is the City Guard investigating the matter?' she asks.

'They came to the House of Webs once, but we haven't heard from them since.'

Irena's face focuses towards me, examines.

'Is that so?'

Valeria makes an annoyed sound to show that she is still present.

'Did you see the attacker?' Irena asks her.

Valeria shakes her head and places hands over her eyes. Then she raises two fingers.

'But there were . . . two of them, you say?'

Valeria nods.

Irena turns to me.

'How was she when she came to the House of Webs?' Irena asks. 'Did she have other injuries, anything else unusual?'

Valeria grasps one hand between the fingers of the other.

'No other injuries,' I say, 'but something else. Do you have any glow-algae light at hand?'

Irena looks at me warily.

'Why do you ask?'

'It's the only way we can show you.'

'As it happens,' Irena says, 'I do.' Her tone is sharp and strange.

Irena gestures for Valeria to take a simple wooden seat at the table. I realize this must be the room where she receives the clients who are coming to get tattoos. There are needles and inks on the table, and intricately designed patterns that could be laid out on human skin. Irena walks to the other end of the room, opens a door in the corner and disappears through it. She returns a moment later, carrying a glow-glass globe.

'Where is it?' she asks.

Valeria turns up her palm and offers it to Irena. Irena brings the glow-glass close to her skin. The shape of my name grows out, white-bright. Irena's face changes, as if the letters mean something to her.

'Invisible ink,' she says. 'My brother was well prepared. Too bad he couldn't foresee everything.'

'Do you know what the letters mean?' I ask.

Irena looks at me.

'Do you know what the tattoo says?' she asks.

'My name,' I say. 'Eliana.'

'Would you let me speak alone with Valeria for a moment, please?' Irena's tone tells me it is an order rather than a request. 'There are a couple of chairs in the room next door.' She nods towards the door in the corner.

I give a slight bow. Valeria nods at me. I step into the other room and hear Irena close the door behind me.

No fires burn in this room, but glow-glass globes hang in three corners. The fourth hook juts bare from the ceiling. The blue shine of the glasses seems to be falling asleep, shrinking. The walls are full of drawings made on paper, but there is not a single picture of the Council. I realize I did not see one in the other room, either, or on the outside walls. That is unusual on the island.

There is also a small bookshelf in the room. I pick up a book and expect to see its pages filled with images. Instead, I find words. I place the book back on the shelf and pick another one. Again, the pages are crowded with words. They describe places outside the island: strange animals, other cities.

Either Irena knows how to read, or she has a lot of clients who do.

The door isolates sound well. I cannot hear anything from the other side. I return the book to the shelf. Time gnaws at the walls, far away the sea clings to the wind and never stops moving. In strange rooms pens scratch marks on paper, fingers run along threads, threads take a different shape and begin to lose it as they do.

Eventually the door opens and Irena invites me to enter the room again.

'I will call for a messenger to take a message to your house-elder today,' she says. 'I will tell her about your visit. I believe, and Valeria agrees,' she glances at Valeria, who gives a nod, 'that the House of Webs is the safest place for her for the time being. If we learn anything else about who might have attacked her, I ask that we keep each other informed.'

'I agree,' I say.

'Take good care of her,' Irena tells me.

I promise I will, although I have not received any of the answers I had hoped for.

We stand in a large hall and wait. Valeria stares at the dark walls, unmoving. The light of the flames burning in the wide fireplace flickers on her skin. I wish I could step closer, reach my fingers towards the heat.

A man in a red jacket steps through the door, carrying an opaque glass urn. It is no larger than a portable glow-glass globe. He hands the urn to Valeria. Valeria's face does not stir, but I hear an unusual weight in her breathing.

'This is both of them,' he says. 'I need your mark here.'

He hands her a piece of paper and a pen. I offer to take the urn, and Valeria places it in my hands. She draws an X at the bottom of the paper. I glimpse the text, but do not let my understanding show. It is important not to look away too fast, or to stare for too long.

'That will be everything,' the man says. 'I am sorry for your loss.'

He holds the door open for us. Valeria does not look at him as we leave the room. The air outside stings and dulls, ice on our bones.

'Is there somewhere you want to go?' I ask.

Valeria takes the urn from me. She stands on the street, her face blank and her eyes turned down. I expect to see tears falling on the lid of the urn, but there are none.

'Or do you want to keep it for now?'

She moves her fingers slowly across the lid. I see dust on her fingertips, lines on the glass where her touch has crossed it. They had not even bothered to clean the urn in the House of Fire after picking it from a dusty storage shelf. Slowly Valeria shakes her head.

'I know a place,' I say.

The black cliff stands apart from the lights and crowds of the taverns, fish markets and loading wharfs of the harbour. From here, you can see the tides beating the shore, and the ships as they come and go. I used to come here with my family, when my parents were still alive. As children, Janos and I would invent stories about the faraway lands the ships were sailing to: blue and bright vaults of ice, forests bathing in rain, hot-baked sand and streets so far inland those who walked them had never known the scent of sea. We used to imagine all the adventures we could have in those places. Now I am old enough to know I will probably never leave the island. Neither will my brother. Few people do.

The wind tugs at our clothes. Valeria kneels on the rock and places the urn in front of her. She is quiet, her movements bare. She does not look at me. I squat down next to her.

'I paid my respects to your parents,' I say. 'In the Glass Grove. I wanted to make sure they had food to make the journey to Our Lady of Weaving.'

Valeria turns to look at me. I can see that she is finally crying. Tears run down her face, her upper lip under her nose is glistening. She hugs the urn with both arms, pulls it close to her, and shakes with sobs.

'Do you want me to go?' I ask.

She grasps my hand and holds it tightly. I stay where I am.

The tall tide crashes to the shore. Seagulls shriek, sharp-winged. I taste salt in my mouth, and water.

Valeria gets up, takes several long steps towards the edge of the cliff, and I feel a jab of chill when her warmth is taken away from me. For a moment I think she is going to continue walking, through the air until the air gives in and the sharp stones and hungry waves below will pull her down. But she stops at the very edge, and with one swift movement flings the urn into the abyss. The lid stays in place all the way. The urn makes a distant splash and floats for a few moments, then the weight of water fills it and it becomes part of the sea.

The wind wraps Valeria's hair into knots. I walk closer and stop. She is only a step away from me, the final one. I take it and throw my arms around her. My heart beats heavy beats, each one of which I feel separately, twining her grief into me and simultaneously cautioning me of a line I may have crossed. I half expect Valeria to push me away, but she does not. Her breathing is a heavy downpour, and she shakes against me. I hold onto her until she is still. A teardrop falls onto the back of my hand. It does not take long for it to cool down.

We stand there for a long time. I feel tiredness from walking in my muscles, and she seems weary from crying. A blister has grown on my sole. The day descends slowly closer to the sea, the sea rises and falls, pulls the night nearer, obeys the swelling and shrinking of the moon. Nothing stops.

It is already dusk when we make our way up the hill through the maze. Winds fray the wall-webs and stones grow a little thinner under our footsteps. Moths stuck to bright glow-glass globes among soft yarns have the shapes of fallen leaves, or hearts embroidered on fabric.

Valeria goes straight to bed. She will not move, or look at me. It is cold in the cell. I pull my own blanket from my bed and spread it on top of her, spread rest and darkness.

'Are you hungry?' I ask. We have not eaten since the light lunch we had before leaving the house.

Valeria is quiet. She curls up more tightly inside the blanket. I touch her shoulder, without weight. Unintentionally my fingers brush her neck. The skin is warm and smooth. I pull my hand away, a little faster than I had intended.

'I will go and see if I can find something,' I say.

I hear nothing but quiet breathing as I leave the room.

We are not supposed to steal food from the kitchen, but everyone does it from time to time. I find a few dry heels of bread waiting to go to the hens, a couple of apples that do not look too maggoty and a bowl of nuts, of which I push a fistful into my pocket. There is nothing warm to eat or drink at all, and the house is as cold as a stone at the bottom of the sea in midwinter.

I head to the sick bay. I find Alva looking sweaty and exhausted.

'Please don't tell me you are catching it too,' she says.

The curtain is slightly open. All six beds are taken, and there are four mattresses on the floor. A violent rash stains the faces that I can see, and the air is thick with coughing.

'I'm fine,' I said. 'I was just wondering if you could make one of your herbal brews for Valeria. She has had a rough day.'

Alva wipes her brow. Her hair is escaping from under the scarf she wears.

'Who hasn't?' she says. 'But you could actually trade in a favour for me. I have run out of poppy. I have water-graphed the Hospital Quarters to send me more, but I haven't received it yet. I know Weaver keeps an emergency supply in her study. Do you know what poppy looks like?'

I have seen her use it often in her medical brews.

'Yes.'

'It will be on the shelf behind the tapestry that shows Our Lady shaping the Web of Worlds from starlight. Third or fourth jar from the left, top shelf. Look inside just to be sure, and bring me five poppy heads.' When I do not move immediately, she adds, 'I will need it for Valeria's brew.'

Without further questions, I go.

The building is full of shadows. Nothing moves in the Halls of Weaving. The door of Weaver's study is closed. I knock. The algae drifts in the glow-glass pipes, its shine nearly gone out. I knock again. When the silence is not broken, I push the door open.

Dusk floats in the room. Far below the window the world is kindled and extinguished again, insects open their wings or close them in the hollows of the coming night. The table is empty, wiped clean.

I find the jar on the shelf behind the tapestry. *Poppy*, the label says. I lift the lid and look into the jar. There are only five heads left. I take them all.

The air remains still. Then, unexpectedly, it moves. I feel the draught on my bare neck.

I know immediately which direction it is coming from. A sharp-edged streak of darkness splits the corner of the room. The low wooden door was still closed when I stepped in.

I could turn away and forget about it.

I walk past the watergraph to the door in the corner, push it open and step into the darkness, which grows around me and embraces me like a long-abandoned home.

CHAPTER SIX

The space is bigger than I had expected. I can sense it from the vastness of the air and the sound of my own footsteps before I see anything. The only source of light in the room is the narrow wedge falling through the chink in the door. The far end fades into a dense darkness in the distance. The walls are bare stone, coarse-surfaced boulders on top of each other, and the ceiling arches into a vault above. A thin smell that would be pungent if it were stronger floats in the air. It makes me think of the cat I had as a child and the dead rats it would sometimes drag into the house.

The length of the room is trailed by webs unlike any I have seen before. They begin somewhere in the thick shadows of the dark end and pour towards me. The translucent threads are arranged into ever-changing patterns that flow, meld and morph into each other. The petrified webs of the Glass Grove surface in my mind. The paths of these threads resemble them, but instead of being frozen and worn away by time, the webs before me are alive, they bend and grow with each moment.

I touch the threads with my hand. The material is exceptionally fine: thinner even than the silk thread of the old tapestries, yet persistent and strong enough to capture a large animal.

Or a person.

The light strands undulate silently in the draught, cold as if it is rising from the guts of the sea, beyond the reach of the sun. The webs are long and narrow, and there are corridor-like chasms between them.

Something moves at the other end of the room.

Everything in me tightens and lapses. The fright settles as a tremor in my legs. My body wants to turn and flee. Yet I remain still, and under the thoughts tensed to a breaking point, others surface. How tired I am to carry my nights alone, to look away from what must remain hidden from the eyes of the island. To pass the doors I wish to enter, to hide my darkness and fear that it will trickle out, for everyone to see. And the webs stretch in all directions around me: who knows how tightly they will pull me into their embrace, if I turn now and get caught in them in my rush?

I keep every step as faint and wary as I can and begin to wind my way among the webs. Their unfamiliar patterns sway spectre-like around me, maps of unknown lands or skies I will never see. I have watched Valeria arrange her yarn. But her patterns are different: impatient or tranquil, careful or constructed in a rush, bound by moment. The webs brushing my forehead, my back, my arms are slow like things long left behind, and no touch can break their calm.

My eyes begin to tire from the effort. The shapes grow ever more unclear, the further from the faint streak of light at the door I walk. A wind blows past me. The webs lash my face. It is only when I hear the whimper of the hinges that I understand what is happening.

The slam of the door is soft, almost as if it is pushed closed gently, and it seems to come from much further behind me than possible. The darkness falls dense and wide. When light is taken away, the space grows vaster, its confines less defined. I hear my own breathing: thin, nervous.

I hear something hit the floor.

It sounds like a heavy sack of grain striking stone, or a wooden beam wrapped in thick fabric. The first thump is followed by several others in a swift succession, like the first drops of starting rain on a roof. The suffocating web of countless threads absorbs their echo. I stand frozen in place. The sounds on the floor are repeated twice, then stop. Whoever or whatever is in the room, he, she or it has been aware of my presence since the moment I stepped through the door. Possibly before.

The creature is close, but I do not know how close. I cannot hear or feel breathing, but I do sense the air moving around me, before me. In the direction where the thumps came from. I stare into the darkness. I know that if there is any light at all, my eyes will eventually discern something, as long as even a wisp filters into the room.

Nothing breaks the blackness.

I try to make my breathing even. There is a low rustling and wheezing in the dark, as if a worker from the House of Fire who has scorched his lungs is giving a deep sigh. The closeness of the sound startles me.

The sound dies, then rises again. I focus and listen. The rustling rises and falls, stretches and falters. I begin to hear a rhythm. I begin to hear—

'. . . True.'

96

Words.

They shrivel and crackle like dry leaves in the wind, or like dead insects crushed under feet. Then they go quiet. Just as I start to wonder if I heard anything after all, the voice begins again. This time I am able to discern a full sentence.

'I suppose you could say,' the creature remarks, 'that we are now equal. But that would not be true.'

The words roll in the dark like waves, their crests clear one moment, the next, gone. I hear my own voice, but it feels like someone else is speaking.

'What do you mean?'

The pause is long enough for me to wonder. About the creature's shape, and size, and strength. If it has a poison sting, or hands to wrap around my throat. Eventually, the rustling returns.

'I am used to darkness,' the creature says. 'You are not.'

My unfamiliar voice speaks again.

'What do you know about me?'

The rustling is like a sigh, or perhaps a hum.

'Are you afraid?' the incorporeal voice says.

'Should I be?'

No response.

'Who are you?' I ask.

The voice lets out another sigh-hum.

'They once called me Spinner,' the creature says. 'But that is the wrong question. The right one is, who are you?'

'I'm a weaver,' I say, although it does not seem sufficient.

'A weaver,' Spinner says. 'And what else are you?'

I am quiet. The rustling grows in the silence again.

'Why are you here?' it asks.

I say nothing.

'This is not a test,' the voice says. 'I will not reward or

punish you based on your response. It has been a long time since anyone in the House of Webs asked so many questions.' Spinner pauses. Despite her words I have a feeling she is expecting something: not just a response, but a particular one. Words she believes are in me but I cannot reach myself. The hairs on my arms and nape of my neck stand up, as if a chilly wind blows across my skin, ready to float me towards the skies.

I wait for the creature to continue. When the silence remains unbroken, I speak.

'I haven't asked anything.'

'Not all questions are made from words,' the darkness replies.

I feel the air move and hear her limbs shuffle, and then something brushes my face. I shiver, not with repulsion or fear, but in surprise. The touch does not feel unpleasant on my skin. When I recover from the first shock, it is as if a light tuft of yarn is wavering against my face in a breeze. It is completely quiet. Thoughts rise in me distinct, their outlines sharp and unsheltered. I think of Valeria's tapestry, its strange, anxious message I do not know how to read. The letters of my name that bind me to her in ways I do not understand. I think of other marks drawn on her, and those that are missing: her bare, smooth skin.

'Humm,' the creature makes a sound.

The thoughts keep coming: the key scratching the stones of the city square under my foot, the empty corridors of the House of Webs and the sounds of pure sleep behind the doors. The black gondolas of the House of the Tainted. The night-maere holding me in place.

'Give me your hand,' the creature orders, and I obey.

The touch does not withdraw from my face. Another limb – or that is what I think, at least – reaches out to feel me. The light bristles study the shapes of my fingers, the lines of my palms, the indentations of my knuckles and the yarn-hardened spots on my skin. Eventually the touch pulls away and a dark silence takes its place. It continues for such a long time that I begin to suspect the creature has fallen asleep – or possibly receded so deep into its own world that my presence has lost all meaning. In my mind I begin to measure the distance to the door. Finally, the creature speaks.

'Just as I thought,' the voice says. 'You do not belong here at all.'

Chill rises from the bottom of the sea, crosses the water and enters the bleak corridors of this house, enters this room. I wrap my arms around me slowly, with caution. I do not know what my fingers might meet in the dark. My voice tries to shrink and vanish, but I chase the words out.

'Where, then?'

'Do you not know?' the creature asks.

I stay silent. I hear a long, swishing sound.

'This island and I,' the creature says, 'we have been here for a long time. Sometimes I hear it bemoaning its maladies to me, and I tell it about the ache in my joints, the fog that never parts before my eyes any more. But most of the time we are quiet and let the surrounding sea jib, grow calm to mirror the clouds and darken again. Winds come and go, and the light in the sky. And then there are you, your kind: your slight lives that flicker and fade in the moment that it takes me to create one thread. I know why you do not sleep at night, but you are only one of your kind. Why do you imagine I would care if you are imprisoned in this house or some other?'

'There are no prisoners in the House of Webs,' I say.

'Is that what you believe?'

'That is the truth.'

'The truth,' the creature says. Her voice wipes sand and dust out of its way, sweeps the stars behind the clouds. 'Do you look at this island and believe you see the truth of things?'

I am still looking for a reply, when the creature speaks again.

'I have upset you,' it says. The limbs withdraw from my skin. The air between us turns empty. 'Why have you come?'

Silence stands in the room, fog-like.

'Go,' the creature says. 'And come back when you are ready to tell me why.'

Rustling, stirring of dry twigs.

I turn and begin to fumble my way back to the door. The long paths of threads sliver the dark. I wonder if the room has somehow shifted its shape, stretched further and grown an infinite maze of webs where I will be looking for a way out forever. The touch of the webs begins to fill me with dread. They fall upon me like hands trying to pull me into an embrace. A couple of times my foot slips into the loops of the webs and I fight panic as I struggle to untangle myself. Not once do I hear anything from the end of the room. Eventually my hands meet emptiness, and there are no more webs ahead. I fumble towards the wall where I think the door is.

The door cracks open before I reach it and a wedge of light cuts the floor. For a moment I am frightened, because it looks much brighter than when I stepped into Spinner's chamber of webs. Has Weaver returned? Then I realize my eyes are betraying me. The light is the same. It simply looks different, because I have spent such a long time in the darkness.

I glance behind me. The other end of the room is pitch-black. Nothing moves there.

When I step through the door into the light, it is as if I feel a light touch against my thoughts, tangible enough to be a moth in my hair. But it could be just air flowing past me.

I take the poppy heads to Alva.

'That took a while,' she says, and begins to grind one of them in a mortar.

'I was looking in the wrong place,' I say.

She raises her gaze.

'Are you well?' she asks.

'Just cold,' I reply and wrap my arms around myself.

Alva stares at me, frowns and places a cauldron on the stove. The dark-boiling liquid swallows the poppy pieces. A strong, sweet stench rises from it that makes me think of rotting fruit and a herb garden roasting in the sun. When the brew is ready, I thank Alva and lift the hot cup with sleeve ends pulled to cover my hands so as not to burn my fingers.

The corridors are cold and quiet.

Valeria raises her head when I enter the cell. She takes the drink from me. I place a piece of bread and one of the apples on her bedside table. I take a bite of the other apple. It is mushy and a little stuffy, but not rotten.

'I'm sorry it took so long,' I tell her. 'Something happened along the way.'

Valeria's head jolts and her posture turns more upright, as if pulled by invisible strings.

'Nothing to worry about,' I say. 'I'll tell you another time.' *When I understand it myself,* I think. The trembling in my limbs is finally subsiding.

She finishes the brew, lies down and turns to face the wall. Her hair falls to reveal the skin of her neck. The light from the glow-glasses catches on the soft fuzz and falls asleep together with her.

Two days later, the squeaking of the air gondola cable blends with the background noises of the morning in the Halls of Weaving. I do not pay particular attention to it. Freight gondolas run between the house and the city several times a week, and not always at regular hours. When the hourglass on the wall has been turned twice after breakfast, a weaver on messenger duty appears in the doorway. She presses her head to the floor, gets up and walks to Valeria.

I do not turn to look, but sense the movement from the corner of my eye. I stare at my moving hands and at the threads before me. Soft footsteps approach across the floor and stop next to me.

'Weaver is asking you to come to her study,' the messenger says. I see Valeria's face behind her, paler than usual.

I place the shuttle on the seat.

The sun behind the window of Weaver's study draws a lattice of light on the floor. Weaver gets up behind her long table, and simultaneously with her two City Guards get up. Captains Biros and Lazaro nod. Weaver points at the hard wooden chairs on the opposite side of the table. I did not even know there were two Scolding Chairs.

'Please, sit down,' Weaver says.

We do. Biros and Lazaro sit down on their chairs at the same time. Weaver remains standing.

'Captain Biros and Captain Lazaro have good news,' Weaver says.

Captain Biros smiles, and it is not an unkind smile. In the bright daylight I see that he is a little taller than Lazaro and there are winter-faded freckles on his face. He directs his words at Valeria.

'We have caught the man who attacked you,' he says.

'He is guilty of other crimes, too,' Captain Lazaro says. His voice is calm and lower than Biros's. He has placed his notebook on the table. A drawing protrudes from between the pages: a gondola against a cloudy sky. 'We have been looking for him for some time.'

I glance at Valeria. Confusion has settled on her face.

'He is a Dreamer,' Captain Biros continues, 'who escaped before he was taken to the House of the Tainted. He has spent several months living in abandoned buildings in the Ink Quarters area.' He looks almost concerned. 'That is where the attack took place, is that not right?'

Valeria nods, but her confusion does not dissipate. I stare at Biros's, Lazaro's and Weaver's expressions. The lattice of light fades and appears again, as a cloud crosses the sun.

'He has confessed to everything,' Lazaro says and crosses his hands on the table. His gaze is direct.

'He is waiting for trial in prison,' Biros continues.

'The verdict of which we will let you know when it has been announced,' Lazaro says. 'Of course, you may be needed as a witness,' he adds and looks at Valeria.

'Just between us, he will probably spend the rest of his life in the House of the Tainted,' Biros says in an ally's voice. 'This must be a great relief to you both. You have of course been released from all suspicion.' He directs the last words at me.

I could stay quiet. That would be easiest. But I must speak. My voice is narrow and cautious.

'I thought Valeria was attacked by two men?'

Valeria nods and raises two fingers. Biros and Lazaro glance at each other. Biros's smile does not disappear. Lazaro blinks once too often.

'You must be mistaken, dear girl,' Biros says.

'The man confessed to everything and emphasized he acted alone,' Lazaro says.

Valeria shakes her head violently and turns her gaze down. Her eyes have begun to redden.

'The situation must have been very confusing for you,' Biros says. His smile melts into an apology. 'A dark night, a stranger who intruded into your home and was much stronger than you are . . . It is not surprising at all that you felt like there were two attackers.'

'She told you there were two of them,' I say. 'How could she be mistaken about something like that?'

'The shock and the pain can delude the mind,' Lazaro says. His fingers fumble with the edge of the notebook. 'And there are those who claim that Dreamers have unusual powers. Who knows what kind of illusions they are capable of creating?'

I draw a breath.

'Valeria is certain there were two of them,' I say.

Valeria raises her eyes and nods again. The corners of Biros's mouth settle into an expression that no longer resembles a smile at all. Lazaro clears his throat.

'Do you perhaps have some complaints about the quality of the investigation?' Biros asks. 'We are only trying to help.'

I turn to Weaver.

'But—'

Lazaro gets up. The chair grates the floor behind him.

'Complaints can be filed directly to the Council,' he says and turns to look at Weaver.

Weaver's body tenses and relaxes, as if the words are

already finding their shape in her mouth but dissolve and let others in to take their place. She breathes deeply, lets the silence settle before disrupting it.

'Of course the City Guard know what they are doing,' she says. Then she speaks to Valeria and me. 'You should both be overjoyed about this news.'

'Precisely,' Lazaro says. He turns to look at me. His face is more angular than Biros's, his smile narrower. 'It is a little surprising you are not more delighted.'

'Perhaps the situation has not yet entirely sunk in, Captain Lazaro,' Biros says.

'It's a relief, of course,' I mumble and bow. I remember what Valeria told me about the invisible tattoo on her hand. I do not wish to cause her more trouble, but I decide to take the risk. 'I just thought you might have found out something about the tattoo?' The question is transparent in my voice, although I do not pose it directly.

Outside, the day is pouring gold and smoke-coloured streaks in the furrows of the walls. Lazaro and Biros exchange a look that is not blank.

'Indeed, the tattoo,' Biros says.

'A coincidence, without a doubt,' Lazaro says and sits down again. His hands drop to rest on the table.

'A coincidence?' I repeat.

Lazaro opens his notebook, moistens a finger in his mouth and leafs through the pages until he finds the spread he is looking for.

'You told us when we questioned you earlier that you had never met Valeria Petros until she came to the House of Webs,' he says. 'How, then, could the tattoo have anything to do with you?'

'Or is there perhaps something you have not told us?' Biros asks. His face is kind again.

'Of course not,' I say.

I look at Weaver, whose eyes elude mine.

'If we agree that the tattoo is mere coincidence,' Biros says and stares at me intently, 'the case is clear, as far as we are concerned.' I nod. He directs his words at Valeria. 'You will be called to the trial, when that becomes timely. It may take a while since the crime is not greater.'

Lazaro closes his notebook and pulls on his gloves.

'It has been a pleasure working with you,' he says.

'A gondola is expecting you at the port,' Weaver tells the Captains. 'Now I would like to exchange a few words with my weavers.'

Biros and Lazaro get up from their seats. Light falls from behind them, draws their shadows within the shadow of the window lattice.

'Thank you for your co-operation,' Biros says. His smile is as pale as his freckles. He too pulls his gloves on. Their fingers are sharp, like claws. 'We will return to the matter if necessary,' he says, to no one in particular and yet to everyone.

They bow and march out of the door. The messenger waiting outside closes it after them.

Weaver sits down behind the table, facing Valeria and me. She takes a rolled-up stack of paper from the drawer and unrolls it.

'It is my understanding,' she says, 'that you visited Irena Petros in the Ink Quarters a few days ago. Would you like to tell me why? It was a working day. You only had permission to go to the House of Fire.'

So, this is the scolding. I look at Valeria. She nods at me.

'Valeria demanded it. She wished to see her aunt.'

'I understand,' Weaver says, 'but you should have requested permission.' She puts her fingers on the stack of paper. 'Irena Petros has sent a letter to me to request that Valeria may stay in the House of Webs. She has shown her skill as a weaver, of course, but this type of rule breaching forces me to reconsider.'

Valeria shifts on the chair next to me. The weight of Weaver's words gathers within me when I understand what they may mean.

'Will Valeria have to leave the house?' I ask. I listen to my body and notice that my shoulders have stiffened, my breathing narrowed.

Weaver's hand rests on the paper, cuts short the words running on it. Her eyes remain on me, examining.

'No,' she says then. 'But I do need to give a warning. After three warnings I must report undisciplined behaviour to the City Guard, and after six to the Council.' She turns to Valeria. 'Make sure this will not happen,' she says to Valeria.

I hesitate, but ask anyway.

'Are you certain that the City Guard have discovered the right culprit?' I choose the words with care. 'I find it hard to believe that Valeria is mistaken.'

Weaver's stare turns slowly from Valeria to me and back. She weighs her words for a long time. Eventually she speaks.

'You heard what the City Guard said. The case is clear.'

Valeria's face has turned into stone. She rises, although she has not been given permission. She takes a brief bow, and does not wait. She turns to the door and walks out.

'You may go now,' Weaver says, and I discern an unfamiliar line on her face. 'Both of you.'

I rise too. Valeria's reaction has made me restless, as if something inside me had been pushed into a small but relentless movement. The words I hear from my mouth surprise me, their sudden will to rise against Weaver.

'May I ask a question first?' I say.

I see Weaver is surprised, too, although she hides it with skill.

'Of course.'

'Irena said she had not received your message about Valeria. I thought you said she had been informed before.'

Weaver's face is unflinching.

'I sent the water-message as soon as I knew who Valeria was,' she says. 'There must have been a glitch in the communications somewhere along the line. That is all.'

'But—'

'That is all.'

That stops the rest of the words trying to get out. I am again an obedient resident of the House of Webs. Yet the restless movement inside me has not ceased, and I do not know if it ever will again. I bow and turn to go. I feel Weaver's gaze on my back, but I feel more intensely what burns behind Valeria's frozen face.

I catch her along the corridor. We are supposed to return directly to the Halls of Weaving and to our work. Instead, Valeria strides into our cell, her mouth a tight line, her stare full of ice. I follow. She slams the door shut, throws the nearly finished ribbon against the wall and pulls all the linen from her bed. When she tears the curtain from the window, light lashes her face and I see the tears running from her eyes and dripping to the floor from the tip of her chin. She grabs the glow-glass globe from the night table. I grasp her wrist.

'If you break that,' I say, 'you'll have to clean it up alone. And I can tell you, it's a rotten job.'

Valeria's arm twitches, as if she is going to do it anyway. Her breathing is heavier than mine. She is standing very close to me. Our chests and sides rise and fall out of synch, brushing each other. One by one I pick her fingers loose from around the glow-glass and place the globe back down on the table. Valeria stirs against me. Then she is still.

'You believe they are lying,' I say.

Valeria pulls away from me. An empty space takes her place. She looks at me, her face as close to spite as I have ever seen. I can almost hear the words, even if I have never heard her voice as it was: *Obvious.*

'But why?'

Valeria does not move, but her gaze is unyielding.

'Could this man be one of the two who attacked you? Did you see their faces?'

Valeria picks a sheet from the floor and folds the edge to cover a part of her face.

'They . . . wore masks?'

A nod.

'Would you recognize them, if you saw them again?'

Valeria stands still for a moment, her shoulders sagging. She whimpers and then slowly spreads her hands: *I don't know.*

'But you don't believe the man captured by the City Guard is either of them?'

A slow shake of her head.

Images flash in my mind, but refuse to connect into a whole: the tattoo, the scar-handed man in the museum, strange blood on stones. Something arises from the dark, withered words from an unfamiliar place.

Do you look at this island and believe you see the truth?

'Is this about something more than just you?'

I can see her thoughts moving, but I do not know how to read them.

'Help me understand,' I say. 'Please.'

Valeria thinks. Then she takes my hand, walks me to the window and points at the view outside.

'The landscape?'

Valeria tilts her head this way and that. *Not quite.*

'The hill?' I try. 'The houses, the canals? The city?'

Valeria raises a finger and nods. She focuses and opens her mouth.

'Eyech,' she says.

'The city, the city . . . the sea . . .'

She rolls her head and gestures at everything outside the window.

'Eyech. Chland.'

'Eye . . . Island? Island!'

Valeria almost jumps into the air and nods eagerly.

'Right. The island. What about the island?'

She stares at me, then turns her eyes to the floor. Her lips open slightly and close again. She looks up and draws a deep breath. She kneels on the floor and pushes her hands under her bed. I hear clattering and dragging, wood chafing against wood, as her grasp finds what it is looking for. Carefully she pulls something out from under the bedframe.

I recognize a lightweight, portable loom that is easy to fold and set up again. It is slightly smaller than the ones we use in the Halls of Weaving, and slanted, rather than vertical. I have seen similar ones in the storage rooms. They were used for making silkweed tapestries when the wall-webs were not the only thing produced in the house. She pitches the loom on top of her bed and I see the patterns I have seen before.

'You did not unravel it.'

Her smile is unexpected, like a falling star.

'How did you manage to smuggle this here?'

Her head tilts. Her smile stays. Of course: all the hours she has spent alone, recovering. No one looking. Not even me. Or at night, when I was walking the corridors. She would have learned my shifts and known when to work in secret.

Valeria points at the patterns, runs her finger along them. The lines are clearer now, they have grown stronger as the work has progressed. She has even woven in different colours, though sparingly. I can see compromises; yarn other than grey is difficult to come by. A palm-wide strip is still missing from the bottom edge of the tapestry. Despite this, I recognize the incomplete outline that floats water-green around the edges. I have seen it before, drawn in the air by Valeria, but now I realize I have also seen it countless times on the walls of the Museum of Pure Sleep, in large paintings and books placed in glass cases that portray the trading routes of blood coral and red-dye. Not a fish or an eye, but . . .

'A map,' I say. 'You are weaving a map of the island.'

Valeria grasps my arm, and one glance at her face is enough to tell me I am right.

At the centre of the tapestry I discern a dark circle from which eight points run towards the edges: the stone sun of the Tower. The highest point is directed at a simple but recognizable human figure that has his arm stretched out for tattooing. The point on the right leads towards a person sleeping peacefully. There is a human figure sleeping under the left point, too, but dark shadows hover over him. The largest has sat down upon his chest.

The annual tattoos, night-rest. Valeria tried to tell me

111

about them earlier. Seeing the Dreamer and the night-maere makes me feel uneasy.

'But why?' I ask.

Valeria points at the dark sun at the centre of the tapestry, then at the unfinished bottom of the hanging.

'It is not ready yet, I can see that.'

Valeria shakes her head and raises eight fingers.

'What is missing?'

Valeria closes her eyes and draws a deep breath. Patiently she points separately at each picture around the centre. She does it again. Her fingers move like celestial bodies, like seasons, but the circle is incomplete and I do not know how to read it.

'City quarters?' I make a guess. 'Canals? Air gondola routes?'

Valeria gives a sigh and turns her palm upward. I see my name glow on it faintly. She points at the letters.

'The tattoo . . . your father made?'

Valeria looks at me, waits.

'Does this have something to do with your father?'

Her expression is complex.

'Not only that? There is more to the pattern?'

She nods. I continue to make guesses, but all I get from her are increasingly frustrated sighs and eye-rolling. We are both getting tired.

'I'm sorry,' I say eventually. 'I'm sorry. But I won't give up. Let's just stop for today.'

Valeria stares at me, her gaze dark.

'Are you upset with me?'

She takes my hand and raises it to her face slowly, asking for permission. I nod. Her lips are dry against my fingers, their touch light as a moth's wing. I close my eyes and hear my own breathing. When she finally lets go, cold catches me again.

'I should return to the halls,' I say. There is an uneven strand in my voice, as if part of it has been burned away. 'Are you coming or staying?'

Valeria pulls the stool from under the window and sits down in front of the tapestry. When I leave the room, her hands are already moving.

The flood bells begin to toll just as I have stepped into the corridor for my night-watch round. I pay no heed at first. Yet when I walk into the first dormitory, I see through the tall windows something that should not be there. It is on the far edge of the view, a flicker in the corner of the room's eye, but it is there, and it moves.

Flames. Far away, but tall and real.

I walk to the window. The view is partially blocked by the wall circling this side of the hill. I am not abandoning my watch, I tell myself; I will come back later. It could be dangerous. It is my duty to find out.

The night air shrouds me with a veil of ice.

I climb on top of the wall outside the Halls of Weaving, and there it is, down in the city. Floods are swallowing the streets, but in the part of the island we all know, on slightly higher ground, a fire burns bright and hungry. The shapes amidst its restless flame-wings are tentacle-like, sharp-toothed like a sea monster's mouth.

The Museum of Pure Sleep is burning

in the gauze of stenches, amidst the fire, where green leaves curl around their edges and darken into bruise-like, there roots push deep into the ground and spread their persistent fingers, listen to the space closed from light and to the traces left there by other creatures. Where all eyes are turned away, the island bleeds into night-water and the landscape grows strange stains. The wings of a moth beat more slowly. A gull quiets, for the tongue has stopped moving in its mouth. People place their hands on their foreheads, or the foreheads of their children, feel the rash spreading on their faces and the invisible claws digging at their lungs; they burn with fever in their beds. Black gondolas carry glass coffins into the burial ground and ashes make murky blotches in the sea where they silently dissolve into the waves, ghosts of breathing cut short.

In the fire that is slower than flames she stays awake, and when sleep takes her, it carries her between unravelling walls, behind darkness-holding doors, over cracked floors, in the rifts of which black water rushes. It hands her words hidden within covers, in which everything is

114

inscribed, but the writing escapes her, and still she turns away. She wants the floors to be unbroken, she wants the walls to be whole again. She wants to step into the map of threads and follow the girl who walks before her, to fill the hole she has always hidden in herself.

She stands on the dream-cliff and raises her hands, and the dream-sea hears the call she does not know is the call of others, long gone. The strands of the Web of Worlds shine around her, made from sky and stars, ready to receive her touch: pull one thread, and all will unravel.

She drops her hands.

Fire swells like flood, eats words in its way, exhausts itself into ashes again, and in their wrap

CHAPTER SEVEN

The drumming begins faint, like the heartbeats of a great and strange beast in the innards of the island. Light remains hidden behind the grey sky. The air encloses my skin between all layers of clothing, from where its chill soaks into bones. I wish I had worn more sea-wool. The bare, darkened remains of the Museum of Pure Sleep jut out on the other side of the square. A dense forest of black City Guard uniforms rises at the root of the Tower. I have never before seen so many at a Word-incineration.

The crowd around us stirs, moves and rustles like foliage shifting in a breeze. Anticipation turns us all towards the archway separating the square from the wide canal. People's faces form a speckled, living mosaic that ripples and flares.

We all stare towards the canal.

It begins as a barely discernible spark, a shooting star sunken into the abyss of the morning, faint enough to be nothing more than an apparition. The rustling of the crowd dies down and the wind withers into calm, until the mute air rests steady and dense. The spark grows, bursts into a tall flame-tree glowing in the wrap of the mist. The music begins with a single long note, and one by one other threads of sound entwine with it, narrow and soft strands weaving themselves into a strange cluster. Slowly, smoothly enough to seem like it is floating in the air, a torch glides out of the mist and after it, ash-white gondolas bearing the scribes of the House of Words.

Soundlessly they tie the vessels to the wharves and step out of them carrying large chests. I search for Janos among them, but their faces are invisible inside deep hoods, and they are as quiet as the stones of the streets. A thin drizzle begins to gather on my garments, rather a veil of fog thickening from all sides than something falling from the clouds.

The procession of the scribes pours into the square in the rhythm of the drumming, an undulating ribbon through the arched gate. They carry the chests to the edge of the incineration field and open them. The chests are filled with words bound in worn leather covers.

These are the Dead Codices: their paper too old and brittle to be leafed. The scribes have carefully copied their words on strong, fresh paper over the past year so their contents would not be lost. When their weight leaves the island as midwinter smoke, the year is ready to turn and new growth begin.

The scribes begin to carry the codices into the incineration field glistening with oil. They tip them over inside the border marked with a red ribbon to make a layer of paper, ink and leather. The threads of the music fray away one by one. The heart-quakes of the drums continue faint. When the final codex is in place, the scribes form a soundless row beside the field. It is the firemakers' turn.

The firemakers move like flames, and they carry the

colours of blaze in their clothing. Their circle closes around the incineration field. They pour liquid on the ground from a large pail on wheels. Some years a rapid and harsh gale blows from the sea, trying to tear sparks from the blaze and fling them all over the square, scatter them around the island. But this liquid raises a wall which they cannot pierce; I have seen fist-sized stars of hell-heat burst and bounce from the flames, and I have seen their way cut short and them being hit back by the fumes.

When the whole field is confined by a narrow streak of liquid, the firemakers step inside.

The sky is dense and grey, the air murky with humidity. It could suffocate the sparks before they can catch. But the firemakers know the ways to feed the flames even in pouring rain. They carry saps and powders on their belts, scatter them on top of the Dead Codices to make certain nothing will interrupt the Word-incineration. A few among them place tall, lidded iron jars on the ground. When all others have left the field, they lift the lids and pick glowing-hot coals from the jars with bare hands. They throw them in the middle of the field, step back and let the flames swallow the codices. The drumming grows louder.

Another anticipation begins.

Every year, they choose their moment with care. The gathering of the people on the square does not move those who occupy the Tower. The music is mere wind to their ears, or creaking of faraway masts. Only the pattern of fire constructed, guided and started with firemakers' skill summons them to show their form. This year the fire climbs the wall of the Tower like a vine, until it reaches the balcony, encloses the rail and grows into a thick, sparkling curtain of fire. The curtain burns bright for precisely the time it takes for the crowd to gasp in awe.

When it goes out with the last drumbeat, the Council is standing on the balcony.

Their masks carved from coral shine in the colours of blood and flames, as if the echo of the fire remains captured in them: eight faceless figures above everything.

The crowd bows. I count to three before straightening my back. Next to me, Valeria does the same. When I get up, the Council is still standing in a row, unmoving. On another balcony below them, a law-reader appears. We wait. A faint chatter begins to grow on the square. Moving as one, the members of the Council raise their right hand, the coral-red palms of their gloves towards the square. The talk quiets at once. The law-reader speaks from the balcony in a voice that echoes in the very bones of the city.

'Today,' the man says, 'a law will come into effect that the Council has seen it best to pass in order to secure the wellbeing of everyone on the island.'

He pauses and glances at the paper he is holding.

'In the past few months the city has been haunted by an illness,' he continues, 'which has touched almost every family and household in some way. You know the symptoms: the rash, the cough, the blurring of eyesight, and eventual death. After a long-running investigation and deliberation, the Council has found out that what we all feared has come true. The dream-plague has returned to the island.'

Next to me, I see Silvi gasp and bow several times with her eyes closed. Her lips move, as she speaks to Our Lady of Weaving. Whispers and rustlings travel in the auditorium.

'Our medical advisers are in uniform agreement that this is a new strain of the illness, more contagious and far more dangerous than any we have seen before. But what is yet of greater concern,' here the law-reader takes a break, letting the audience hold their breath, 'is that there is a secret movement of Dreamers spreading the illness in our city. Their actions are ruthless and purposeful, and they pose a real threat. Their aim is to contaminate everyone, until life on the island can never be the same. They were responsible for the fire that scorched the Museum of Pure Sleep to cinders.'

An unrest sweeps through the crowd again, a wind tugging at anxious trees.

'According to the new law, anyone suspected of dreaming tendencies must be reported to the City Guard and imme-diately isolated from other islanders. Until now, we have believed that only Dreamers suffering from night-maere possession are dangerous, and their kind has been dutifully delivered to the House of the Tainted every year. As of this day, however, all dreaming must be treated as a threat. Protecting a Dreamer is a punishable crime, because it endangers the security of the whole city. The Council has spoken.'

The law-reader rolls up his paper, bows and vanishes from the balcony into the Tower. The Council takes one step forward. The crowd bows again, and when we straighten our backs, a vast cloud of smoke drowns their dark-clad figures. When it dissipates, the Council is gone.

I want to reach out and take Valeria's hand. I want to look at her to see if anything has changed on her face. Instead, I clap my hands together with the crowd and lose myself in the surge of ovation. I wonder how many others are hiding in it with me, afraid to close their eyes at night.

The fire on the square is still devouring words.

The blaze does not wear out until only a silent layer of ashes that have shed all colour remains.

* * *

A slightly bittersweet scent of ashes and burnt herbs floats in the air, wrapping the streets in a thin gauze that shivers in the early afternoon like a butterfly's wings. The weather is calm, and the smoke has not yet dissipated in the direction of the sea. Weavers stand around the field, scooping ash into large sacks. This year it is the turn of the House of Webs to gather the ashes. I find a place at the edge of the field and open my sack. The ash crumbles into a fine powder in my fingers, smoother than clay. Silvi, who is scooping it next to me, looks at me and her movements stop for a while.

'Are you well?' she asks.

A short distance away, Valeria bends down to collect white ashes from the ground. Some cling to her clothes, like mist or traces of a dream.

'It is just the smoke stinging my eyes,' I say. 'I never get used to it.'

I wipe a streak of tears from my cheek and feel the stain left on my skin by the blend of ash and salt water.

A girl of perhaps twelve threads her way through the ash-collectors. She stops to speak to Viola further away. I see Viola look around. Her gaze falls upon me. She turns to the girl, says something and points in my direction. The girl gives a slight bow to say thank you and starts walking towards me.

'Are you Eliana?' she asks.

I tell her that I am.

'One of the scribes sent you a gift.' The girl hands me a ball of yarn and waits, with her hand extended. I take the ball and dig for a coin in my pouch. I place it on the girl's palm. She curtsies and sprints towards the edge of the square. Viola winks at me. I ignore the gesture and look at the ball of yarn. It is coarse sea-wool dyed pale-green, sold by many market stalls. I push the ball into my pocket.

If the sun was not far behind the clouds, the shadow of the Tower would fall where I bend towards the ground.

Night wind is metal-sharp on the wall next to the air gondola port, a numb, salt-crusted finger brushing my bones. I am not on night-watch, but I do not want to sleep tonight. I left Valeria breathing deeply under the covers, moving like those who are not awake move. The Glass Grove glints in the distance under the half-moon; the clouds have parted, and the island is a rippling oval of soft silver lights, like a deep-sea creature mariners sometimes see in the dark before losing it again.

I turn the piece of coral hanging around my neck between my fingers. Its surface is coarse and porous. I hear footsteps and turn to look. The white hem of Alva's coat folds, wrinkles and unfolds against the sea-green of her thick overcoat, flipping in the wind. She climbs on the wall next to me. Silence hangs between us. A stretch of sea ripples on the horizon where I see dark specks, glimmers appearing and going out in them: trading ships anchored around the island.

'How are things in the sick bay?' I ask.

Alva's sigh drifts into the wind.

'Quiet, at long last,' she says. Weariness weighs her brow, the curve of her mouth. 'There are no new infections.'

Some twenty weavers have been taken from the House of Webs to the Hospital Quarters. A few of them have lost their eyesight, and others complain they see worse than before. Yet most have returned to work, and the illness has not killed any of them.

A cloud moves on the sky and the light of the moon

draws visible the hulls, masts and sails of the ships. The crews will have already seen the harbours, emptier than usual. They will have sent scouts to land and heard the message about the rash that tightens flesh from the bones, about the cough that scorches lungs into shreds. They will have heard about the fog that settles into eyes and will not dissipate. At dawn, if the wind blows from the right direction, the ships will turn back and carry their cargo to other cities.

'Do you think trading ships will stop coming to the island altogether?' I say.

Alva looks out to the sea. The shine of the glow-glasses on the wall falls on her face.

'Blood coral is too valuable to be abandoned,' she says. 'But there will be ever fewer ships.' She quiets and turns to me. Glow-glass lights stir in her eyes like thoughts.

'No one wants to carry home the . . . disease that they call dream-plague.'

She pronounces the last words slowly and with care, as if choosing them with great consideration. I stare at her. She does not avoid my gaze. She waits.

I have known Alva since I came to the House of Webs. She is probably the only one of its residents I am able to think of as a friend. She does not know everything about me, but still more than most others. Now I feel like she is leading the conversation to walk on a ground we have not visited before, reaching out a hand to see if I will take it.

That they call dream-plague.

The thought does not come for the first time.

Alva's gaze is alert. I too choose my words with care, offer her something to grasp.

'How do they know it's dream-plague?'

The moon disappears into clouds. Alva's cheeks twitch, her eyes narrow and open wide again.

'What do you mean?' she asks in a low voice.

I mean the night-maere on my chest, the suffocated moan on Mirea's lips. I mean the paintings of the Museum of Pure Sleep that now lie in ashes, and the tales of the guide: dark tumours on the skins of the diseased, death that came in mere days and from which few of those contaminated were spared. Not a word about a shattering cough or weakening eyesight.

'I mean,' I say, 'that I haven't seen anyone show the same symptoms we have been taught to look for and keep an eye on.'

Alva turns to look at the sea. Her voice is steady.

'You have noticed it too,' she says.

The silence widens between us again. She has spent weeks and months in the sick bay among those who have caught the disease. If the symptoms were the same as in dream-plague, she would have seen. I wonder how to take the conversation one step further.

'Why would the Council call it dream-plague,' I say, 'if it is something else?'

'Yes, why?' Alva says. The words linger in the middle of the silence, floating and growing.

'Do you believe them?' I ask.

Alva takes a breath, another. She pushes a wind-flung strand of hair under her scarf. She turns her face back to me and looks me directly in the eye.

'No,' she says. 'That's what you wanted to know, isn't it?'

We both know she has said something she should not have.

'Are you going to report me?' Alva asks. 'A healer who

124

doubts the word of the Council?' Her voice seeks lightness, but her shoulders are tense, her neck rigid as glass.

'I know how to keep a secret,' I reply.

Alva observes my expression. Something on her face changes. Stiffness does not dissolve from her body. She speaks again.

'I know.'

I shiver. A cold wind whistles through me, tears thoughts with it. Her tone raises a memory in my mind.

During my first winter in the House of Webs, I spent a week in the sick bay with a cough and shortness of breath. One night, throbbing images pulled me under the surface of sleep against my will. I woke up to chilling cold and a strangling feeling, but it was not the cough. It was the night-maere sitting on my chest. When it fled, I saw Alva standing nearby, holding a strong-scented, steaming bowl of water and a towel. I knew my eyes had been night-maere black and dream-song had sounded on my lips mere moments earlier.

She pulled me to a sitting position, placed the water bowl on my lap and covered my head with the towel. The bright, herb-infused scent of the steam rising from the bowl brought tears to my eyes and scorched my nostrils, but I was able to breathe again.

After that, I was wary in her company for months. When she never said a word about the episode, I eventually began to believe she had not seen my eyes. That she had imagined the dream-song to be breathing, wheezing with cough.

'How long have you known?' I ask.

She could still deny it, pretend she does not know what I am talking about. If she does not, I can. We could bury the matter in silence. The choice is hers. The choice is mine.

Something shifts in Alva's eyes. Her breathing runs fiercer.

'Don't misunderstand me, Eliana,' she says. Her voice is hoarse. 'I want to help.' I study her face. Its expression is bare and true. 'I've been trying to find a way. Every time someone has been taken to the House of the Tainted, I have wanted to raise my hand against it. But there's nothing I can do alone. If I had proof, and others to support me . . .'

Her voice trails off. The night is dark, the dawn still impossible somewhere beyond the horizon.

I nod slowly, once, twice. She has made her choice. I make mine. I am surprised by the tears that rise to my eyes when I make the decision to step in a direction from which I cannot turn back.

'I've never told anyone,' I say.

I wipe my face. Alva's expression does not ask, does not reject.

'Now you have,' she says and squeezes my shoulder lightly.

I sigh: out of relief, out of exhaustion.

'You should sleep,' I say.

Alva closes her eyes.

'You're right.'

She opens her eyes and looks at the piece of coral hanging around my neck. She takes it between her fingers.

'That is entirely useless,' she says. 'For you and everyone else.'

'I know.'

The light of the glow-glasses flares on Alva's face. She lets go of the necklace. It falls back onto my neck.

'Will you help me help you? And others?' she asks.

'How?' I say quietly.

Alva looks at me. She looks at the sea, and at her hands, and eventually at me again.

'I don't know yet,' she says slowly. 'But I'll tell you when I do.'

I nod.

'Thank you,' I say.

Alva smiles. It is like a flame behind her face blazes higher.

'You are right,' she says. 'I should sleep. And you too.'

I smile back. Alva waves her hand goodbye, turns. Her white coat flutters and flutters, and vanishes into the night. Winter-chilled stars shine like silver coins sinking into the sea, sprinkling their faint light on the streets and canals.

There is yet another hour less left of our lives, but something has changed while it passed.

I knock on the door four times, softly, so I would not wake Valeria. I pause and repeat the knock. We have agreed on a sign so she would have time to hide the tapestry when someone else is at the door. After a moment I hear four knocks in response from the inside. Valeria opens the door to a cell where the algae-light of the glow-glasses is awake. She has spread the tapestry on the bed. Eight masked figures have appeared in the simple map of the city under the dark centre: the Council. The bottom edge remains unfinished.

'What do you need to finish it?' I ask.

Valeria sits down on the edge of the bed and looks at me. I cannot read her expression. I sit down next to her.

'If you need more yarn, other colours or materials, I can try to get it for you,' I say. 'If—'

Valeria lets out a deep sigh and closes her eyes.

'I'm sorry,' I say. 'I just wish I could help.'

Valeria smiles: a weary smile, but not impatient.

'I can't sleep either,' I say.

Valeria takes my freezing fingers between her own. I feel like I could sense the invisible glow of my name on her skin if I shut my eyes. She rubs my cold hands and slides them into the pocket of my jacket, her own hands still around them. The woollen fabric is rough and encloses our fingers in a hidden space, quiet and dark and warmer than the air.

Our hands hit something at the bottom of the pocket.

I pull out the ball of yarn the strange girl gave me at the Word-incineration. I had forgotten about it. I turn it around. It looks like an ordinary ball of sea-wool yarn, the kind from which people knit scarves for winter. Unless . . .

Janos and I used to hide things from each other as children, and then give hints on how to find them. Whoever found the chosen toy or small stone or piece of ribbon with fewer hints, won the game. One of my best hiding places had been a ball of yarn. It had taken Janos days to find the piece of coral I had hidden inside it.

I feel the ball with my fingers. At first they meet nothing but the prickly softness of the yarn. But then, something rustles and crumples, presses a different surface against my thumb. I push the yarn aside and find a piece of paper rolled tightly and wedged at the centre of the ball. I manage to grasp the edges, and I keep the movement unhurried as I pull it out.

I unroll the note. It has been years since I have seen his handwriting, but I recognize it immediately. A simple map is drawn on the paper. There is also a time written on it, and one word: *Seashell House.*

Janos never sends written messages.

Whatever it is, it must be important.

128

'My brother wants to see us both next week in Seashell House,' I say.

Valeria has frozen to stare at me. The sheen from the glow-glass lights one of her cheeks and part of her chin. It leaves her eyes in the dark, but I see a chasm has opened in them.

'Is all well?' I ask.

Valeria raises a hand and puts two fingers up. She brings them close to my face and points at my eyes. Then she points at the piece of paper in my hand. Her lips have bent into a hard arc.

I do not take the meaning immediately. When she begins to repeat the gesture, I understand. Blood floods my face and it is too late to mend what has been broken.

I have forgotten to look at the words as if they mean nothing to me.

It would be useless to lie any longer, so I tell the truth.

'Yes, I can read,' I say and observe her expression. 'I learned as a child from my father's books, while I was looking at the pictures. I was not trying to learn. It just happened.'

Valeria is still.

'My brother knows. And now you. No one else does,' I continue.

Valeria turns her head very slightly. The blue shine of the glow-glass reflects in her eyes, stirs. A low, slow voice emerges from her throat. Her lips open, sounds push towards the roof of her mouth, attempting to make words without the guidance of the tongue that is not there.

'Ch-ee . . .'

She gives up, draws a deep breath and tries again. I follow the movements of her mouth, trying to imagine the tongue shaping the sounds.

129

'Ch-ee-' She swallows and forces the final letters out.
'-chh. Chh. Chee-ch . . .'

I want to place a hand on her knee to encourage her,
but I do not know what she wants. Her face struggles.

'Mmwee.' She sees I do not understand, and tries again.
'Mmee. Chee-achh mmee.'

She waits.

'Teach?' I say.

Valeria nods. I hesitate.

'Mm . . . me?'

Valeria nods again. Light spills in her eyes.

'Teach me?' The meaning of the words begins to unfold
for me. 'You want me to teach you . . . to read?'

A nod. A line surfaces on her brow and disappears.

'And – to write?'

Another nod. She waits for my answer, her face in half-
shadow, ready to turn to me, or away.

This time I nod. I realize how much easier everything
can be for both of us. And the most important thing,
which is written all over her expression: with the word-
skill she will finally be able to tell what happened to her.

'Of course I will teach you,' I say. At the same moment
as the words fall between us I understand it is the only
response I can give. Valeria knows things about me that I
am used to hiding alone. Now she must hide them with me.
I do not wish to ask it of her, but I have no other choice.

My fingers tremble a little as I loosen the cords of the
coin-pouch hanging from my belt and push my hand into
the pouch. I find the metal edge I am looking for. I pull
out the flat key with one end shaped like an eye. I place
it on my palm and offer it to her.

'Here. Take this as a pledge.'

Valeria breathes deeply and stares at the key, then at

my face. The shine of the glow-glass flashes off the key as she takes it from me. She gives a thank-you nod. She picks up the ball of yarn I have placed on the bed and unravels an arm's length of yarn. She breaks the yarn with her teeth, threads one end through the key and knots the ends of the yarn together. Then she puts her head through the loop. The yarn settles around her neck. She squeezes the key in her hand, looks at me and slides the key under her clothes.

I feel like she has not only accepted my offer. She has also offered a pledge of her own.

When we go to sleep, I imagine the warmth of her skin gathering around the key out of sight.

I walk in a narrow corridor where the floors are stone and walls are web, gauzes woven from silver-grey yarn which a draught sways like water does dead plants. My footsteps make an echo as they hit the stones: *tap tap tap*. The ceiling arches into a high vault and vanishes into dusk.

Behind the wall-web a shadow moves at the same pace as me. The sound of its footsteps is an echo of mine, *tap tap tap*, and its shape is not unlike my own. I touch the web and move my fingertips along the threads. The shadow on the other side does the same. I feel the touch of its fingers against my own.

'Valeria?' I ask.

The shadow withdraws, stops. I hear its breathing. It begins to move forward. The sounds of the footsteps fall on the stones in a swift succession, like the first drops of starting rain: *tap tap tap*. I follow the shadow.

Something clatters to the stone floor behind me. I turn to look and see a metallic shimmer. I take a few steps towards it. It is the same key I gave to Valeria, and yet it is not: a dream-key, shifting its shape before my eyes. A metal chain threaded through it leads to the other side of the wall.

The chain pulls the key slowly towards the wall. The key scratches the stones, begins to slide behind the bottom edge of the web. I grasp it. Someone on the other side of the wall yanks, and the key comes loose from my grip, disappears from sight. I am on my knees on the floor. A shadow whose outline could be mine has knelt behind the web. I grasp the web and rip it. The wall-web of waking would never give in under my hands, but in dreams my strength is different, and the web splits in two. Behind there is another web-gauze, and through that I discern a shadow. I tear this web away too, and behind is yet another. I shred layers of web, and my fingers grow sore and my arms ache until I remember my dream is mine to command. I want the webs to vanish and the shadow to show itself.

The shadow is in front of me, its back turned to me. In the half-light of the dream its clothing is black, or perhaps sea-green. I hear the shadow's rustling breath. The shadow moves, begins to slowly turn its face towards me, and I see it does not exist. It is the face of the night-maere upon which light never falls and the features of which I can never discern. It looks directly at me, and its name is darkness.

The night-maere raises a hand towards me. I get up and flee. I run along the narrow dream-corridor, an undulating alley of webs, and the footsteps of the night-maere echo after my own, *tap tap tap*. I want myself out of the corridor, and the corridor is gone, a hall in its place, dusk-clad, tall enough for its roof to be the top of a tower. On the edges of the hall stand people. Their eyes are

132

closed, their faces unmoving, and their skins are etched with tattoos, like wounds, like chains.

The night-maere stands at the centre of the hall and approaches me. I want the walls to fall away, I want an open landscape and light. But the escape has worn off my strength, and the dream does not obey. I push the wall with both hands, I want it to be air through which I can step, but there is only stone on my way that does not give in, and the touch of the night-maere is only a step away from my skin.

I open my eyes in a cell where the glow-glass shines in the dark, faint as a moth's wing. Valeria's face is discernible as a light, sleeping patch across the room. The night-maere is away, but I can still sense its touch.

I do not sleep again before morning.

CHAPTER EIGHT

The building must have been beautiful once. Its husk still stands tall among the ruins of the neighbouring houses, on a stretch between the Ink Quarters and the sea, where waters run deep grey-brown and their stench turns people away. The seashell-shaped chimneys are tinted green and white with algae and seagull droppings. We follow Janos's map: a narrow alley turns left and ends in a wall. There, hidden behind a thick growth of grapevine and thorny bushes, is a small door from which the paint has peeled off almost entirely.

I push the door. Then I push it harder. The wood swollen with humidity creaks, and a decayed strip drops to the ground from the top of the frame. I stare into a dark room where dust floats like sand above the seafloor. Valeria is close behind me. We step in.

The light of our glow-glasses falls upon piles of rubble floods have gathered into the room. The floor feels steady enough under our shoe-soles as we walk among the odd broken piece of furniture, fallen roof tiles blocking the way and dislodged pieces of a stone handrail. This must have been a sitting room once. A wide stairway rises at the centre. I am about to set foot on the bottom step to try its strength, when the shine from our glow-glasses grows bright enough to show the highest step. It ends mid-air, with nothing but a fall into darkness behind it.

We stop at the bottom of the ghost stairway, not knowing where to go. Valeria notices a jarred-open door in the corner and points at it. Before I have time to respond, a dark shadow detaches itself from the wall and begins to move towards us. Valeria gives a start, takes a step back and raises her glow-glass high.

The shadow stops and pulls back its hood. The light of the glow-glass falls on Janos's face.

'Valeria, this is my brother Janos,' I say. 'Janos, this is Valeria.'

Janos's expression is friendly as he bows at Valeria. Yet I see his shoulders have stiffened and his smile is wary. I realize I have made a mistake. He had hoped I would come alone. He eyes both of us.

'There is more light in the other room,' Janos says and nods towards the jarred-open door in the corner. He glances at Valeria again and I see he intends to say something, but does not.

The other room is nearly as tall as the first one. I discern a figure carved on the stones of the ceiling where the vault peaks: Our Lady of Weaving and her eight limbs holding the threads of all cardinal directions. A few of the glass panes of the skylight have broken. Misty daylight filters through from the outside. Shelves that have fallen out of joint in many places run across the walls, and dark-green algae drips from their edges like the hair of the drowned. Some have crashed to the floor into piles of cracked, twisted wood. I glimpse a slumped shape in the corner

135

and my breath catches, until I realize it is probably a water-gnawed sofa or armchair. On the floor lie shrivelled, torn covers and mushed, yellow-white scraps, like dirt-speckled wet feathers.

'This used to be a library,' I say. I can imagine the shelves, straight and steady, and the bright glow-glasses and candelabras in the bruises of the walls. I can imagine my finger running across the spines of the books, contemplating and choosing, picking a volume, weighing it in my hand.

'Yes, a long time ago,' Janos says. 'The house has been uninhabited for a hundred years at least.'

The story of Seashell House is one of the ghost tales of the island. The members of the merchant family that lived in the house perished one by one in strange accidents, by drowning themselves or from what was said to be the dream-plague. The last of them was sent to a Dreamers' colony during the Reverie Revolt, and Seashell House fell into disrepair, because it was believed to be cursed. This does not seem to have stopped looters. As far as I can see, there is nothing left of any value.

'We could both have got in trouble because of your letter,' I tell Janos. I cast the note into the canal on the way, because keeping it did not seem like a good idea.

Janos looks ill at ease. Tension has not disappeared from his shoulders.

'I know,' he says. 'But I couldn't think of another way. This could not wait until next month.'

Janos looks at Valeria. Valeria understands the situation and looks at me. She raises her hand and points at herself, then at the doorway to the other room. She stirs to leave. Janos's expression is annoyed and apologetic at once.

'Wait,' he says. 'You don't need to go. It concerns you as well.' He clears his throat. 'I think.'

Valeria manages something akin to a smile. She stops. I nod at her and send a look in Janos's direction I used to silence him with as a child. Valeria steps back beside me.

Janos pushes a hand inside his cloak and pulls out a bundle of fabric approximately as wide as two palms. As he begins to unwrap it, I see a leather spine I recognize as part of a codex. I see the word painted on the cover.

A cold wave travels through me, like an aftershock of stepping into chilled water. Valeria's body tenses next to me.

'What's this about?' I ask. My voice scratches the walls.

Janos has produced the whole codex from inside the fabric. I look at the leather covers holding the contents of the book. Apart from the one word there is nothing special about them. They are worn and brown, and could belong to any of the hundreds of codices that are spread on the square every year to be incinerated. Valeria stares at the volume intently.

'The cover has my name written on it,' I tell her.

A line appears between Valeria's eyebrows which looks deep in the light falling from the ceiling. I notice her fingers bending towards her palm, where the tattoo has woken to glow. Shadows are dense in the corners of the room.

'This codex was on its way to be incinerated,' Janos says. 'I saw it on the morning of the Word-incineration, when I was brought some volumes to add to the Dead Codices at the very last minute.' He pauses and ponders. Before he speaks again, I know he is thinking of his work. Scribes are expected not to share too many details about the practices of the House of Words, just as weavers are sworn to keep details about life in the House of Webs to themselves. Janos chooses his words with great care.

'Each codex in the House of Words is given a name

137

and a number. The name is dictated by the nameday calendar. I was moving the codices to the gondola, when I noticed.'

Not all scribes may have spotted it. Janos knows, of course, that my name is rare enough not to be on the calendar. As a child I sulked so many times because of it that our parents eventually began to celebrate my nameday the same day as Janos's.

'At first I thought that someone had simply made a mistake, or picked a name outside the calendar as a jest,' Janos continues. 'But then I read the contents.'

'What's in it?' I ask.

'I think it's best if you read it,' Janos says and offers me the codex.

It is surprisingly heavy in my hands. Valeria takes the glow-glass from me so I can get a better grip of the volume. I open it. The first spreads are empty. I turn the pages until I see pictures run along them.

The drawings are simple coal drafts of everyday life on the island: a fish placed on a table next to vegetables, a bread stall at the market, a butterfly landed on a flower. Hands winding yarn, a fishnet spread to dry, a canal disappearing between houses. In some drawings I recognize the Ink Quarters, and one is a hasty sketch of the edge of the web-maze among the stone walls of the city. A few pictures tell short stories: a flock of seagulls fights over fish in the harbour until a clowder of cats frightens it away and begins to brawl over the catch.

I raise my gaze. Janos stands quiet, the shine of the glow-glasses a distant light in his eyes. Valeria has frozen completely in place. Her breathing seems to have stopped.

'Are you well?' I ask.

The sound rising from Valeria recalls the night she

arrived at the House of Webs. It is shapeless and wordless, like springing from an animal. She puts down the glow-glasses in her hands so quickly their water storms and tugs the codex away from me. For a moment I think she is going to tear it to pieces. Janos shifts towards Valeria, but I stop him. Valeria kneels on the floor covered by wood and paper and places the open book on her lap. Her hair falls and hides her face. She follows the lines of the drawings with her finger, turns the pages so fiercely that I am afraid they will rip. The spread on which she stops portrays a room with a large desk and papers covering it. Patterns and writing are visible on the papers. There are also numerous bottles of ink on the table and a device I recognize as a tattoo needle: an inkmaster's workshop.

I see a tear fall on the page, then another. Valeria sobs.

I lower myself to my knees next to her. A woodlouse slips out from under a piece of plank and runs into a crack in the floor.

'Have you seen this codex before?' I ask quietly.

Valeria sweeps the hair from her face and nods. Janos bends closer, his eyes full of alertness. I take Valeria's hand.

'Where?'

She draws a breath. Her lips move and her expression focuses as she tries to form the word.

'Mmuh . . . Mye. Fah. Cher.' She closes her eyes, her brows frown and frustration twists her mouth. She turns her palm upwards and points at her tattoo.

'Your father?'

Valeria nods. I place my fingers on the spread.

'Is that your father's workshop? Did the book belong to him?'

Valeria nods again. Janos crouches on the floor next to me and examines the picture.

'It sounds possible,' he says. 'Jovanni Petros was an inkmaster. I found the information when you asked me to look into Valeria's family.'

Valeria glances at me surprised, cautious.

'I asked for it because I wanted to understand why my name was tattooed on you,' I say. 'I was afraid I'd get in trouble with the City Guard.'

Valeria stares at me and then seems to accept the explanation. She squeezes my hand, turns back to the codex and leafs through the pages as if looking for something on them. I have time to notice that among the light-handed drafts are more intricate, detailed drawings that have clearly taken longer. Some of them are drawn with ink. A spread emerges with an image of a woman sitting in front of a loom with a child. Valeria bends toward it. Tears gather in her eyes again. She places a finger on top of the drawing and points at the child. Then she points at herself.

She is much younger in the picture, but I recognize her regardless. Curly hair and pale skin, grey eyes in a face that is no longer as round. The woman of the picture has similar hair, woven into a long braid. She has turned to look at the child next to her with a smile on her face.

'Is that your mother?' I ask.

Valeria closes her eyes and nods. She sniffs.

'Mihaela Petros was a weaver,' Janos says. 'She learned her craft in the House of Webs.' He pauses for a moment and then asks, 'Valeria, are you familiar with the contents of the codex?'

The light of the glow-glasses sparkles in Valeria's eyes when she opens them. She begins to turn the pages again, finds what she is looking for and points at the drawing that makes me gasp. I recognize it.

The spread is filled by a map of the island, at the centre

of which a dark sun reaches its rays in eight directions. In the north a human figure is seated for tattooing; in the east he sleeps without dreams, in the south the Council observes the events. In the west the dream-images approach the sleeper on whose chest a night-maere sits.

'Your tapestry,' I say. 'You've tried to weave something of the contents of the book into it.'

Valeria's expression is victorious and her nod emphatic. Janos looks confused. I tell him about the tapestry. Valeria turns back to the beginning of the codex and hands the volume to me.

'You want me to read it from the beginning?' I ask.

Valeria nods. I look at Janos. It seems to me that he is trying to hide his excitement. I take hold of the codex and begin to turn the pages again from the beginning.

The inkmaster's workshop recurs in many of the drafts. In some there is also a master at his table: Valeria's father. Of the more detailed images drawn in ink the first one portrays the same man sleeping. The expression on his face is calm, and there is nothing but a dim glow-glass next to the bed in the room. A few words are written on the margin of the page.

'*Sea-apple, buckthorn berries, powdered sap, rainwater. Two weeks,*' I read. 'What does it mean?'

'Those are ingredients of ink,' Janos says. 'The time most probably refers to the time that the dyes are soaked in water.' He glances at Valeria.

Valeria smiles and nods. I remember something about her earlier fierce leafing through the codex. I find the next ink drawing. I bend very close to the page and tilt the volume so the light filtering through the skylight would fall on it better. I compare two drawings with each other.

'The inks are different colours,' I say. 'Look.' The lines of one drawing have a dark-green hue, the lines of the other dark-red. The difference is so small it would be easy to miss.

Janos draws closer.

'You're right,' he says.

In the drawing made with red ink the writing is smaller and less noticeable. The words have been embedded as part of the image, but when I look closely, I discern them among the lines. *Charcoal, beetle powder, vitriol, resin, vinegar.*

'Your father developed different inks, then?' I ask.

Valeria confirms this with a nod.

I continue to turn the pages and begin to realize that whereas the drafts portray sole everyday events, the more detailed drawings tell a continuous story. The inkmaster is shown at his desk, drawing, mixing different inks. In one picture he sits at the Ink-marking as the tattooist, in another he is being tattooed. A woman who occasionally vanishes into the web-maze enters the story. A spread-sized ink drawing shows the man and the woman sitting next to each other in a gondola decorated with garlands and ribbons. The woman wears an embroidered gown and holds a bunch of flowers.

A few spreads later the man and the woman board a ship together which carries them away from the island. The eight figures of the Council follow the journey from the Tower. The man sits at his desk again, but the cell is different now: lighter, arranged in a different manner. The woman weaves fabrics and tapestries, winds wefts and yarns. In one drawing she spins yarn from sea-wool. The point of the spindle is as sharp as a tattoo needle.

'Did your parents travel to the continent?' I ask.

'Mm,' Valeria confirms.

'Why?'

Janos's expression changes. I have seen it many times.

He is searching for things in his memory, building bridges between this moment and what he has read somewhere.

'About twenty years ago people could still leave the island on the condition that they returned once a year for the Ink-marking,' he says. 'At the time many inkmasters, scribes and healers went there for learning. Perhaps he left in order to study dyes that were not known on the island.'

I look at Valeria. Her face and the movement of her head accept the explanation.

I turn my gaze back to the codex. The woman holds a baby in her arms who smiles at her. The baby sleeps. The baby does not sleep. The baby stares from the pages again and again, her eyes wide open with wonder. Yet another part of the story: the man and the woman stand with their travelling chest ready to go, when the man falls to the ground. The man lies in bed. There are abscesses on his skin and his forehead trickles with sweat. In the direction of his blurred vision a ship carries the woman and the child back to the island. While the woman sits at the Ink-marking getting her tattoo, the man still lies in bed.

The woman returns from the island with the child. The abscesses disappear from the man's skin. He gets out of bed and settles at his desk again. The images of everyday life continue for a while, but then new ones begin to appear between them.

The man and the woman lie in bed. The woman sleeps, her face calm, the emptiness of night-rest around her. The man sleeps too, but he is surrounded by restless images rising from himself. There are still drawings portraying everyday life, but more and more drawings depicting dreaming grow around them. The man sleeps, and animals and plants and buildings rise from him, entire worlds alien to wakefulness.

And then a picture that confirms everything: a night-maere sitting on top of his chest, a faceless shadow against the fragile sources of light in the room.

I look at Valeria. Her face is quiet and pale.

I turn to a spread on which the man travels back to the island. He sits at the Ink-marking, getting his tattoo together with his wife and young daughter. This is followed by a spread on which the man sleeps again without dreams. Yet his expression is not calm.

While awake, the man sits at his desk and draws. Images spring from his pen showing islanders queueing for the Ink-marking, carrying dreams and night-maeres with them. After the Ink-marking they are gone, replaced by nothing but emptiness. But the tattoos drawn on them begin to shift their shape: they transform into abscesses and bruises, etching their skin like wounds, like chains.

The man sits at his desk and draws. The Tower rises behind him, and on top of it the Council. Page by page they move closer until their dark shadows grow on the wall of the man's cell.

I arrive at a spread, one half of which has a drawing of an inkmaster dipping a tattoo needle in an inkpot. Under the picture is written:

charcoal
burnt olive oil
diluted vinegar
??
??

The other page is blank apart from one sentence.

After that there are only blank pages.

I raise my gaze from the codex.

Valeria looks at me. Janos looks at me. His lips move. He is about to read the sentence aloud. I shake my head as unnoticeably as possible. His mouth goes still.

'Tell me if I'm interpreting this incorrectly,' I say to Valeria. 'Your father fell ill while living on the continent and couldn't return to the island for the Ink-marking. While sick, he began to have dreams.'

I remember the conversation with Alva.

Why would the Council call it dream-plague, if it is something else?

Yes, why?

Valeria nods. I see the final sentence of the codex which she cannot read bothers her.

'And when he returned to the island with you and your mother, the dreams disappeared again.'

Shadows stir on Valeria's face. She drops her chin into a nod.

'She . . .' I go quiet. This I am least certain about. But the thought fits with everything depicted in the codex, it fits with Valeria's tapestry. If she had wanted to tell one thing, the most important of all, would it not be this one?

I speak the thought out loud.

'Did your father suspect that . . . the annual tattoos had something to do with dreaming?'

Valeria's gaze turns darker and denser. She turns back to the codex spread which her tapestry imitates. She points at every picture in turn. I follow the movement of her hand.

'Ink-marking brings a calm night-rest,' I say. 'The Council watches over to make certain that it will happen repeatedly. If dream images appear . . .' I hesitate. 'The Ink-marking will take them away again?'

Smile spreads in Valeria. She nods, closes her eyes and

takes a deep breath. I know I have finally interpreted the pictures correctly. I also see the message in their order now, in the movement of her hand: the cycle remains the same on the island year in, year out.

Janos looks at me. His face draws into contemplation.

'But some people dream anyway,' he says.

I have thought of it myself. It is the piece that does not fit.

I return to the spread where ingredients of ink are listed. I point at the list.

'Maybe Jovanni Petros was not only trying to develop new inks. Maybe he was trying to find out the composition of the ink used in the Ink-marking.'

I see Janos ponder the suggestion.

'Why would he have done that?' he asks.

'Because he wanted to know why it doesn't work on everyone,' I say.

Janos is silent for a long while.

'If he knew all this,' he then says quietly, 'that explains the last sentence of the codex.' He looks at me.

An expression has risen to Valeria's face that I would not wish to see. She points at the sentence. I take her hand and look her in the eye. She stares back, wants to know, and she has the right to. I take a breath.

'*They plan to kill me*,' I read aloud.

Light clings to Valeria's skin, makes her look much older than her age for a moment. The corners of her lips twitch and her fingers press around mine.

We are all quiet, and thoughts rise around us like tall shadows growing on the walls, like mist rising from canals. The face of Our Lady of Weaving above us has crumbled, but her web still circles the room. Its threads run as embossed figures on the walls, spiral around the columns carrying the ceiling. Seagulls meow outside and water wears the shore down. In the distance a cable screeches. Wood creaks in the structures of the house like ships in the wind. Strange and dangerous forces are shifting out of sight, and my hand is slight against them, easily crushed under their weight. Valeria is still next to me, does not make a sound. Yet I feel like I can sense every word and sentence ravaging inside her, the scream she is holding fastened within silence.

'What do you want to do?' Janos asks eventually.

'I think,' I say, 'that we should meet again. In this same place. A week from now.'

I look at Valeria to be certain, and she nods. Janos nods slowly.

'That's what we'll do,' he says. 'I will see if I can find out how the book got among the Dead Codices.' He pauses. 'The two of you go first. I will stay behind and leave when you have had a head start.'

We give a slight farewell bow. The shrubs of thorn part like a dream, then fall back, dense and wide enough to cover what they must.

It is the evening after, or the frayed edge of day brushing last threads across skies. I sense a new core under Valeria's grief, grown since we read the codex. The weight of sorrow has turned into something sterner, more restless. It stirs in her and seeks, and I feel like I could feel it turning if I placed my hand on her skin. We are seated next to each other on Valeria's bed. She has a scrap of fabric in front of her, on top of which we have formed the alphabet from short pieces of thread. There are still a few threads left. I am teaching her to read and spell her own name.

'*Va*,' I say. 'Which letters do you need for that?'

Valeria picks up two pieces of thread. She shapes one into a *v* and the other one into an *a*.

'Good,' I say. 'What about *le*?'

I feel Valeria's breath on the skin of my neck when she bends closer to pick the last two thread-lengths. Her side presses against mine. Her hand brushes my bare wrist. The touch remains glowing under my skin, an invisible trace. Valeria forms the letter *a*, then her fingers begin to place the thread in the mirror image of *e*.

'Almost,' I hear myself say. 'Are you certain about the *e*?'

Valeria puts her head on my shoulder, watches the thread letters. She turns the points of the *e* downwards.

I shake my head slowly. I feel the arc of her body by my side, the weight of her hand on my knee.

Valeria looks at me and turns the points to the right.

'That was a guess,' I say. 'You would have tried turning the points upwards next.'

The window of the cell behind Valeria frames the darkening evening, and a star has come out about her hair. The light of the glow-glass softens the frolicking of her smile. Her lips are smooth, their bruises have faded long ago. She looks at me, so close I discern every eyelash, the winter-pale freckles on both sides of her nose.

I turn my gaze away.

'What about *ria*?' I say. My voice clutches, flows again. I wonder if she notices.

There are no more unused threads. I wait for Valeria to pick one from the alphabet row. Instead, she places her hand on my wrist and begins to roll up my sleeve, baring my arm. She does it slowly and taking her time. I understand she is giving me the chance to refuse, to pull away or show in a different manner I want her to stop.

I do not want her to stop.

Her fingers brush the bare skin of my arm lightly, back and forth. I notice my breathing has grown narrower, as if it was being pulled tighter from both ends. Valeria looks me in the eye, asking for permission. I do not stir. She places her fingertips inside my forearm, where the row of annual tattoos marks me as belonging to the island. Her fingers are pale against my own brown skin. She draws a letter that breaks the line of the annual tattoos on purpose.

R.

I am only able to nod. I am molten glass inside, and small flames that reach towards her. She pauses, lifts her fingers from my skin, and then draws another letter.

I.

I take a deep breath. I know she hears the pauses in my breath, the weight and burn behind it. She draws the final letter.

A.

'Just like that,' I whisper, and although I have everything to lose, I lift my hands onto her neck and kiss her.

Valeria's arms settle around me and she presses closer. She is warm and smooth and slick, and her arches and angles fit mine. Slowly, slowly she guides my hand, and we are both learning things we do not know how to do yet.

149

CHAPTER NINE

Irena stares at the last spread of the codex. Janos glances at Valeria, who glances at me. We are sitting around a circular table in Irena's house. Candles burn orange and white and yellow on the walls. Their smoke gathers into a skein high in the ceiling. The glow of flames ripples on the paper.

'It reads—' Janos begins.

'I can read,' Irena interrupts. She places her fingers on top of the codex and raises her gaze. There is bright-polished grief in it, and something else.

'Why did you bring this to me?' she asks. The words crackle into the dusk of the room.

I sense Valeria's warmth next to me when she stirs. Her leg presses against mine. I stop the smile that is already growing inside me.

'We thought the contents might interest you,' I say.

Irena's face looks smoother in the soft light, and yet there are sharp angles under her skin.

'Has it crossed your mind that the codex may be a mere fiction?' she asks.

'We talked about it,' Janos says. 'Why would your brother have gone to such trouble? And how would he have been able to foresee—' He glances at Valeria and goes silent.

'His death?' Irena says. She fixes her stare on Valeria.

'Did Jovanni know you had seen the drawings?' she asks.

Valeria shakes her head. The scent of the candles is pungent and the smoke stings my eyes.

'I thought as much,' Irena says quietly. Her fingers brush the words on the last page.

'Do you believe the codex is a fiction?' I ask.

Irena does not respond immediately. She looks at each of us, looks at the book before her again.

'No,' she says. 'I believe there are people in this city who would pay a royal reward for finding that codex. Even more for destroying it.' Her hand squeezes into a slow fist. 'And most of all for reporting the persons guilty of keeping it in possession.'

Shadows throw themselves closer and retreat again in the flare of the fire. Valeria's fingers seize my wrist under the table. Janos's face tenses. I remember our first visit to Irena, the feeling that she left things untold.

'Do you know something about this?' I ask. Valeria's grasp is soft and firm on my skin, like a tightening knot of silk yarn.

'How do I know I can trust you?' Irena says.

'We have just given you something you could use against us if you wanted to,' Janos says. 'Is that not enough?'

Irena looks at each of us in turn. Her eyes are black and glistening, like a bird's.

'And how do you know you can trust me?' she asks.

'Valeria does,' I say. Valeria nods to confirm this. 'That is good enough for me.'

151

Two deep lines appear between Irena's eyebrows. Her fingernails press onto the skin of her palm. She takes a breath and lets out a sigh. The corners of the room are dark cracks in the world, and flames fumble for air. Irena turns to Valeria.

'I made your father a promise not to tell,' she says. 'But every reason behind his request has now been made void.' She places her hands on the table and spreads her fingers like roots. The narrow tendrils of vines run over her knuckles and spiral on her skin. 'The truth is that I have been looking for this codex. I thought it had been destroyed.'

Janos's face is a surprised shift in the half-light, Valeria's a pale, alert patch. Her fingers squeeze tighter around my wrist.

'Did you know about the book?' I ask.

'I did,' she says. 'But not of its contents. Jovanni was afraid, but he would not tell me why. At the time I thought he did not trust me. Now I think he believed he was protecting me. He feared for his family.'

'Did he ever mention his dreaming to you?'

The voice belongs to Janos.

'No,' Irena replies. 'Perhaps he didn't wish to burden me with the secret. He only talked about the inks used on the island and implied he had discovered something important. He had been trying for a long time to acquire the membership of the guild that manufactures the tattoo ink used in the Ink-marking.'

'You said you thought the codex had been destroyed.' Valeria's fingers slide between mine. 'Why?'

Irena looks at me. Her cheeks are bony, her gaze sharp in its hollow.

'My brother told me that if something happened to him,

Valeria would come to see me and bring a message.' Irena
turns her gaze to Valeria. 'I was to convey it forward to
someone in the House of Words. Jovanni told me he had
hidden a notebook there.'

Valeria shifts, and I see surprise run through her.

'But Valeria did not come,' I say.

Irena shakes her head. The shadows move back and
forth.

'When my brother died, I looked for her everywhere.
No one seemed to know anything. I began to believe she
had been killed and thrown into the sea, or perhaps
captured. I feared she might have been sent to the House
of the Tainted. And then, weeks and weeks later, the two of
you appeared at my door.'

She pauses, looking at Valeria and me.

'You showed me the tattoo, but I did not know what
it meant,' she continues. 'Then, when I spoke to you alone,'
she says to Valeria, 'you seemed to know nothing about
a message. And that is when I made the connection. If
Jovanni had wanted to send me a message without anyone
else noticing, tattoos are the way he would have done it.'

'Why did he use my name?'

Irena shakes her head slowly.

'That I don't know.'

Janos shifts on his seat.

'I haven't told you,' he says. 'I went through the record
of Valeria's family again. You are the only person on the
island who shares the exact same birthday with her.
Perhaps her father chose the name because of that.'

Valeria looks at me. Her hand squeezes mine under the
table.

'That's exactly what Jovanni would have done,' Irena
says. 'He meant it as nothing more than code. He couldn't

have predicted you would ever have anything to do with each other.'

One of the candles on the wall burns out. The tall flame shrinks into a blue spectre and goes out entirely. Orange glows in the remains of the wick for a moment, until there is nothing but black left.

'Did you convey the message to the House of Words?'

'I couldn't,' Irena says. 'The scribe to whom Jovanni had asked me to send the message was taken to the House of the Tainted immediately after his death.'

Janos's expression grows more alert.

'Ilaro Matis,' he says. I remember he mentioned it when we visited the Glass Grove.

The stench of the burnt-out candle drifts in the room.

'So someone else may have read the codex, too,' I say.

Janos thinks about it.

'I don't believe it likely,' he says. 'Ilaro was responsible for the storage room where the Dead Codices are kept after they've been copied. No one reads them again at that point, so it would have been easy to hide the book among them. He probably intended to move it elsewhere before the Word-incineration.'

Slowly Valeria's hand withdraws from mine. We are all silent. Winter chill emanates from the walls of the room, besieges us like a skerry amidst sea, and somewhere far away a rising storm gathers strength.

'What do you want to do with the codex?' Irena finally asks.

I look at Janos. I look at Valeria. We spoke about this before we came to Irena.

'We must find out if the claim about the connection between the tattoo ink and dreams is true,' I say. 'And if it is, islanders must be told.'

154

Dusk breathes around us. Irena watches us. After a long moment she speaks.

'How do you plan to succeed?' she says.

I glance at Valeria and Janos.

'We haven't really thought about it yet,' I say. The words sound fragile, ready to bend in the first wind.

'You were all at the Word-incineration,' Irena says and crosses her arms on her chest. 'You know what the Council says about Dreamers. That they are deliberately spreading the plague. That they burned down the Museum of Pure Sleep. How will you get people to believe the word of a Dreamer?'

Janos opens his mouth but says nothing. Valeria drops her gaze and frowns.

'You will need allies,' Irena continues. Her voice is low and emphatic. 'Where will you find them?'

'There must be other Dreamers on the island who are not yet in the House of the Tainted,' I say.

The words have left my mouth before I have had time to consider them. Irena looks at me carefully. I feel the beating of my own heart and the tightness in my breath. Yet I do not turn my eyes away.

'Interesting,' she says. 'And true.' Her bright bird-eyes are still fixed on me, wary under the dark brows. 'They hide because they must, but they have always existed.'

Valeria has frozen still next to me. Janos's voice is calm, without colour.

'How do you know this?'

Irena's gaze turns slowly from me to Valeria and softens a little.

'A few years ago, clients started coming to me requesting invisible tattoos,' she says. 'The kind you can only see in glow-algae light.'

Valeria makes a sound, another. I think I can pick the words in them.

'Like Valeria's?' I ask.

'Like Valeria's,' Irena says. 'I began to pay attention to it because they all requested to have the tattoo on their palm, which was an unusual place.'

I sense Valeria's unrest. I know she is thinking about the tattoo on her own palm.

'I also wondered why there were so many who wanted a similar tattoo who nevertheless seemed to have nothing in common,' Irena continues. 'They came from all trades and age groups.'

Again I remember the tattoo I saw at the Museum of Pure Sleep, the scar on the strange man's hand. I nearly mention it, but Valeria's hand drops onto my own, squeezes my fingers as if knowing and wanting me to keep silent. Irena's voice does not break off.

'When people had been coming to me to get these tattoos for a while, I began to hear rumours about things happening on the island.'

'What kind of things?' Janos asks.

'Long-outlawed Dreamer symbols began to appear on buildings in the deep of the night,' Irena says. 'On the cliffs of the shore, on bridges. Once, even on the City Guard's weapons.'

Janos stiffens in his chair.

'There was an incident in the House of Words last year,' he says. 'When we went to work in the morning, a symbol resembling an eye was drawn on each one of the unfinished codices in the Halls of Scribing. They all had to be destroyed and started anew.'

'Why do you think it has anything to do with Dreamers?' I ask.

'The eye is an ancient Dreamer symbol. They have others, but that is one of the best known.'

'Another group of people could be using the same symbol,' Janos says.

'That is what I thought,' Irena says, 'until I was recruited.'

I cannot hear my own breathing, or that of the others. The flames of the candles burn straight and tall, without the slightest stirring of air. A narrow smoke disappears from them into the dusk of the room.

'What do you mean?' I ask.

Irena blinks and new lines cross her expression. She gets up and pushes her chair back. The wooden legs screech on the floor. She walks into the other room and returns carrying a glow-glass she places down next to the codex. Its light blends with the amber glow of the flames as she walks to the niche in the corner of the room, pours water from a jug into a pewter cup and brings the cup to the table. She sits down again.

The surface of the water in the pewter cup evens out to reflect the faint lights. Irena turns her palm upward. I see now the barely discernible scar tissue runs on her skin. Irena pulls a handkerchief from her pocket, dips it in the pewter cup and wipes her palm with it.

A shining-white tattoo is drawn visible in the light of the glow-glass: an open eye.

We all stare at Irena. Valeria lets out a sound.

'A secret for a secret,' Irena says in a quiet voice. 'I'm not a Dreamer, but I work for them.'

I remember how the tattoo I saw at the Museum of Pure Sleep disappeared from the skin of the scar-handed man. Of course: a way to reveal the tattoo, a way to hide it from sight where needed. A resistance movement.

'How . . .?' Janos begins, but the sentence trails off.

157

'They have ways of announcing their existence,' Irena says. She closes her fingers around the tattoo. 'The contents of that codex might give them – us – the weapon we have been longing for.'

Two of the candles burn out. Their smoke gathers over the table, floats as a veil before our eyes. Its scent brushes my nostrils. Somewhere sand flows through narrow hourglasses, one grain after another, until there are none left, and the glass is turned again. The smoke lifts, clearing the air between us.

I ask the question to which we all need an answer.

'Do you think they can help us?'

'Yes,' Irena says. 'I also think I will need your help.' She lets her gaze circulate on all of us. 'First of all, we need more knowledge of the tattoo inks.' She points at the drawing on the last spread of the codex and the words written underneath it: *charcoal, burnt olive oil, diluted vinegar*. 'This is a common recipe,' she says. 'My own inks are based on it. But Jovanni suspected that in the Ink-marking something else is added to the ingredients.'

'If you can blend me a small amount of ink with this recipe and get a sample of the one used in the Ink-marking,' I reply slowly, because the thought is only just taking shape, 'I may know the right person to look into it.'

Valeria's face is brighter than it has been in ages. Janos's thoughts move behind his eyes, arranging knowledge and the world and seeing new possibilities. Irena speaks again.

'And now, we need to talk about a plan.'

I wash my hands in a tub filled with soapwater, one of which has appeared by the doorway of almost every tavern in town. The water is murky and I feel like it leaves my hands dirtier, but this is the only way we will be allowed in. Tavern-keepers are too scared of the dream-plague. I shake water off my hands while Valeria and Janos wash theirs. We step in. A sticky smell of fish stew, malt and unwashed bodies pours in our faces. A picture of the Council watches everything from the wall. The venue is full. I do not see any customers dressed in the uniforms of the City Guard or the colours of the Houses of Crafts. This is a place where fishermen, butchers and the crew of midden ships come to drink and eat. There are no black-clad family members of Dreamers in sight, either. Many taverns in the city no longer admit them.

I point towards the corner where a piece of plank has been nailed to the wall to serve as a table. Janos goes to the bar. Valeria and I head for the corner. She has tied her hair back, and a strip of the skin of her neck is visible between the coat and the hairline. It is difficult for me not to step closer and brush it with my fingers. I still feel the traces of her touch where her hands moved last night and this morning. The disguise is successful: I would not guess she is a woman if I did not know. She has changed the sea-green coat of the House of Webs for a brown, hooded jacket and loose men's trousers. I wonder if my own disguise is as credible.

Usually fires burn in taverns, but here glow-glasses have been placed beside them to light many of the tables. The globes look new, freshly made by glass-masters. I have seen similar ones elsewhere in the city recently. I almost say something to Valeria about the matter, but just then Janos threads his way through the crowd to us, carrying three tankards of hot cider. He places them on the makeshift table. We have rehearsed this frequently, but this is the first time we have an audience.

I can hear the conversation at the nearest table. They must be able to hear us, too.

'I heard something the other day,' I begin. I lower my voice as much as I can.

'Tell us more, friend,' Janos says.

'About Dreamers.' I say this louder on purpose. A man wearing clothes that have been patched repeatedly glances in our direction.

'What about them?'

Slowly the man turns his eyes away, but I notice that he and his companions have gone quiet, perhaps in order to listen.

'A strange thing happened,' I continue. 'There was a withered old man sitting by the square and telling a story. I was buying vegetables from the stall next to him, and I couldn't help hearing. He chatted that a long time ago everyone on the island had dreams. And that it wasn't a disease at all. That dream-plague doesn't exist.'

'A village idiot, no doubt,' Janos says. Valeria hums in agreement.

'That's what I thought,' I say. 'But he was dressed in healer-white. He said that more and more people on the island have begun to have dreams, and there will be a time when it's a normal part of life again. When people will understand there's nothing to fear about it. That many on the island are already talking about it.'

'I haven't heard anyone say such things,' Janos says. He is good at playing suspicion.

'Me neither,' I say. 'But that's what the man said.'

'The City Guard could arrest you for such talk,' Janos says. 'Why would you tell me this? You're not one of them, are you?'

'Of course not,' I reply and take a gulp from the tankard.

160

'Besides, I'm not saying I believe the old man. I'm only telling you what I heard.'

The men at the next table are silent.

'Rather bad, those shoe leathers they've been bringing from the continent lately,' Janos changes the subject.

'You said it,' I reply. 'Good luck to anyone trying to make footwear from those. And don't even let me get started on the fabrics . . .'

We continue our chatter about shoemaking, tailoring, the weather and other insignificant matters. The men at the next table return to their own conversation. An hour or so later we leave the tavern.

Perhaps none of them will remember afterwards what they heard. Perhaps someone will, and tell someone else. The rumour has been sown. I hope it will not need much in order to start growing. If it returns to us one day, either in the same shape or changed, we will know everything is proceeding as it should.

If anyone asks them to describe the customers who spoke about Dreamers, they will remember three young men in the corner of the tavern. Cobblers, maybe, or tailors. Two dark and one pale, in brown jackets, like most people in the city. No particular characteristics.

The first phase of the plan is in action.

A week later Alva invites me to see her. The curtains between her workspace and the sick room are closed. It is silent on the other side. The water in the medusa tank casts a reflection on the thick fabric, a flickering ghost of moving light. I glance at the tank and see that it is empty.

'I should ask you where you got the inks,' Alva says, 'but I will not.'

'Did you find out anything?' I ask.

'A whole lot of interesting things,' Alva says.

She opens a cupboard and takes out six glass jars, which she places on the table.

'I did a series of experiments,' she says, 'and concluded that one of the inks has three components that are missing from the other. One of them is a mineral powder used in making red-dye. Another has been extracted from a species of passionflower. The third I could not identify. I tested the impact of the inks on glow-algae.' She points at the glass jars. 'I added ink to each jar of algae, doubling the dose with each one. Would you cover those glow-glasses, please?'

I pull fabric hoods over two glow-glass globes hanging from the ceiling, leaving only one bare next to the singing medusa tank. In the diminished light I see clearly that each of the algae jars is dimmer than the previous one. In the first one the algae shines almost normally, but the last jar has barely any glow left.

'Does it kill the algae?' I ask.

'Eventually,' Alva says. 'The larger the amount of ink and the longer the contact with the algae continues, the worse the algae fares. The ink seems to damage it in ways which prevent its growth and renewal.'

'Could the ink have an effect on people?' I ask.

Alva looks at me strangely.

'It is hard to say for certain,' she says. 'Like I said, I cannot recognize all the components, and algae does not necessarily react the same way a human would. Passionflower deepens night-rest. The mineral powder might cause something akin to symptoms of poisoning. It depends on many things. People have different tolerance levels.'

I stare at her.

'Are you certain?'

'Of course not,' Alva says. 'It would need to be tested, preferably with large numbers of people and for many years. But that would be highly questionable, of course.'

'Of course,' I say.

Alva reaches to remove the hoods covering the glow-glasses.

'I wrote a completed ink recipe for you,' she says and digs a piece of paper out of her pocket.

I stare at the note for a moment. I sigh and take it.

'You know all my secrets, don't you?'

The corner of Alva's mouth lifts.

'Is there anything else I can do for you?' she asks.

'Perhaps a time will come when you can,' I say.

Alva smiles in the growing light.

'Do you think it will come soon?'

'Yes, I think so,' I reply.

'I promise to be available.'

I hear Alva collect the glass jars from the table behind me as I leave the sick bay. I imagine her writing down in her remedy notebook everything she has discovered, filling the spread with small, knife-sharp letters that have the power to cut open the surface of the world.

I run in the narrow dream-corridor where the floor is stone and the walls are webs, gauzes woven from silver-grey yarn, persistent and far-reaching. A dark wooden door stands tall at the end of the corridor. The night-maere is always a few steps behind me, the echo of my every movement. I want the dream-walls to vanish, I want the night-maere off my heels. Yet the escape has worn my strength small and my will does not bend the shape of the dream into another. I reach the door and want it to be mist-thin, but it is solid and robust under my hands, does not give in. I turn to look at the darkness of the night-maere. Cold gathers around me, and silence. Terror floods into me, carries icy metal on its crest, heavy chains I have no strength to break. The face of the night-maere burns as a lightless hole at the core of the dream. I tell myself to wake up, but the web of the dream will not yield; its threads tie me in place. The night-maere reaches its hand towards me.

The touch sends a bright current through me that fills me with strength.

I draw a breath.

I want the door to be mist-thin again, and this time it lets me through. I fall to the other side. The door settles between us, translucent as glass. Behind it I see the night-maere that has also fallen to the floor. It rises together with me. The power kindled by its touch still sparkles in my body, tingles in my palms and glows in my veins. On the other side of the door the threads of the wall-webs have begun to shine faintly.

Go, I tell the night-maere without words.

It stands and watches me in silence and does not turn away.

The threads of dream let go under Valeria's touch. It is still early, the night behind the window without the edge of light. The glow grows and diminishes, grows and diminishes in me still, as Valeria moves, wraps around me like a vine.

Slowly I transfer the glow onto her skin.

The creaking of the cables carries to the Halls of Weaving when the hourglass has been turned for the sixth time after lunch. My hands continue to work, but my hearing clings to the sound, because visitors are rare in the House of Webs and the cargo of the day arrived earlier. After some time, heavy footsteps approach along the corridor.

We all cease to work when four City Guards step into the Halls of Weaving. I do not remember seeing any of them before. A few weavers get up.

'You may sit,' the tallest of the guards says. His hair curls grey above his ears. He nods at another guard who steps forward, takes a paper from his pocket and unfolds it. He clears his throat.

'The following weavers are to come with us,' the City Guard says and begins to read names from the paper. 'Viola Matia, Sisi Ditos, Kiela Lanero.'

Viola and Sisi look at each other, startled. Kiela stares in front of her. She is one of the weavers who returned from the Hospital Quarters having lost their eyesight. The City Guard continues to read names.

'Nita Lupolis, Reia Nieves, Leli Nuntio.'

The tallest guard interrupts.

'Get up from your seats,' he says.

The other guard reads more names and one by one those whose name has been read aloud get up in front of their looms. Sisi stands closest to me. Her eyes are red. My breathing runs superficial and panicked; I am afraid I will hear my own name. Yet I am beginning to realize it will probably not come. The weavers whose names are on the list have one thing in common.

Agitated footsteps sound from the corridor. Alva appears on the doorway with the weaver who is on messenger duty.

'What is going on here?' she asks in a voice that clangs against the stone walls.

All four guards turn to look at Alva. The City Guard

reading the names goes quiet. The tallest guard steps towards Alva.

'We are under orders to take all weavers carrying dream-plague away from the House of Webs,' he says.

Weaver appears at the door too.

'To where?' Alva asks.

None of the guards speaks, but I read the answer on their faces. So does Alva. Her expression thickens like a storm cloud.

'No,' she says. 'They don't belong there. They are all completely healed. Every last one of them returned from the Hospital Quarters to work weeks ago.'

'There is no cure for dream-plague,' the tallest guard says.

Alva turns to look at Weaver.

'This is senseless,' she says. 'I can guarantee they are healthy. A few of them don't see as well as before, but it has had no impact on their ability to work. Their hands know the routes of the yarn.'

The tallest City Guard stares at Weaver. Weaver's dark gaze is steady, but eventually he turns it towards the Halls of Weaving and says, 'According to the new orders from the Council, all carriers of dream-plague must be isolated from other islanders.'

Sisi stirs uncertainly. Reia too.

'Move,' the tall guard says.

The weavers treated at the Hospital Quarters begin to move towards the door. Those who do not see walk in short, cautious steps. Others, whose names have not been called out, get up to support and guide them. They settle in a row. I see Sisi holding back tears. I see Weaver look away.

Alva turns her back. Her footsteps beat the floor of the

166

corridor steady and sharp, like wind beating at windows it is ready to break.

We are not permitted to follow the progression of gondolas or to interrupt our work. Yet that evening we do. We gather on the wall outside the gondola port and watch twenty-three torn away from the rest of us sit on board. Their faces are turned towards us.

One of them raises a hand, so far away I can no longer discern who it is. Slowly we raise our hands in response. The rest of the weavers in the gondola do the same. We know most of them cannot see us. We keep our hands raised anyway until the gondola has disappeared from sight.

I only begin to wonder at supper where Valeria is.

She has not been to the Halls of Weaving all day, because she is on kitchen duty. The last time I saw her was at lunch. Silvi thinks she may have seen her doing the washing up afterwards; Ania claims she was feeding the hens in the garden just before supper. When I visit the sick bay, Alva tells me she saw Valeria on her way to Weaver's study, but cannot remember exactly when.

I approach Weaver's study in order to ask her if she knows about Valeria, when I hear sounds behind the door. Two male voices speak softly, and I cannot discern the words. Between them, under them, behind them a third voice comes and goes, trying to make its way out, but lacking words and a way of shaping them. A voice without a tongue.

I stand in the empty corridor, frozen in place, and try to determine what to do. Maybe I do not have time to get help. Maybe I am putting myself in danger if I step inside.

I hear Valeria again. I gather my courage, stride to the door and tug at the handle.

Weaver's study is locked. She never locks it.

I knock on the door. The sounds pause for a moment, then begin again. Their rhythm is now more fervent. Words are still formless on the other side of the thick door. I knock again. When no one opens, I begin to bang on the door.

There is a screech from the room, like a heavy piece of furniture being moved. Then a clank, like something falling to the floor.

'Valeria!' I cry out. 'Valeria!'

The door remains closed. My strength alone will not open it. I turn around and run.

I find Weaver outside on top of the wall.

'There is something happening in your room,' I tell her. 'Could you come and open the door, please?'

Weaver turns to look at me and her face is in the shadow. It is too dark for me to see her expression. Her voice is night-coloured.

'What on earth are you talking about?'

'Valeria,' I say. 'I think she is in your study. I heard noises from there, and the door is locked.'

Weaver is still, like a doldrum in wind, and then she begins to move. She strides down the steps and into the building. I follow. We walk the length of the corridor, past the Halls of Weaving, to the tall wooden door.

It is wide open. There is no one in the room.

'So there was someone in here?' Weaver asks.

'I didn't see anyone,' I say. 'The door was locked. But I heard the voices. Valeria was here.'

Weaver's gaze is stone and sky, unmoving.

'Why would Valeria lock herself in my study?'

'She was not alone,' I say. 'I also heard two men.'

'Two, you say?' Weaver raises her eyebrows. When they

168

come back down, her expression considers, decides. She stands steady enough to be one of the walls of the building, perhaps the one that supports everything else. 'When the City Guard came to the house today, they probably checked the cells and dormitories.'

Weaver waits for my reaction. Our Lady of the Weaving in the wall hanging in the corner raises her hand, in invitation or warning. The door behind the tapestry is cracked open, so slightly it might be my imagination, a gateway into dark.

My voice does not falter. My face shows nothing. I can do this.

'Valeria is not a Dreamer,' I say.

'How do you know?' Weaver says. 'Would she have told you?'

'What do they think they will find?' I ask. 'If someone were a Dreamer – someone not known to carry dreamplague – how would they know?'

'According to the new law, they do not need to know,' Weaver replies. 'It is enough if they find something that can be interpreted as suggesting dream activity. Tattoos depicting Dreamer symbols. Books or clothes bearing their colours. Amulets or rings. Anything that could be connected with Dreamers in any way.'

A thought that casts me frost-cold takes shape in my mind.

Without waiting or asking for permission I begin to stride towards the cell. I take a shortcut across the square. The air is like invisible rime on my skin. I do not care if Weaver follows me or not. I step into the cell, kneel on the floor and begin to feel under Valeria's bed. My knees ache against the stone floor. Weaver's long shadow appears in the doorway. My hands meet nothing but wooden slats and between them the coarse underside of the mattress, the tangles of dried seaweed stuffed inside the fabric. Inch by inch I go through the bottom of the bed despite already knowing I will not find what I am looking for. I turn and lean on the edge of the bed. It presses my back painfully.

Weaver stands in the doorway of the cell.

'It is gone,' I say.

Weaver steps into the cell and closes the door behind her.

'What is?' she asks quietly.

'Valeria's tapestry,' I say. 'The one you told her to unravel. She continued to weave it in secret.'

Weaver's lips squeeze tighter together. She straightens her back.

'Why was it important to her?' she asks.

I realize I may have said too much.

'I . . . don't know,' I say. The words leave my mouth hesitant, slow. 'Maybe she just wanted to weave something else than wall-webs.'

Weaver gazes at me with dark eyes into which the light of the glow-glass draws cold specks.

'What did the tapestry portray?'

I wonder if it is wiser for me to lie or to tell a careful half-truth. I decide on the latter.

'The island,' I say. 'It was a map of the island.'

'Was there anything else in it?'

'Just people,' I say. 'And the Council.'

Weaver's head turns a little.

'The Council?'

'The patterns were simple,' I say. 'I think she was just imitating a tapestry she had seen in the Museum of Pure Sleep, for her own amusement.'

170

'Could she have hidden the tapestry somewhere else?' Weaver asks.

'I don't know why she would have,' I say. 'She—'

My hand hits something on the floor, next to the leg of the bed. I hear metal scrape stone.

That is when I understand.

I should have seen the connection much earlier. It has been in front of me all this time.

The item is not heavy, yet I can feel its weight in my whole body when I slide it to sight along the floor and pick it up. I turn it before my eyes.

The light refracts dimly off the dark-stained metal with a broken piece of grey-green yarn hanging from it. At the centre of an oblong eye shape an eight-pointed sun stares at the world, all-seeing.

The key Valeria carried around her neck

out of sight, in the dark grow things that bear the greatest weight and burn, for in light everything grows slighter. Sometimes strands spend a long time seeking each other, fumbling without light, and interweave without knowing that it is exactly what the web wants.

The door is mist-thin, the door is solid and robust, the door is translucent as glass and time behind it is dream-time, where the threads of the web shine faintly. There wander all those who have begun and ended and gone; their thoughts are open towards dreams every moment, and the threads tremble at their touch, becoming something else under it. The strands twist into painful knots and stretch to a breaking point, they settle next to each other and take a new shape that shatters the world in order to rebuild it. And time, dream-time, is brief and endless, is here and yet not, it is already out of thoughts' reach although it only just began. A moment or countless ones have passed, and no one else moves the threads any more.

Mist gathers around the island, it fills the streets and fills the houses, it drowns as dregs into the sea and wraps *all things alive and dead, clings to the threads as weight that will not wear away. Mist encircles the beds where people carry each other across the sea of night, encircles what must go and what must stay. But dreams will not submit to chains; where the weight and burn are greatest they still roam free. The dream-cliff is ready. The dream-sea is ready. The dream-threads are silent and ready, and deep under the sea one can already sense what is coming. A story that must be carried far away so it would not disappear.*

I stand in the broken darkness that is her gate and my home.

The world is ready to drown. The world is ready to rise. On its surface walk creatures who have forgotten their dreams, and only rarely do they remember that their hours are brief and their days are brittle, and there will not be many chances at happiness.

Quiet,

CHAPTER TEN

Weaver places the key on the table in front of me. Darkness presses heavy against the corner window. She ordered me to go to sleep for a few hours that I spent awake. It is such early morning that light has not yet broken through the edge of night.

'Where did Valeria get this?' Weaver asks. 'She did not have it when she arrived at the House of Webs. Who gave it to her?'

Glow-glass light paints the metal with a pale-blue sheen. Looking at the key turns a cold blade inside me.

'I don't know,' I say. 'She just began to carry it around her neck. I thought maybe it was an amulet, like pieces of coral.'

Weaver stares at me intently, reading every movement on my face.

'Do you know what it is?' she asks.

'No, but I think I can guess,' I say. That at least is true.

'Dreamers use these to recruit more people,' Weaver says. 'Carrying one of these is a serious offence.'

I understand now why the woman on the square dropped the key at my feet. I feel my eyes well up.

'Perhaps Valeria didn't know,' I say. My voice is faint and dissolves into the shadows. A lump of stone grows in my throat.

'In any case, it was found in her possession,' Weaver says. 'Together with the tapestry it gives the City Guard more than enough reason to detain her.'

I have tried to turn what I heard into images so I could understand: Valeria's wordless voice, the bangs and creaks. And I have driven the images away, so I would not need to see them. I look at Weaver.

'Is that what you believe happened?'

'You are intelligent enough to draw your own conclusions,' Weaver says. Her gaze is even more serious than usual.

I close my eyes for a moment and draw a breath. If this were a dream, I could turn everything around. I could make Valeria step through the door unharmed, will the key out of existence. Take back what happened. But the moment around me is not a dream-moment, and I have no power over reality.

Weaver must see the struggle on my face. Her expression changes barely at all, but I hear compassion in her voice when she speaks again.

'Eliana,' she says. 'How well do you know Valeria?'

I wipe my eyes.

'We have shared a cell for three months,' I say and realize it does not sound like much.

Weaver's face is dark and unreadable. She looks at her hands on the table, then at me again. Thoughts move across her expression.

'There is another possibility,' Weaver says. She considers her next words for a long time. 'Could she have run away?'

I have thought about it myself. Of how little Valeria

has been able to tell me about herself. Of how much time she has spent by herself, avoiding even me. And yet also of the way she raises her eyes to look at me in the middle of weaving, as she arranges the threads in order to find the right form for her secret image. Of her endless focus when I have taught her letters and words, the arc of her body against mine.

'She wouldn't have left without telling me,' I say.

Weaver sits still, like a statue behind the table.

'Maybe she had her own reasons to leave,' she says.

'What do you mean?'

'There are Dreamers on the island outside the House of the Tainted,' Weaver says. 'It is known that they have sent spies around the city. To the Hospital Quarters, Ink Quarters, Museum of Pure Sleep. And the Houses of Crafts.'

'Do you believe Valeria is a spy?'

Weaver's face is stone-smooth.

'Do you believe it is impossible?'

I think about it. After all, what do I know about the Dreamers' movement, beyond what I have heard from Irena? I have not met them. I do not know how they work. But if Valeria is with them, she is not in danger. I almost want to believe it.

'No,' I say. 'But I find it hard to believe.'

Weaver's head stirs, only slightly.

'Why?'

I look her in the eye.

'I feel like I know her,' I say.

Weaver nods slowly.

Yet the thought stays, bothering me. The City Guard did not take Valeria away together with the other weavers. I cannot think of an explanation for it.

'I can see that Valeria means a lot to you,' Weaver says. 'I promise to do what I can.'

'There is something I have been wondering about,' I say. 'I don't understand which way she took out of the House of Webs. No one saw her walking in the web-maze. And no air gondolas have left the port since yesterday morning.'

Weaver raises her eyebrows. Her thumb taps the edge of the table. The sound is faint, like a beetle hidden in the walls.

'You have been asking around,' she says.

'If I knew where she was,' I say, 'I'd go after her.'

Weaver looks at me intently, as if pondering the truth of my words. Eventually her mouth turns into a slight smile.

'I understand,' she says. 'You may have heard stories about the past of the island. Maybe even this one. Not necessarily from me, but from someone else.' Her voice proceeds deep and knowing its direction, like waters in the canals. 'A rumour tells there are secret routes on the island, long-abandoned passages. Only a few know of them. Yet it is said that the Dreamers have rediscovered their locations and put them into use again.' She goes quiet for a moment. 'And I have heard that one of those routes begins at the House of Webs.'

Hope begins to shine within me like algae in a glow-glass.

'Whereabouts?' I ask. My voice sounds breathless.

'If I had to look,' Weaver says, 'I would look somewhere people rarely go. An unnoticed and dusk-covered corner.'

In the House of Webs, everything is on display. In the dormitories you sleep under the eyes of others; the cells are shared, and the washing rooms and dining halls are communal. There is no shelter from looks in the Halls of Weaving. Only Weaver's room is often empty.

I remember the webs, the rustling voice in the dark. The limb that studied me. The chill rising from the core of the sea, an abyss where no warmth could reach.

'If there was such a route,' Weaver continues, 'it might not be the safest, and it is difficult to tell where it would take you. Anyone who does not know the way would do wisely to consider carefully whether to follow it.'

Weaver's face has paused to wait. Her hand rests still on the edge of the table, the other one in her lap, hidden.

'I think I understand,' I say.

'My study will be empty tonight,' Weaver replies. 'You may go now.'

I get up to leave.

'Why are you telling me this?' I ask.

I think I see something on Weaver's face that resembles sorrow, or perhaps regret, but in the dusky room it is hard to be certain.

'Because I must,' she says.

As I walk through the door, I feel the stares of twelve of Our Ladies of Weaving on my back. Weaver may have turned hers away, or not.

I have all day to consider it. I think of the unfamiliar hands that have taken speech away from Valeria, of the sharp weapons of the City Guard. I imagine the House of the Tainted, its high walls covered by thorny vines and its gates which prisoners never exit. I feel the weight of the key I gave to Valeria, which she carried above her heart, against her skin. I think of her hands on the smooth surface of the shuttle and on my skin, of her face in the dusk and the story hidden in her tapestry.

By nightfall my decision is made.

If Valeria is with Dreamers, she cannot be in great danger.

If she is somewhere else, she is there because I gave her the key.

Either way, I must find her.

I dress in several layers of sea-wool. The shoes are easy to pick: I only have one pair. I place some dried fruits, a piece of bread and a wineskin filled with water in the middle of a shawl, then tie it into a knot. I pick up a glow-glass from my bedside table. I go and refill it from the shimmering algae pool in the square.

The final thing I do is find the only piece of paper I have. I am now glad I have carried it in my coin pouch at all times and not left it in the cell for anyone to find. I already know by heart the ink recipe Alva wrote on it. I scribble a few sentences with a charcoal pen on the blank side.

I have gone looking for Valeria down the path marked by Our Lady of Weaving. If I do not return within a week, ask Weaver to show the way and get in touch with my brother in the House of Words. E

I cross out the ink recipe on the other side, fold the paper and write 'Alva' on it.

On my way to Weaver's study I stop by the sick bay and slide the note through the gap under the door.

Our Lady of Weaving watches me from the wall. The threads at the ends of her many fingers tighten, shift, loosen and tauten again as the fabric undulates. Without looking I know that the low door in the corner is cracked open.

I step through it with the glow-glass in my hand, into the place where everything looks different.

The strange stench that reminds me of dead things surges stronger over me than last time. In the growing light of the glow-glass I see now that darkness had given the room a different scale. On my first visit, the height resembled that of a great hall, the distance between the walls felt like the width of many Halls of Weaving, and the end where the ancient creature lives was as far as the sea or sky. I see clearly now that the room is barely larger than Weaver's study. The far end is still draped in shadows, the webs persistent and far-reaching, and the figure waiting amidst them is big – several times my size – but not enormous, not too much for the mind to comprehend. In light, many things lose their impossibility and turn into a conceivable part of the world.

I see other things I did not see the first time around. On the edges of the room, there are hanging lumps wrapped in silk yarn. None of them is large enough to be a human. Most are the size of small birds. A few could be goats, or maybe dogs. Someone must have brought them here. Weaver, perhaps. A mild nausea runs through me.

Spinner stands there, in the broken darkness that is her home and my gate. Her limbs have stopped, but the movement still sways on the web she is spinning.

I wait for her to speak. When the silence continues, I address her.

'I came back,' I say. 'Do you know why I am here?'

Spinner is quiet. A draught moves in the threads.

'Do you know who I am?' I continue.

A voice materializes from the shadows, put together from sounds that are not produced by a human.

'Of course I do,' the creature says. I am not certain if

180

she is answering both of my questions, or just one. 'Do you?'

My words are small and feeble before her; they vanish into dark corners.

'Because I believe you can help me,' I say, although that only answers one of the two questions she may have posed.

'Yes,' Spinner says, and her voice rustles like dried seaweed. 'The girl who weaves a different pattern. Who turns the threads into her own map. You wish to step into it and follow.'

She goes quiet. Silence intrudes me, encircles my thoughts and draws them clear.

'Have you seen her pass here?' I ask.

'Interesting,' Spinner says. 'I can see your outline more clearly. Before, your spirit hid and wandered without direction. Now it has chosen its path.'

She moves one of her long limbs. It brushes softly against the stone floor.

'There is a secret way out of the House of Webs,' I say. 'Is there not?'

A limb rises towards me and falls on my chest, before I have time to yield. Terror thrusts through me and settles as a fluttering in my muscles. The limb does not press or push, but I sense its strength precisely. One swift movement, one merciless wrench that would require less of her than plucking a loose thread from a fabric would of me, and I would never talk again, or move.

'Even if you were right,' Spinner says, 'why would you wish to walk that way?'

I imagine Valeria vanishing among the shadows of the earth, her red hair disappearing around the corner, her coat-hem waving, my own hand reaching for it and meeting nothing but empty air. My voice curls somewhere under my chest, will not rise to the lips. My heart beats red and slippery in my breast. The only thing between its movements and the strange, stark limb of the creature is fragile human bone and a strip of thin skin. I feel Spinner's mind probe my thoughts.

'Is she the only reason?' Spinner asks.

I do not understand the question.

'What other reason could I have?' I respond with words more fragile than webs.

Spinner stares at me with all her eyes, and yet stares only into her own darkness. A memory turns in me, another. A dream I have half-forgotten. They slide away, drift apart in the dusk. Spinner is quiet. Her mind draws further. Cold gathers around me, and silence.

'It does not matter,' she eventually says. 'My mind has travelled in the world for a long while. Sometimes it wanders and seeks what no longer exists.' Her voice ripples into the dark and goes quiet.

'I only wish to find Valeria,' I say. 'Will you show me the way?'

Spinner is silent and still. Then a great sigh moves across the room, rouses winds to blow above the sea. The weight withdraws from my chest. The limb falls to the floor without a sound. I breathe evenly again.

I see the creature move towards the wall. I hear a click. A breeze blows into the room from the shadows behind Spinner, colder than winter sea and cutting like the edge of broken glass.

'Go,' Spinner says. 'The hours of your kind are brief and your days are brittle, and there will not be many chances at happiness.'

I pull my shawl tighter around me and shiver. I walk

past Spinner between the webs. I do not look at her directly, but I sense her heavy presence next to me. I step through the doorway that has opened in the wall, and hear the door close behind me. I do not stay to see if I can open it again. I do not need to.

The glow-glass is delicate as an insect's wing against the unmoving storm of the darkness. In its light I discern my own arm, the tattoos on my wrist poking from the sleeve end, and a few steps before me. I am standing on top of a stairway. The steps deepen into the earth. There is no other way ahead. I begin the descent.

The stairs are steep, smooth-worn, and the stones do not shift under my weight. I listen to the space. Sounds from the House of Webs or the city do not carry to the passage at all. I hear a distant sighing and roaring, which I imagine to be the sea, a wind that moves atop water and gathers waves into tall, sharp folds. I soon give up on trying to maintain a sense of direction; the stairs circle around their own axis like wool on a spindle.

There is nothing to indicate whether the route was last used yesterday or a hundred years ago. My senses seek a footprint, a hair stuck to a wall, a scent still floating in the stagnant air or a human voice far ahead. The stones keep within what they know, do not stir to reveal and tell.

When I do not expect it, my foot meets a level floor, hits it too hard because it is closer than I anticipate.

The floor spreads ahead of me like the frozen surface of a pond. It is only slightly wider than the staircase. I raise my hand. It hits the ceiling. The walls only allow one direction, so I continue along the passageway. Dark ribbons of algae run along the borders like dark upside-down flames flaring towards the innards of the earth. I discern oozing humidity, as if the stones are sweating. Yet the air is cuttingly cold.

Eventually the passage opens into a wider space.

The first thing I see is a faint sheen on the walls circling the darkness. The ceiling above rises to form a high vault that vanishes into the shadows. The rock floor before me is sleek, as if washed pure from all human traces. Across, I discern a black doorway leading deeper into the dark. I step towards the wall and raise the glow-glass close to it. Carefully I run my fingers along the wall. It is smooth under my hand, its surface glass-clear and orange-yellow. I recognize it as amber. I take a few steps and let my hand continue following the wall. The smoothness morphs into sharp edges. The light of the glow-glass hits the shining-white objects.

Seashells.

Most of them are barely larger than my fingertips, and their glinting mother-of-pearl insides are turned outward. They have been arranged next to each other in patterns, but there is not enough light for me to see the whole.

I follow the curve of the cave. Approximately halfway I see a niche in the wall. Inside, there is a small pedestal, like the base of a statue. Above the pedestal a round, convex disc is attached to a chain, its surface apparently formed by several circles within each other. I bring the glow-glass closer. The disc hangs yellow-orange and translucent in the stagnant air.

Amber.

When the light from the glow-glass hits the disc, it refracts onto the walls of the niche and seems to brighten.

I place the glow-glass on the pedestal and pull the amber disc cautiously downwards. Somewhere higher up there is a metallic creak. The chain moves. The amber disc descends to cover the glow-glass.

I turn to look at the hall and my breath catches, as if a night-maere had sat down on my chest.

The amber lens grows the light of the glow-glass brighter than the sheen of full moon. It falls on the mother-of-pearl of thousands and thousands of seashells, draws their patterns clear. It pierces the smooth, honey-coloured surface of the walls, showing what is hidden in them.

The creatures stand still in their translucent amber shell, taller than me, slim limbs arched. I immediately think of Spinner. The bodies of the creatures have the same build, but these ones are larger, and their jaws look wider. The fangs are sharp and the look in the black eyes bright.

My heart flutters inside me. I try to get my breathing to calm down. These creatures have not moved towards or away from anyone for thousands of years, not raised a limb or wrapped anyone in their webs. Amber has caught them during a time so distant that I have no words for it. But they do not look forgotten or hidden away, not like obscure figures on the edges of the senses. As I walk closer and study the creature that is separated from me by nothing more than a thin layer of translucent wall, I see each bristle on its limbs and body, each round and glistening eye. The posture in which it is frozen. As if to attack.

Others like it float in the halted time of the amber. One has curled its limbs into a tight knot. One limb of another creature is broken at a joint. Some are tensed, wriggling their way out, at strange, anxious angles. One holds prey in its jaws: an animal no bigger than myself, and not very different.

The cave is roughly circular. Carved by the sea and reshaped by human hands, I think. Someone must have polished the amber to reveal the creatures within. And many hands over many, many years have collected the seashells, sorted them by colour and attached them to the walls. At first their patterns look in my eyes like a word I have known but forgotten, or a dream dying at dawn. But as I stare at them for longer, I begin to see more than parts of something bigger. I begin to see threads that have each their place.

The parts tie together and I understand.

The seashells form the Web of Worlds, surrounding and enclosing the room. Stars glow blue at its knots where the strands meet, and small moons that grow from slim sickles to full globes and shrink into tiny claw-slivers again. All strands run towards the centre, a shape that I first take for the sun, made from silvery-white and pale-yellow seashells. Its eight points reach in all directions. As I stare at it for longer, the points morph into arms, the rays shooting from them into threads holding earth and sky and sea together.

It is the sun and Our Lady of Weaving at the same time, and she is not just holding the threads, she is spinning them and arranging them and weaving the tapestry of life itself. I now see that some of the patterns are not images, but there are words too: none that I know, their language long forgotten, but the letters I recognize and know they spell something with a meaning.

There are small human characters shaped around Our Lady of Weaving. Threads run to them from her fingertips, and from their fingertips start other threads. They grow into trees, buildings, clouds and sea animals.

I do not understand what I see, but as I gaze at the patterns, it feels as if a long-unmoving knot begins to unravel inside me.

I walk a full circle around the hall to make certain there is no other exit that might have gone unnoticed. The only ways out are the passageway from which I came, and the other across the room, which I must follow.

I pick up the glow-glass. The light goes out in the hall again and the images sink under the dark surface. The eye closes.

When I come to the doorway, something shifts behind me. I turn to look. All I see is my own shadow, which follows me, climbs onto my back and wraps itself around me.

I take it with me. The chill of the sea emanates as a veil through the doorway onto my skin as I step into the passage.

Behind the doorway the walls turn into dark and coarse stone again. The passage descends deeper under the island. I have walked a few hundred steps, when my eyes brush the bare slice of my wrist at the sleeve end. I hold the glow-glass a few palm-widths away from my skin. The tattoos do not show as clearly as earlier. I wonder how long I have been walking in the passage. It cannot be longer than an hour or two since I left. I filled the glow-glass with fresh algae water just before I stepped into Spinner's chamber. It should last at least a day, maybe two.

I continue and count my steps. After three hundred I raise the glow-glass again and look at my wrist. The light has grown dimmer than before.

I quicken my footsteps.

I am grateful for the simple route, for the passage which does not branch in many directions. I force myself to proceed without looking back. I begin to wonder what will happen if the glow-glass loses its light entirely. Perhaps

I could find my way back in the dark, feeling the way with my hands. But who would hear me, if I ended up behind the door to Spinner's chamber? Would Weaver let me back into the House of Webs? Would Spinner know, or care?

The glow is dying fast. Only a few pale-blue speckles float in the water. I can barely discern my hand carrying the glow-glass, and a narrow stretch of the wall beside me. I realize that when the last of the light goes out, I will be completely alone. The algae is a living being, but it is dying next to me, and there is nothing I can do to stop it.

I fumble onwards until darkness comes.

Time disappears into the cracks of the stone floor and freezes as puffs of breath in the air. Maybe the world above does not exist. Maybe there is no island or city, no House of Webs. No Valeria. Maybe this is the only existence and everything else is a dream. I wonder how far below the city I am, and another, far more terrifying image takes shape in my mind: what if I am under the sea?

I imagine the stone ceiling above me ripping apart, the weight of water crashing in and filling the passageway, swirling to the stone steps and enclosing me in its lightless embrace. No one would know where I am, or ever find me – not Weaver, not Janos, not Alva. Not Valeria. Perhaps she would float in the darkness of water somewhere ahead of me, and the currents would carry us closer to each other, intertwine our limbs, and we would move in a strange, soundless embrace, unseen by anyone. Water would tug off the garments floating about us, and we would sleep forever on each other's skin without knowing it ourselves. Perhaps we would be washed to the storming sea, where waves would tear us apart again. And we would not know that, either.

The darkness pulls me deeper. The passageway is still descending. My fingertips meet moisture on the walls. In the distance I discern roaring, a sound of welling water. Maybe I am on my way to the bottom of the sea, where the drowned wail and long for the daylight they will never see again. Maybe I should stay here and wait for them to come for me.

Weariness weighs in my limbs. *I am caught in your net,* I think to the drowned. *Come and claim me.*

And then, light.

Not bright or all-changing, but nevertheless: the thin outline of a rectangle-shaped door far ahead. I walk towards it with cold-stiffness and ice weighing down my bones. The distance is long, but finally I am in front of the doorway. I have hung the glow-glass from my belt long ago. I place both hands on the surface of the door and feel it. The warmth surprises me. The surface is wooden. I run my fingers across it. There is no handle of any kind.

I draw a breath, press my palms against the door and push.

Light floods in my face and stabs behind my eyes. Warmth descends onto my skin.

'We have been waiting for you,' a voice says.

CHAPTER ELEVEN

I have not yet had time to get used to the light, when I am gripped by my upper arms and wrenched through the doorway. Someone larger than myself steps behind me and captures my wrists in a severe grip. The glow-glass slips from my belt and breaks on the floor. I see flames reflected in the water spreading into a pool at my feet. I try to tear myself free, but I realize I am shivering, and all my limbs feel as fragile as empty husks.

I begin to see the shape of the room at which I have arrived. There are no windows. Instead, a large fireplace is blazing on each of the four walls. Their burn emanates onto my skin, but the chill of the passage still smoulders in my bones. *This is how cold the dead are,* I think, *when nothing moves in them any more. When all has stopped and nothing will ever change again.*

The only piece of furniture is a table with a skein of rope on it. A man stands in front of one of the fireplaces, his back turned to me. He picks up a coal poker and trims the fire with it. A cloud of sparks bursts into the air and withers in front of the fireplace like a swarm of dead insects.

190

The man turns to me. He does not put the poker down. I recognize his City Guard uniform only a moment before I recognize his face.

I cannot bring myself to make a sound. The words stick to my tongue. The spikes of the poker are knife-sharp. A voice speaks next to my ear.

'The new arrival looks somewhat surprised,' it says. 'Would you agree, Captain Lazaro?'

'You are undisputably correct, Captain Biros,' Lazaro says.

He nods at Biros. The fingers around my wrists tighten their grip and Biros shoves me forward. I almost lose my balance. Words return to me.

'Wait,' I say. My voice moves coarse and taut in the room. 'What is this place? Where am I?'

Lazaro gives a slight nod. Biros stops forcing me forward.

'You will see soon enough,' Lazaro says.

In my mind, I go through the underground route again. I look for doorways I might have missed, exits I may have passed. I find nothing. It is not impossible that there might have been a fork in the passage somewhere. I walked the last stretch in complete darkness. But Lazaro and Biros were expecting me. This means someone somewhere knew there was only one route and one destination. That I could only end up here, if I ended up anywhere at all.

Anyone who does not know the route would be wise to consider carefully whether to follow it, Weaver had said. Her hands on the table, untarnished from work. Her closed gaze, brushing the door in the corner just enough for me to notice.

'Why am I here?' I ask.

Lazaro places the tips of the poker onto the floor. He moves them sideways, just a little. The hard metal screeches against stone.

'Orders from high places,' he says and smiles, a sharp smile of fire-glow. 'Would you like me to take over, Captain Biros?'

'I am quite pleased with the way things are, Captain Lazaro,' Biros says. 'But maybe you could lend me a helping hand.' I feel him bend my arms a little, so Lazaro can see my wrists.

'With pleasure,' Lazaro says.

He places the fire poker onto a stand in front of the fireplace and moves to the table. He picks up the skein of rope and begins to slowly unravel it as he walks closer. Biros is still holding my wrists, when Lazaro wraps several layers of rope around them and pulls it tight. The rope bites into my skin. Its fibre prickles.

'Thank you, Captain Lazaro,' Biros says.

'The pleasure is all mine, Captain Biros,' Lazaro says. 'Are we ready?'

'All ready,' Biros replies.

He pushes me towards the door in the corner between two of the fireplaces. It is difficult for me to turn to look while I stumble across the room, but I can feel Lazaro's eyes following me. When Biros stops me to open the door, I turn my head far enough that my neck hurts. I speak over my shoulder into the room.

'Where is Valeria?'

Lazaro's face twitches, but he remains silent. Biros pushes me to move. The door is open now. Biros's mouth is so close to my ear that I feel his breath on my skin. A shudder runs through me. I try to suffocate it. He shoves me into the faintly lit corridor. The door closes behind us. We begin the long climb up stairways. He is too close behind me on every step.

Cold settles around me again now that the fires are left

behind. The corridors are bare, windowless, and the walls are close. They catch the echoes of our footsteps and cast them into the surrounding silence. Torches paint quivering spheres of light along the way, and between them the dark crawls onto the skin. We stop several times to pass through locked gates. Biros has a key to every one of them. I feel like I am walking towards the centre of a maze that keeps moving further away. Biros does not talk to me during the journey, but his grip of my arms feels forged from metal and the points of his boots hit my heels repeatedly. Intentionally or not, I do not know. He would not hesitate to hurt me if I tried to escape. And where would I run? A stretch of corridor between two locked, barred gates would not take me far.

Eventually we turn to a corridor at the end of which stands a guard dressed in a uniform that carries the sun emblem of the Council. I am surprised to see that she is a woman. The City Guard does not allow women to join. A long whip with a thick handle is hanging from her belt.

'This is her, then,' the guard says.

'Yes,' Biros replies. 'I trust you know what to do with her.'

The guard regards me, her face impassive.

'The instructions were clear,' she says.

'She is yours,' Biros says.

The guard-woman nods. Biros steps back. The guard takes my arm and opens the door. It is thick and makes a metallic sound.

'We do not have all night,' she says.

I walk through, listening to Biros's footsteps behind me. They do not follow.

The next corridor opens wider. We walk past several closed doors with only a small hole at eye level. I see

193

nothing but unmoving dusk behind the holes. Behind one door there is a tense, stretching sound. Like someone pulling a narrow string tight, or moaning.

'Keep your gaze turned ahead,' the guard-woman orders.

We climb one more flight of stairs. Behind yet another gate a smell pushes against us that is not very different from the House of Webs, only denser. It is the odour of people and bodies. Here, a strong stench of drainage blends with it. I breathe through my mouth so I cannot smell it.

The cells only have bars instead of solid doors. I catch glimpses as we walk past. Some of their inhabitants are lying on plain bunks. Others are curled up in the corners, either sitting or lying on the floor, face buried in hands. I realize most of them are probably trying to sleep. Everything is lit by glow-glass pipes along the corridor. The guard pokes at me to walk on. She stops near the end of the corridor, opens the door of an empty shell and begins to loosen the rope around my wrists. She yanks the rope off and pushes me in. The key creaks in the lock.

'Your number is 505,' the guard says.

'Wait,' I say. 'What is happening? Where am I?'

The guard is silent. She pushes the key into her pocket and leaves. I hear her footsteps draw further away in the corridor.

I stand beside the bars. I see the prisoner in the opposite cell get up from the corner, walk to the bars and push her face against them. Finally I understand where I am.

The tattoo is clear in the middle of her forehead.

The mark of the Tainted.

A loud bell begins to clang. I have not slept a wink. I ache all over, my neck and back are stiff from lying on the hard bunk and my throat feels like I have tried to swallow shards of glass. I am still cold. The clanking of the bell is followed by rustling and whimpering in the cells. Heavy footsteps enter the corridors, and there are creaks and clangs as the doors are opened. When the light changes, I think for a moment there is a window somewhere and daylight, but then I realize the guards have brought torches with them.

Eventually, a bored-looking guard appears outside my barred door. She lets me out and orders me to join the queue. There are another twenty or so prisoners already standing in it, herded by three other guards.

'Move!' one of them shouts.

I look around in the dining hall. There are maybe a couple of hundred people sitting at the long tables. They are all girls and women. My eyes fall on a girl who looks familiar. I realize it is Mirea: the ten-year-old weaver who was taken from the House of Webs a few months earlier because of her night-maere. The tattoo on her forehead is still fresh, its lines sharp. The wrists revealed by the too-short sleeves are narrow as fish-backs. She does not see me. Like most prisoners, she is staring at the thin porridge on her plate without looking around.

Next to me, an older woman whose hair is woven into a long, white braid gives me a glare. I turn my gaze to the porridge, but cannot help noticing that her hands are covered in scabs. The skin of the fingers looks like it has broken and grown back repeatedly without ever having time to heal properly. There are long, lighter scratches running across the backs of her brown hands. A woman sits opposite who cannot be much older than me. The skin of her hands, too, looks broken and only half-healed.

I let my gaze slide along the surface of the table and

see that everyone's hands are scarred and scabby, even those of the very youngest. In addition to this, many have visible patches of rash on their faces and arms.

I do not see Valeria. Apart from Mirea, I also do not see any of the weavers the City Guard took away from the House of Webs because of dream-plague.

There is still porridge on my plate when the clanging of the bell begins again. Everyone gets up and forms a long line. A guard opens the door, and the prisoners begin to march out of the dining hall. I join the line and follow the others, worried that I will do something wrong. The guards keep their hands close to their whips.

I notice that it is not only the prisoners who carry the tattoo of the House of the Tainted on their foreheads; a few guards do, too.

The line walks into a long and narrow room with pigeonholes on the walls. Everyone seems to have their own. Women around me begin to undress and put on the garments folded on the pigeonhole shelves.

I stand at the centre of the room, not knowing what to do.

'Excuse me,' I say to a middle-aged woman covered in dark moles who is changing next to me. 'I'm new. I don't have a pigeonhole.'

The woman looks at me, expressionless, and then inclines her head towards the nearest guard. Uncertainly I approach the guard. She wears a house-tattoo on her forehead, already slightly faded and blurred on the edges, although she looks like she cannot be older than thirty years. She must have lived in the house since she was a child. I conclude she must be a woman, because I have not seen any male guards. Yet her build is angular in a robust way, and her face looks sexless. Her short-trimmed hair barely shows from under the guard's cap. There is a strange familiarity about her face, but I am unable to place it.

'Excuse me,' I say. 'I don't have a pigeonhole.'

The guard turns to look at me. Her expression is not kind, but it is not threatening, either. Her eyes fall on my forehead.

'You are new, are you not?'

Her voice is low. I nod.

'What is your number?'

'505,' I say.

'Follow me,' the guard orders.

I walk after her to the back of the room, where she unlocks a cupboard and pulls out a set of garments, which she hands to me.

'If it is so big it falls off or so small you cannot fit in it, ask for another one,' she says. 'Preferably ask me.' She locks the cupboard. 'There are some unused pigeonholes at this end.'

She nods towards an empty pigeonhole with no one standing next to it. I thank her.

The others have already changed and are shivering in short trousers that end above the knee and in sleeveless, loose tops. Even in summer, the outfit would be unusual. At this time of the year, it is a mere undergarment.

'No loitering!' a guard shouts from the other end of the room. I realize she means me. Quickly I tear off my layers of clothing and put on the outfit that provides no warmth. I barely have time to push my own clothes into the pigeonhole, when the line is already moving out of the changing room. I wrap my arms around myself and follow.

'Hands on the sides!' the guard shouts. I straighten my arms and notice their hair standing up.

I recognize the place where we are taken along stairs and corridors. Last time I looked at it was from the other side: the old, secluded harbour where spectres pass and vanish without a trace, visitors from the land of dreams and death. Now I am one of the spectres. From this side I see the city that does not look back, because I no longer exist under its gaze. None of us do.

We are marched onto ships, packed below the deck. I smell sweat and the sea, the dirt and humidity inside the ship.

The hold is divided by rails running across it. Some prisoners slump down to sit or squat in the corners. Others stand. There is little light. Only a few glow-glasses hang in the corners. I thread my way to the edge of the crowd. There are no guards down in the hold, but one of them comes to see us at repeated intervals.

When the guard is not around to hear, a faint chatter grows to surround me. No one talks loudly, and no one talks to me. I look for Mirea. Eventually I see her leaning on a curved wall near the back of the hold. Slowly I start moving towards her. The sea is not harsh, but I am not used to the swaying floor under my feet, and I need to hold on to the rail so as not to lose my balance.

There is an empty space next to Mirea where I settle. She does not look at me.

'Hey,' I say.

Mirea does not seem to hear. Her face is pale, almost blue in the dusk of the hold. The bones of her cheeks jut out from under her skin. She says nothing.

'Do you remember me?' I ask. I keep my voice low.

Mirea turns to look at me, surprised that someone has spoken to her. I see a slow recognition on her face, but not the slightest delight.

'Yes,' she says. 'You let them take me.'

I remember her tears in the dusk of the dormitory, the distress in her expression, when she understood. My chest tightens.

'I know,' I say. 'I'm sorry. I was afraid. That they would take me too, if I tried to help.'

Mirea stares at me, her eyes cold.

'And they did,' she says.

'Yes,' I say. 'They did.'

Not the same way they took you, I think, but adding that would be meaningless. The outcome is the same.

'Good,' Mirea says and turns her face away from me. She stares ahead, into the shadows at the low end of the hold.

I have nothing to say to that. We listen to the roll of the waves and the creaking of the wood.

Eventually I break the silence.

'I know you're mad at me,' I say. 'And I deserve it. But I'd like to ask you something.'

Mirea continues to stare ahead of her without looking at me. Her breath flows back and forth. Her ankles are no thicker than a few of my fingers together. They are covered in purple rash.

'Ask,' she says.

'Where are they taking us?' I ask.

'To work,' Mirea says.

I look around. I find it hard to imagine what kind of work we can do in the cold of winter in our underwear.

'What kind of work?'

'You will see,' Mirea says.

She still does not wish to talk to me. I cannot blame her. In her place I would probably have got to my feet and sought somewhere else to sit.

Mirea's narrow fingers scratch her instep. The sound of the waves rises and falls ceaselessly.

'But it doesn't kill you,' she adds after a long pause.

'What doesn't?'

'The work,' she says.

I nod. I am not certain if she sees it, because she still stubbornly refuses to look at me.

'I have another question,' I say.

Mirea does not respond. I do not take it for assent, but neither for rejection.

'Have any others arrived lately, or am I the only new one?'

Mirea's gaze circles the dusky space.

'503 came last week,' she says. 'The grey-haired one sitting by the opposite wall. About midway.'

I look. A woman is squatting on the floorboards with her gaze turned inward, palms pressed together. Her lips move soundlessly. Maybe she is talking to Our Lady of Weaving. The tattoo on her wrinkled face is red-edged and fresh.

'Is she the only one?' I ask.

'Another one arrived yesterday. 504,' Mirea replies. 'She's maybe as old as you. Or maybe a little older.'

I have looked around so many times I am certain I would have seen Valeria if she was in the hold. Yet hope rises in me, light and heavy at once.

'What does she look like?' I ask. 'Is she here?'

'Next to the hatch,' Mirea says. 'Black hair, a little shorter than you.'

I look and I see the girl whose curly hair has fallen to cover her forehead. She notices me looking and rolls her eyes. Embarrassed, I turn my gaze away.

'Are all prisoners brought here to work?' I ask. 'Or is there another place where prisoners are kept?'

'There's a later shift,' Mirea says. 'They eat after us, and their ships go to a different place.' This knowledge makes me feel a little better. Perhaps Valeria is in the house after all. The second shift also explains why I have not seen any of the others taken from the House of Webs. 'And there is the men's side, but I have never seen them,' Mirea continues. 'And then there's the solitary confinement. Sometimes the new ones are taken directly there.'

I remember the dense, thick doors past which the guard walked me, their small peekholes. I nod.

The hatch opens and a guard looks in. The chatter is cut short.

After the guard has gone, Mirea says, 'If you want to talk again, don't do it anywhere but here. Talking gets you in trouble.'

She moves away from me and joins a group standing by the opposite wall, where someone is telling a story. I only hear stray words of it. I look at them laugh, but do not know what it is at.

The journey is long. The rocking of the ship makes me nauseated. It is difficult to estimate the passage of time in the hold, but when we are ordered to the deck, I can see from the angle of light that the morning has turned to day. The ship is anchored near a cluster of islets scattered in the sea as if by a giant's hand. The nearest islands are small mounds on the horizon, and I cannot see the tall buildings of the city on them. Then again, I do not know if they would be visible from this distance; I have never been so far from the island before.

I begin to understand what is happening when the prisoners begin to line up behind daises next to the ship's rail. There are only enough of them for about twenty at a time. The rest of us remain in queues behind them. A cold wind sweeps the deck. My teeth clatter and my stomach churns.

We are all given light, tight-woven baskets. I watch the others tie theirs to their waists and do the same. One of the guards rings a bronze bell hanging from a hook and turns an hourglass. The sand begins to measure time. The first prisoners dive into the sea from the daises. I now understand the meaning of the garments: the outfits are light so they will not hinder swimming. But at this time of the year the seawater is cold as frozen glass.

The waves fold and spit salt into the air. A seagull takes wing from an islet of rock. Every hair on my skin stands sharp, like a bristle. The first divers surface. One or two of them are holding something white in their hands, like branches paled by a silver-burning sun.

Bone coral.

For a moment I am perplexed. There is bone coral everywhere on the island: in the amulets people wear around their necks, and hanging over doorways to keep night-maeres away, and in the buttons we sew on our garments. Great amounts of it wash onto the shores every month. Why would we be sent to gather it from faraway waters?

The women throw the branches into a small boat floating on the waves that is tied to the ship with a rope. They pull out more from the baskets tied to their waists.

'Wrong colour!' one of the guards shouts. 'The white ones are worth nothing.'

'This is all there is,' one of the women shouts back.

'Keep looking,' the guard shouts. 'There is sand in the hourglass yet.'

I understand then. It is not bone coral we are expected to find, but blood coral. The Ink Quarters have ground it into red-dye and ships have carried it to faraway lands throughout my lifetime. I have always imagined the seafloor thick with forests of it, only waiting to be thinned so they could grow back.

The prisoners draw a deep breath and vanish underwater again.

I am next in line. From the corner of my eye I catch glimpses of the sand flowing towards the moment when I will have to cast myself into the sea. The divers keep springing to the surface and throwing their modest catches into the boat. I notice them glancing at each other, clearly hoping that someone might have found a coral haul of which they could have their share.

The sand flows to an end. The bell begins to clang. The prisoner who jumped into the sea ahead of me comes back to the surface. Her lips are colourless. Her hands are empty.

The guards throw the rope ladder into the sea, and the divers climb on board, shivering with cold. One of the guards, the same I spoke to earlier, begins handing them blankets they wrap themselves in as soon as they reach the deck. I decide to turn my thoughts towards that moment.

I step onto the dais. The other second-round divers jump into the water. My feet do not budge. My weight does not move. The water below furrows, grows teeth-like edges on its surface.

A harsh hand presses onto my back and pushes.

My breath stops short from the blow of the collision and cold. I hit the water half-sideways, and the collision feels like a sore slap on my skin. I paddle up to the surface to breathe. The air is no warmer than the water.

'You! Back!' one of the guards shouts when she sees me. 'There is no place for freeloaders on this vessel.'

I fill my lungs with air and try to keep moving so the chill wrapped around me will not paralyse me completely.

The sea encloses me, faint and soundless. I swim deeper and fumble with blind hands. My fingers meet sharp-edged stone and soft, slippery seaweed. Something slithers away from under my touch. Then I feel something hard and forked in my hand. I squeeze my fist around it and begin to kick my way to the surface.

My lungs seem to be running out of breath. I blow out air through my nose, and my chest aches with the need to breathe in. My head pierces the surface of the water and ripping-cold air flows into my lungs. The cold prickles my limbs. I look at the branch I am holding, and I nearly cry. It is only a tree branch covered in seaweed, probably from one of the stunted pines growing on the islets, low and twisted.

I place the branch on the water for the waves to claim.

The guards are throwing glances at me from the deck. All I can do is draw breath and dive again. This time I force my eyes open under water. I have little hope of finding coral; with my eyes closed, I have none. I need to blink, because the salt stings. Everything is blurred.

Slowly I begin to discern shapes: the dark, oblong form of the ship behind me, the ridges sloping into the sea from the islets until they open into cliffs and deep caves. I need to return to the surface to breathe again. Yet I am almost certain about one thing already. The blood coral, if there is any, grows in the caves and on the lower surfaces of the deep-reaching cliffs that are hard to get to.

I also realize now why divers are used for gathering the coral. The gathering devices of the coral ships are four-branched, slightly bigger than anchors. But if blood coral now only grows in places where the device does not reach, in nooks and crannies requiring precision, hidden in the folds of rock, then only human hands will do.

During my next dive the assumption is strengthened. Most others head directly for the dark holes in the rock and the undersides of the cliffs so deep that I have no courage to try to swim to them. There is porous reef visible on the stone ridges, but when I swim closer and try the surface with my hand, I notice that it has probably not grown for years. There are few branches, and those are simply short, death-white stubs. Worth nothing. My hand raises a rust-coloured cloud of sediment into a slow movement from the reef.

I no longer know how many times I have dived. I know I will not be able to do it many more times. Feeling is vanishing from my hands and feet. The cold only cuts occasionally now. Just as I am ready to sink into water again, the bell begins to clang and the rope ladder is lowered. I find it difficult to move my body, to pull my own weight up the side of the ship. My fingers slip off the rope. I look at them in confusion. They simply no longer obey my order to hold on. Sea-floor sediment clings to my skin. A guard grasps my wrist and drags me over the rail with a pained look on her face. My legs give in when I reach the deck. A blanket is wrapped around me and a mug of hot, faintly herbal-smelling water is placed in my hand.

I hear the splashes as I am being herded into the cabin close to the brazier. I think of the sand pouring in the hourglass unstopping, and I wait, my heart colder than anything else.

I shiver in the cabin, and the warmth of the brazier is nothing more than a puff of breath on one's skin on a chilly day, only warming for a moment and leaving an even deeper cold behind. I see the short-haired guard look at me and say something to another guard. The other one shrugs without looking at me.

The ship does not head back to the island until dusk.

Back in my cell I am still shivering. Although I have been allowed to change into dry clothes and eat a meagre evening soup, the blanket around me feels thin and my bones have turned into ice. Broken glass sinks deeper into my throat every time I swallow, and my breath does not want to flow. I close my eyes and try to sleep, but it is too cold. I shiver in a drowse where I lose my sense of time.

My spirit sends me wandering in the stony maze of the House of the Tainted, behind the closed doors. I place my hand on the surface of each door to sense if Valeria is on the other side. I whisper into the opening on every door to call her to me, but she does not come.

Much later a burning eye appears in the half-dark. Looking at it makes my eyes hurt. I try to remain in the small, stiff coil into which I have curled, but I am pulled off my bunk. I try to speak, but only whingeing and wheezing comes from my mouth. The scorching eye glows in front of me all the way along the corridor. In the pupil I see the sun flaring on top of the Tower, staring back at me, red and ready to burn the world into ashes. I want to throw the Tower off its roots, sprain the bones of the earth underneath, but that power I do not hold. I want to tear down the stone sun, but it is too far above. The sides of the Tower are smooth and without foothold, and the stones below spread hard and merciless in all directions.

CHAPTER TWELVE

The waters of sleep part around me. I let them wash over the weight of my body and try to sink back in, but my lips feel dry, my nose is blocked and an ache throbs on my brow. I open my eyes. The bedsheets cling to me, and I can feel the wetness under my armpits. The room is unfamiliar. A woman dressed in a healer's white coat sits in the corner, darning a sock. I croak. The woman glances at me.

'Thirsty,' I say. The sound that comes out is not a word.

The woman seems to understand, however, because she gets up, picks up a jug from a small table and pours some water into a cup. She brings the cup to me. I wriggle into a sitting position from under the clammy sheets and drink. Water drips down my chin. Without asking questions the white-coat fills the cup again. Three cups later I begin to feel tolerable. The sheets are soaked with my sweat, and I am glad I cannot smell my own stench, but my throat no longer hurts. I remember short moments of wakefulness: hot herbal brew, salty broth I had barely been able to swallow. Humiliating squatting over the chamber-pot, supported by someone in a white coat – perhaps this woman, perhaps not – because my own legs would not carry me. A damp cloth on my forehead, and small red dots floating before my eyes.

I fall asleep again.

A pressing urge to go to the privy wakes me up. The white-coated woman walks me there, wearing a doubtful expression. She seems relieved when I do not slump along the way. As we return, I stop at the doorway. Someone in a guard's uniform is waiting for us in the room. At first I think it is someone from the City Guard, but then I realize the uniform is slightly different and bears the emblem of the Tainted. The guard turns. I recognize her as the same short-haired guard who gave me my diving outfit on the first day.

I remain standing, uncertain what is expected of me.

'Go back to rest,' the guard says. 'This won't take long.'

I sit down on the bed and try to look as formal as I can in my white gown. Cold air brushes across my chest. I shudder. The guard gives the healer a glance. She stares back for a moment that freezes and shatters, then collects her needlework and leaves the room. We are left alone.

The guard pulls forward the healer's chair from the corner and places it before me. She removes her cap, sits down and regards me.

Her skin is slightly darker than mine. Every feature of her face is strange to me, and yet there is something familiar about the shape of it. Her short hair curls against the arc of her skull. She watches me in silence. A broken cobweb floats on the wall. I discern the square of light of a narrow window near the ceiling. The passing shadow of a bird grazes it. Eventually the guard reaches out a hand and takes hold of my wrist. She turns the back of my hand upwards, pointing at the tattoo on my arm.

'You are from the House of Webs,' she says.

'Yes,' I say. I want to pull my hand away.

'I have always wondered what it is like there,' the guard says.

I wait for her to continue, but she does not.

'Have you visited any other Houses of Crafts?' I ask to fill the silence.

'Have you ever seen people who wear the mark of the Tainted walking around in the city?' she asks, an edge in her voice.

I think of the Ink-marking, the Dreamers standing on the dais before all eyes who only have two routes ahead of them: a return to the House of the Tainted, or banishment from the island.

'No,' I say.

The guard lets go of my hand.

'Tell me about the House of Webs,' she says.

So this is a questioning, then. I wrap Valeria in silence, tuck her at the back of my thoughts, turn her into hollow letters of a name I can barely spell.

'What would you like to know?' I ask.

'Anything,' the guard says.

It is a strange request. Frowning sends a crack of pain across my brow. I do not remember hitting my head, but I must have.

'Anything?'

'Anything,' she confirms.

A trick to get me talking against my better caution, perhaps. I scour my mind for something irrelevant, something safe.

'There's the smell of bread in the mornings,' I say. 'Not

every day. Twice, maybe three times a week. It doesn't carry all the way to our . . . my cell, but when I open the door to go for my wash, it wafts along the corridor, and I know there will be fresh, warm bread at breakfast. The kind with a crust that grates the roof of your mouth if you're not careful, and white insides that are like sun-baked clouds on your tongue.'

'We get freshly-baked bread here once a week,' the guard says. 'But it is always brown, hard before it is out of the oven. And by the end of the week there are white stains growing on it that taste like dirt water.' She crosses her arms. 'Tell me something else.'

'When the work has not yet begun in the Halls of Weaving,' I say, 'the unfinished wall-webs are like mist in the light sifting through the windows.' I can see them before my eyes: soft and pliant and yet made stronger than many a house built from stone. 'And as we come in, we bow to Our Lady of Weaving, who watches us from the wall.'

I speak of crammed mornings in the washrooms, of air gondolas docking at the port and of rooms where inside and out are not opposites, but one and the same. I talk about weaving, hanging and unravelling the webs. I pick and choose things that cannot possibly interest the guard: cleaning the chicken coops, the scent of rosemary and lavender in late-summer heat, the soft lights of the city flicking and fading like deep-sea creatures. I speak of the pool at the centre of the square, the brighter-than-world colours of the old silk-weed wall hangings in the Tapestry Room.

The guard listens to me in silence, as if memorizing everything I say.

As I speak, a realization grows within me.

I walked the long corridors of the house for years. I hid behind the closed door of my cell, and day after day I picked up the threads that sometimes weighed like chains. But the washrooms smelled of home, and the slow-blue fires of glow algae showed me the way after darkness had fallen. Now I would run my fingers along every surface, breathe in every smell and memorize the shape and size of every room like I once learned the paths in the web-maze, if I ever could return. There may have been days and nights when I wished to tear down the walls, but those walls were also my shelter and my skin, giving me the shape into which I grew. Without them I stand alone and terrified on a slowly drowning shore under a crumbling sky.

A stinging-hot bubble bursts in my chest and a clenched sob falls out of me. I cease to speak.

The guard looks around, seeking. She grasps a wrinkled but clean-looking rag lying on the table next to the water jug.

'Wipe your eyes,' she says and offers the rag to me. 'And your nose.'

I take the rag and blow my nose on it. My eyes leave damp stains on the fabric. When I look up again, I see the guard staring at the floor and something that could be a trace of kindness fading away on her face.

'You have said nothing about your house-elder,' the guard says and raises her eyes. 'What is she like?'

I see Weaver's tall figure walking along the corridors, standing still at a doorway. Is that what this is about? Her loyalty, or betrayal? I choose my words with caution.

'I have always thought she was fair and kind.'

The guard watches me, studies my face.

'Did something change?' she asks.

I see Weaver sitting at her table in the half-dark. Pointing the way with steady hands, speaking the words in a snare-smooth voice. I do not know what will spare or condemn me, or if anything will. I may as well speak the truth.

'It's her fault I am here,' I say. 'She sent me.'

A strange expression flashes on the guard's face, like a lightning so swift you cannot be certain if you saw it. I expect more questions. I think I can see them taking shape on her tongue and crowding her mouth until there are too many to hold.

But she gets up and says, 'Rest. You will return to work tomorrow.'

She moves the chair back into the corner of the room. The legs scratch the floor. She turns and stares at me. The light falls on the tattoo on her forehead.

'You are not here because of your house-elder,' she says.

I wait. She seems to weigh her words, rehearse them in her mind the way people do when they wish to share a secret. I hear someone pacing outside the door. Probably the healer.

'You are here because you carry the dream-plague,' she continues.

She puts her cap on and opens the door. I am almost certain that she intended to say something else. I wonder if she knows that what she said is not true. I cannot see behind her words and gestures.

After the guard is gone, the white-coated woman steps back in.

My forehead itches. I scratch it. Some skin comes off under my nails.

'I will put ointment on it,' the white-coat says. 'The wound will take a while to heal.'

'What wound?' I ask.

She begins to open the lid of the ointment jar.

'Sometimes the needles cause infections,' she says. Then she sees my face. 'Is everything fine?'

'Can I see?' I ask. My voice cracks.

There are no mirrors in the room, but there is a small metal plate on the side table. The white-coat hands it to me. Something passes across her face. I recognize it as compassion. In the surface of the plate I see my reflection, unclear and dim, but the features are just about discernible. And on my forehead, where it cannot be missed, a tattoo darker than my skin. I understand the red dots swimming before my eyes, the stinging above my eyebrows. Drops of blood on a damp cloth.

I hand the plate back.

'I do not want ointment,' I say.

The white-coat tilts her head, curves her lips downward and screws the lid of the jar back on. I wrap myself in the blanket and turn to the wall. I taste the salt of my tears as they trickle into my mouth.

I stand on the dream-cliff looking over the island and the sea. The mark on my forehead burns. I rouse a grey-gleaming torrent of rain from the dream-clouds that is like a wall-web cast over the world. The canals swell and wash the streets and doorsteps and bedrooms, where people sleep, unknowing. I call the dream-waves to come closer and shove them away again, I carve their crests with my hands and thrust them towards the sky, until no ship can survive in their steep, perilous desert. I dig ever deeper: I seek the roots and veins hidden under the seabed, buried in rock and coral and layers of mud. I tug at the bones and sinews of the earth far below and feel the sea rolling faster and faster, rolling towards the city and covering it with a wide stroke that sweeps everything off the skin of the island: the towers reaching for the sky, tall and low rooftops, gondola-carrying cables, people's thin lives.

Only the dream-cliff remains. It stands still amidst the waves, as they slowly settle to cover the horizon-wide silence.

Then I am awake and exhausted, and every last drop of strength has been drained from me.

The next morning I am taken back to my cell before dawn, packed on a ship again with other prisoners and shoved into the sea. I still feel like a trampled-on wineskin that someone filled with muddy water, but pain has turned into dull discomfort, and my head weighs a little less than the day before. The water wraps me with freezing fingers again. Again I fumble around with blind hands and aching lungs. I climb on board with the sediment of the seabed on my skin and drink the tasteless brew. The bell clangs, the hourglass turns, and it all begins anew.

At first I expect the short-haired guard to come and ask me more questions. But time drags on and she does not approach me. The guards who wear the tattoo of the Tainted eat in the dining hall with the rest of us, whereas the untattooed guards never do that. There are many of them, but I give names in my mind to those I see most often: Octopus is tall, robust and dark, and never hesitates to grab or shove us. Turtle is slow to move, but sees everything. Oyster is grey all over and says little. And there is a pale-eyed, red-haired guard whose orders are sharp and whip-hand swift. I call her Stingray.

The tattooed guards I name after insects. Mantis is bark-coloured and so narrow she seems ready to snap in two anywhere. Ant is short and walks as if she has more than two legs. Bug has shiny, black eyes and hair and is often kinder to us than the others. The short-haired guard I decide to call Moth.

The tattooed guards are responsible for herding us in tasks like cleaning our cells, washing the pots and plates, and emptying our chamber-pots, whereas the untattooed ones give them orders. Once I see Stingray argue with Bug on the ship. She pulls out her whip and hits Bug's bare hands with it, twice. It leaves a red mark. Bug lowers her head and accepts the punishment.

After following the rhythm of the house for a while I am convinced that the tattooed guards are prisoners, like the rest of us, but with some privileges. The more I think about it, the less I understand why Moth would have been sent to question me. Sometimes I catch her watching me with an unreadable expression, and I turn my eyes away.

I have begun building two maps of the House of the Tainted in my mind: of its space, but also of its time, the way the days are shaped within. I look for hidden openings, cracks I could slip through. I need to send a message to Janos, but I do not know how. I have nothing, except my clothes, my blanket, a chamber-pot and a bar of soap. I have not seen anyone in the house use pen or paper. There must be a watergraph somewhere, but I have seen no indication of it being used, either, so I am growing increasingly certain it must be on the men's side of the building. Occasionally we see the prisoners of the second women's shift from a distance: boarding a ship in the harbour, arranging themselves in a line behind a barred door as we are leaving the dining hall. Too far away for me to recognize Valeria, even if she were among them. The male prisoners are separated from us completely. The building is divided in two with only a passageway in between. The only time I caught a glimpse of them was when we boarded the ships one day and a silent line of them carried full coral cages further away.

I learn about currents under the surface, the push and pull of tides arranging the pieces in the house. One day I notice I am floating alone in my strip of sea. Everyone else has gathered into a dense cluster. I swim the same way and see a short, wide-shouldered girl who is around my age, maybe a year or two younger, emerge with a basket full of deep-red branches. She throws them into the boat. As I dive, I see it: a patch of blood coral, dense enough to see but too deep to gather with ease. The girl is fast and dares to dive deep. The rest of us try and follow, but her catch is the largest of the day by far.

That evening at supper we queue for vegetable soup with little more than cabbage and seaweed in it. The wide-shouldered girl stands in front of me on the line. The cook looks at her and slips something into her soup while the guards watch. The aroma of roasted meat drifts into my nostrils and my mouth waters. It smells of goat, or maybe lamb. The last time I felt no hunger was at the House of Webs, before Valeria disappeared. The girl takes the bowl and sits down at the long table. A guard moves close to her. No one takes another glance at her portion, although many must have seen what happened.

As the chain of days grows longer, I get further confirmation that there are rewards for the best coral-hunters. I see a guard offer a spare blanket to a woman whose hands are strong enough to pick branches that no one else can break, and another give new shoes to a young girl whose arms are long and thin enough to reach into hollows that are too narrow for the rest of us.

I learn to hold my breath for longer, and wounds open in my hands from tearing off coral. Rash grows in blotches onto my arms and neck and legs. But I am never faster or stronger or nimbler than the others. Hunger never goes away, and cold never goes away, and the sores on my fingers and feet never heal.

It is the evening of an overcast day, drab and dreary. Heavy drops of water lash at the walls around us and, somewhere, at the streets where people walk free. Hunger tears my insides, an emptiness around which my body wraps itself and which gives form to my every thought and movement. We are eating thin soup once again. With it we are given a slice of bread each, dark in taste and colour, and hard before it was out of the oven. Just like the guard I have named Moth said.

Mirea is seated next to me. I have tried to speak to her once or twice since our first conversation on the ship, but she has given curt answers, or no answers at all. I gnaw at the edge of my bread slice. I can sense its hardness at the very roots of my teeth. I place the bread on the table and tilt the soup bowl to my lips.

A crash from the other end of the table catches my attention. I see an older woman bend to pick up the pieces of a soup bowl from the floor. I hope the bowl was empty before her arm swept it off the table by accident. She will not be given another one.

When I turn back, my bread is gone. I have barely had time to notice, when Octopus, the dark and robust untattooed guard, strides towards the table.

'You!' she says, a raised whip in hand. 'Give it back. Now!'

I stare at Octopus. Then I realize she is not talking to me. She stops beside the table, looking at Mirea next to me.

217

'I saw you,' Octopus says. 'We are waiting. Or would you rather go into solitary confinement?'

Mirea looks defeated. She pushes her hand into her sleeve and pulls out the piece of bread on which I have already nibbled.

'There's been a misunderstanding,' I say, addressing Octopus. 'Everything's fine. I told Mirea she could have my bread. It's too hard for my teeth.'

Mirea looks at me, her eyes wide. Octopus appears suspicious.

'Are you telling me she didn't steal it?' she says.

'It's hers,' I say. 'I gave it to her.'

Stealing is harshly punished, but sharing food is not forbidden. I have seen prisoners do it before.

Octopus still does not look convinced.

'Try to look a little less like you're doing something forbidden next time, lass,' she says.

Mirea gives a nod.

'Eat your bread then,' Octopus says.

Mirea begins to chew on the corner of the slice of bread. The guard watches for a few moments, then turns her back on us. Mirea glances at me, but says nothing. I say nothing either.

A week later I am ordered to laundry duty. I have been in the House of the Tainted for well over a month, and this is the first time I see laundry being washed. My clothes have taken on the same smell as everything else here: of tears and sea and sweat, salty things that give the threads a feel of rotting against my skin.

The sticky stench of lye rises from the copper at the end of the room and cuts into my nostrils. The steam concentrates at my hairline, making the tattoo sting as sweat runs down my forehead in small streams. I am scrubbing yet another swimming-shirt against the slanted stone in the sink before me. On each side of me, I see dozens of others doing the same. Next to me Mirea is focused on removing a stain from a pair of trousers. Moth paces around the room. Her gaze stops on me for slightly longer than it needs to.

When she has turned away, Mirea's quiet voice swims into my ears.

'Why did you do it?' Mirea says without raising her eyes from the stain.

I take a quick glance around. Her words have dissolved into the splashing of water, unheard by others.

'Do what?' I ask, staring at my own washing. I keep my hands moving.

'Why did you help me? When I stole your bread.'

Guilt spreads in my guts, a dark pool that settles into something heavy and strangled.

'Because you needed it more than I did,' I say. 'You've been here for longer.' And it's my fault, I almost add.

Mirea is silent for several moments. She pulls the dripping garment out of the sink, wrings it and drops it into a tub behind us. She picks another pair of trousers and begins to rub it against the stone.

'Thank you,' she says.

I wring the shirt and throw it into the tub, taking the chance to look around. The guard is at the other end of the room. I reach out and give Mirea's hand a quick squeeze: a gesture I should have made long ago, in the dormitory when her night-maere had just visited. She looks surprised, but not displeased.

'I spoke to someone who was moved to our shift,' she says, still staring ahead of her. 'About that girl you asked about on the ship.'

Hope sweeps through me, light as a dream-wind that lifts me off the ground.

'She is about my age,' I say. 'Red hair. Pale skin. She cannot speak. She was . . . hurt.'

'It's probably not the same girl,' Mirea says. 'Or else she is kept hidden somewhere.'

I am heavy again, full of weight of water and worry.

'Thank you anyway,' I say. And then, just because I want to feel her name on my tongue, I add, 'Her name is Valeria. Valeria Petros.'

Mirea's face freezes. Her head makes a tiny movement. I realize Moth has stopped behind us. She stands close enough to raise her whip and lash at me, or Mirea. But she does not. She remains still and says nothing.

I do not know if she has heard us. After a while she continues to walk around the room, but Mirea and I do not speak again.

The sinks are drained and the laundry hangs on lines outside, on a roof landing surrounded by high walls but baked by the sun on bright days. The tubs are lined to dry against the wall of the laundry room. Smoke from the burnt-out fire clings to the air. We stand in a row, ready to leave. Moth inspects the room with Oyster.

'I will need two prisoners to clean the floor,' she says. '505 and 317, stay behind.'

I watch as the others walk past me. Oyster gives her nod of approval and leaves the room with them. Mirea and I are left alone with Moth.

'The buckets are in the corner,' she says and gestures towards the back wall. 'Use water from the copper.'

The floor is covered in puddles of lye and dirty foot-prints. We begin to mop it with rags. Wipe, wash, wring

220

and wipe again. My already sore knuckles are chafed from all the scrubbing, and the lye-water stings. Moth watches us closely.

'Is laundry very different in the House of Webs?' she asks.

I run possible answers through my mind. Did she hear me talk about Valeria, and is this a way of turning the conversation to her? But again, why would Moth be sent to question me instead of one of the higher-in-rank guards? And why would she arrange to do it in secret, rather than as a disciplinary action, a display of power in front of other prisoners?

'We wash it more often,' I say, with caution. I watch Moth's reaction. She looks calm, even kind. Sincerely curious. Why would she want to know about something as mundane as the laundry?

'Once a week with cold water, and twice a month in a large copper heated on fire,' I continue. 'The bed linen, too.'

'How do you dry it?' the guard asks.

'The same as here,' I say. 'We hang it outside in the sun, or if it rains, we leave it outside but under a roof.'

'What do weavers wear in the House of Webs?' the guard asks.

Mirea stares at the floor, at her hand wiping it.

'Sea-green coats and long grey skirts under them,' I say. 'You may have seen them on weavers who have been brought here.'

'Yes,' the guard says. 'In fact, I took a closer look at yours. Very fine fabric.'

'Sea-wool,' I say, although the image of her taking my coat and feeling the texture makes me uneasy. 'Our house-elder is very specific when it comes to our clothing.'

221

'Interesting,' the guard says.

She steps close. Her boot is right next to my hand. She could break my fingers by stepping on them.

'I think that is enough,' she says.

As she walks us into our cells, I wonder what she wants. I still do not know.

Days unravel around me, and nights string the days together, for they bring the dreams. I walk in passageways where no light falls, holding a hand I know to be Valeria's. Every morning my fingers close around emptiness. When the ship rides the waves, I imagine myself on stable ground to push the sickness away, and the roll of the sea still lives in my limbs when I lie down in my cell at night. Yet a part of me is grateful for the sailing, because that means the sky is not sealed out of reach. I scan it for the moon to keep track of time. Our Lady of Weaving has unfolded her fingers to reveal the silver coin in her palm, closed them and begun unfolding them again. I have been in the house for just over two months.

I save a piece of bread and slip it to Mirea whenever I can. She seeks a place next to me in the dining hall and on the ship more and more often. Sometimes we speak. Usually we sit in a shared silence. Moth has not spoken to me since the laundry day, except to give the orders she gives everyone. A warmer wind brushes the winter breezes now and then, although spring is still far off. It is yet another evening when the ship is carrying its cargo to the island: blood-coral branches, weary bodies and torn fingertips. Mirea is slumped next to me: her dark hair, her twig-thin limbs.

'Have you heard what they're saying?' she asks after a while.

My first thought is that she has heard something about Valeria.

'What do you mean?' I ask.

'It's not about that girl,' she says.

A heaviness settles into my chest again.

'What is it, then?'

'It's so strange,' Mirea says. She lowers her voice. I lean a little closer, keeping an eye on the hatch so I can pull away swiftly if the guard looks into the hold. 'I've heard some of the girls talking. Saying things about dreaming.'

'What kind of things?'

Mirea hesitates.

'That it's not a disease. That you can't catch it from others, and that you can't die from it.'

'Who was saying it?' My heart moves faster. The glow-glasses on the ceiling look brighter. 'Where did they hear that?'

'243 and 111. 479. Many of them.' She brushes off a piece of seaweed clinging to her leg. 'They said they heard from the newcomers that people outside are saying it. But it can't be true, can it? Everyone knows we're sick. That's why we are here.'

People outside. New prisoners arrive at the house every day, bringing scraps of news from the outside world. If the people of the city are talking about dreaming, it means the Dreamers are still working on the plan we devised.

'What if it were true?' I say in a quiet voice.

Mirea does not turn to look, but I see the shift on her face.

'How could it be?' she says.

'Think about it,' I say. 'We were all sent here because

of dream-plague, but have you seen night-maeres visiting here any more often than elsewhere in the city? Do you see anyone getting ill from anything other than cold, or lack of food or washing?'

I can see she is thinking about it. We would know: all sounds carry from one cell to the next, and most cells have three or four people in them. We can hear each other snore and cough and urinate and moan quietly into our blankets. A night-maere would not go unnoticed.

I glance around. No one is paying us attention. I lean closer to Mirea and lower my voice into a whisper.

'Mirea,' I say. 'You are not sick. None of us is.'

Mirea's head twitches slightly, but nothing else reveals her thoughts. She stares at her feet.

'Do you remember when I said it's good that they brought you here?' she says.

'Yes,' I say.

'It's not good, really,' she says. 'I wouldn't want anyone to end up here.'

'Neither would I,' I say.

Mirea's eyes move in the dark. The only person at a hearing distance is prisoner 503, but her eyes are closed and she is speaking her soundless words again: to those lost to her, to Our Lady of Weaving. No one knows. Maybe she does not, either.

'I'd set everyone free if I could,' Mirea whispers.

'So would I,' I say.

Mirea is silent for a long while. The hatch opens with a creak. A guard's dark silhouette appears against the bright daylight, then disappears. Eventually Mirea speaks again.

'If everyone knew that we're not sick,' she says, 'if even the guards knew, do you think they'd let us go?'

I glance at her from under my brows. I feel my own smile, uninvited, but it makes me lighter. I let it stay.

'I don't know,' I reply. 'Maybe.'

Mirea smiles back at me, and for a moment I imagine her roaming free, picking seashells on the shore, turning her laughing face to the sun and growing like a tree.

The rumours are spreading. The Dreamers are still working to proceed with the plan. For the first time in weeks hope runs through me like quicksilver, liquid and many-shaped and shimmering the Council is seated at a round stone table in the Tower, their mute faces turned towards each other and away from their crumbling surroundings; they sit without making a sound. A lizard runs across the table, turns swifter than water, is startled by the approaching footsteps at the door and disappears into a crack in the wall. Its tail wriggles on the table, twitching, prey caught in a web, until it comes to rest still, dark as a rock or the shadow of a rock.

The Council around the table does not pay attention to it, does not turn its gaze, does not say a word. Other creatures live in the cracks of the humid Tower too, they cross the room now and then. No one will raise a hand for just one.

The door opens and a servant carrying a torch steps in, bows in the direction of the table. He walks from one window to the next and kindles the torches on their racks outside the windows, the eyes of the Tower that watch the island when darkness falls. Before leaving the room he glances at the sea, sees what the Council does not.

A grey-gleaming torrent of rain falls from the clouds,

lashes at the landscape, moves the waters and whips into movement the sediment clouds that rest as a heavy, rust-coloured ring where life is supposed to stir. The roots of the seabed and the bones of the earth stir, ready to sweep everything off the skin of the city: the towers reaching for the sky, tall and low rooftops, gondola-carrying cables, people's thin lives. The dream-cliff stands silent amidst the waves and the movement of dream-threads still continues; it is ever stronger, it unravels into the world

227

CHAPTER THIRTEEN

Torrential rains and wild winds have been flinging the ship every day for over a week. I am grateful that the sea has finally calmed down a little. I sit near the hatch of the hold and watch the golden sunlight discernible around its edges. Mirea has slumped down to the floor with an arm bent under her head. Her breathing runs smooth, and every now and then a faint snoring steals into it. I lean my head to the wall and close my eyes. I waken when someone pokes my arm.

I open my eyes. 479 squats next to me. She places something in my hand, raises a finger quickly to her lips and starts moving toward the back of the hold.

The guard has just checked on us, so I dare to take a closer look at the object. At first I think it is a bundle of fabric, it is so soft. When I begin to unfold it I realize it is a long strip of paper folded into a leaflet, opened so many times its surface has worn shabby and linty.

I have seen the contents before.

The images have been copied recognizably, but roughly. Many details have been left out. Yet they still tell the same

228

story: about an inkmaster who left the island, fell ill on the continent and could not return for the Ink-marking. Who began to dream and suspect the tattoo ink had something to do with dreaming. And whom the Council began to stalk. I notice a few new pictures have been added in order to make the story clearer. The Council breaks the cable of the air gondola, and the gondola carrying the inkmaster falls to the ground. Dark sludge leaks from the Ink Quarters into the sea, where it kills plants and singing medusas. On the final page of the leaflet is a picture of an eye with an eight-pointed sun as the pupil.

Many memories from the recent weeks posit themselves in a new manner. A cluster of prisoners in the corner of the hold gathered around something. A loose piece of a conversation heard in passing, in which an inkmaster was mentioned. One of the prisoners handing something to another and hiding it quickly, when the hatch of the hold was opened. All things possible enough to happen for other reasons, too, but collected over such a short time, now given a meaning.

I hear the chain of the anchor begin to clang on board and the anchor splashes into the water. The ship glides on for another moment, but the sounds are a sign that the guard will soon come to herd us to the deck. 479 has made it nearly to the back of the hold. I think about what to do. I do not want to be caught with the leaflet in my hand. Yet I must talk to her. Hastily I push the leaflet in the only hiding place I can think of, under the waistband of my trousers.

I catch 479 under the glow-glass swaying in the corner. We are too close to the other prisoners, but I must ask.

'Where did you get it?'

479's black eyes flash in the faint light of the glow-glass. She glances at others and says in a half-whisper, 'You must be quiet.'

'This is important,' I say. 'I've seen the same pictures elsewhere.'

Footsteps and cries carry from the deck. 479 glances towards the hatch, but it remains closed.

'It has been circulating hand to hand for two weeks already. Don't you dare tell the guards.'

'Of course I won't,' I say. I begin to take the leaflet out from under my waistband.

My hands do not find it.

I search again, but the leaflet is gone. It must have fallen along the way. I look behind, and two things happen at once.

I see Mirea spread the leaflet before her eyes. The hatch of the hold creaks as it opens, and a slanted, sharp light flares in through it. The shadow of the guard appears in the hole.

Mirea startles and tries to push the leaflet behind her back, but the guard has already seen it. And it is not Bug or Oyster or even Moth. It is Stingray.

'You. What is that?' she asks.

Mirea is speechless. I am frozen in place. I do not dare to look at 479.

'Bring it to me,' Stingray says. 'Right now.'

Mirea begins to move. She climbs the steps to the hatch of the hold and hands the paper to Stingray.

'Get out,' Stingray snaps. 'The rest of you too!'

Other prisoners gather between Mirea and me. She is already on the deck. As I stand there on the dirty floor and wait, there is commotion ahead. Wind swallows the words waving outside. Eventually I climb through the hatch. The day is glass-clear, burnished with bright-spun sunlight. Apart from Stingray, Octopus, Moth and Ant are among the guards today.

'Keep moving!' Octopus shouts and gives a push to a couple of women to make them walk faster.

Stingray is standing next to Mirea. Her hair glows orange like straw on fire, and she is studying the pictures in front of her eyes. Prisoners are gathered around them.

'Who gave you this?' Stingray demands.

Mirea stares at her feet and remains quiet.

Stingray crumples the paper in her hand, drops it and crushes it under her boot. Her fingers fall to the handle of the whip.

'Its contents are lies,' she says. 'And blasphemy. Just like the rumours circulating in the house, which without any doubt originated from this piece of paper.' She leans close to Mirea and speaks in a voice that is soft, yet taut at core. 'Why are you all here?' she asks.

Mirea's lips move, but I cannot hear the words.

'Louder,' Stingray says. 'Tell everyone.'

'Because we are sick and tainted,' Mirea says in strangled sounds.

'What are you tainted with?' Stingray continues.

'Dreams,' Mirea says.

'And why does the Council in its great mercy let you live?'

'Because we work,' Mirea says.

'Correct,' Stingray says. She straightens her back, stands tall and gleaming in the early afternoon, and looks around. Her voice hits us clear and metal-hard. 'Dreamplague will claim the lives of each of you in time, and the only way to deserve your place in the House of the Tainted in the meantime is work. And honesty.' She turns back to Mirea. 'Now, will you tell me where you got this piece of rubbish?'

Mirea does not look up. I begin to feel terror. I did not wish for her to get in trouble. I should have been more careful. This is my fault.

'Will you tell me?'

I cannot get my mouth open.

Mirea is quiet. Stingray raises her whip. I think she is going to lash it across Mirea's face. Mirea still says nothing.

'Very well,' the guard says. 'Back to work, all of you.' She keeps the whip raised. 'You will be among the first to dive today,' she says to Mirea. 'Take your place.'

Mirea looks up and begins to move towards the nearest dais. Stingray lowers her whip.

The rota starts: the first row dives and the hourglass is turned. They bring their harvest, blood-red branches and some white ones. They dive again. When the sand has settled at the bottom of the hourglass, the guards throw the rope ladders down. The divers begin to climb. I step on the dais, waiting for my turn. When Mirea tries to climb over the rail to the deck, Stingray stops her.

'Not you.'

Mirea stares at her. I glance around. Octopus is watching in silence, her face still. Moth is handing blankets to shivering prisoners. I catch the movement of her head as she turns away.

'You are going back,' Stingray says. 'Unless you have something to tell me.'

Understanding spreads on Mirea's face. Her mouth opens and closes again. She does not look my way. Without a word she looks down and jumps back into the water.

Words gather within me heavy and cold. Still I do not speak.

232

It is my turn to dive. Before I do, I take note of where Mirea is. Moth prepares to turn the hourglass. She is looking into the water, too.

The sea is cold and heavy and pulls me in. I seek Mirea with stinging eyes until I see her. Her movements are slow, weighed down. Through the thick sediment I spot a cluster of blood coral further away. The reef is turning white, but deeper there are still branches that spread like tendrils of hot blood. I try to estimate whether they are too far. I see others wondering about the same, making tentative swimming movements towards the branches that would certainly buy a better meal or warmer night, then deciding against it. They are just out of reach; even if we could get special permission to use long-handled hoop nets instead of baskets, we might not be able to reach deep enough.

I kick back to the surface to breathe.

During the following dives I keep an eye on Mirea and only manage to collect a few thin branches. Eventually the bell begins to clang, and it is time for the rope ladder. Shivering, I climb up the side of the ship. Mirea climbs behind me. I step onto the board, and the blankets Moth is offering are already close. I think of the hot herbal drink, which has hardly more taste than water but restores warmth to the body for a moment.

Then I hear Stingray again.

'Back,' she tells Mirea. 'Unless you have changed your mind.'

Mirea's body is blue with cold and all colour has vanished from her lips. Words slither within me, they are slimy and swollen inside.

I hear a splash as Mirea plunges back into the water. Moth is offering me a blanket. My hand is already touching it.

I turn back.

'It was me,' I say.

Stingray spins around and stares at me.

'What did you say?'

'Let Mirea back into the ship,' I say. 'The leaflet was mine. I lost it and she found it by mistake. She barely had time to glance at it. Please let her out of the water.'

'You,' Stingray says. 'In that case, you'd better go and fetch her.'

I look at the guards. I look into the water. My hands and legs tremble with cold and the weight of the heavy words. I jump into the sea.

Salt water floods into my eyes when I open them, but the stinging is no longer as unbearable as it was on the early dives. I turn around until I see Mirea, and my heart knots into a tight twist.

She is swimming towards the deep-growing corals.

Don't do it, I think. *Those rewards will not save you. And they don't need to; I have taken the blame, as I should.* But she does not hear me.

I go after her. She has been in the sea for too long. She does not have enough strength left for a dive that even the most experienced of us do not dare try. She swims deeper and deeper, and is always just ahead of me, slightly too far for me to reach. Once I manage to grab her ankle, but she slides from my grasp in the water, slippery as a fish. I feel the pressure in my chest and swim to the surface for air. I expect her to do the same any moment.

When I break to the surface, I take deep breaths until I am no longer gasping.

'Where is 317?' Moth yells at me from the deck. I am still waiting for Mirea to appear on the surface. I begin to understand she is not coming.

I dive.

She is there, deep enough to pick the blood-red branches next to her, but no longer able to do so. I see immediately that her limbs are cradled by the sea, back and forth, not moved by any will of her own. I swim towards her, kicking hard and not moving fast enough. I need stronger lower limbs and larger feet, webbed like a seagull's, and wide fins to replace my hands. I need a chest that will hold the breath of a dozen men, so I can give her half of it and make her move of her own will again.

My head begins to feel like it is squeezed by invisible hands, inside and out. Shadows float before my eyes, and lights, and their embrace is deep and silent. I am close enough now. I wrap an arm around Mirea, clutching her tight against my chest so the hunger of the sea will not tear her from me, and kick as hard as I can towards the surface. Strength is bleeding from me, whatever little there is left. The water no longer feels so cold. I continue to swim, but I hang in the water-space now without weight to pull me down or lightness to lift me up: suspended, like a bird with a great wind under its wings. A shred of seaweed, ready to be claimed by the waves, until fish and time tear it to dust.

Shadows grow denser and wrap around me, and I am theirs.

Then someone is pulling me up, into the air where my body weighs like a thousand stones, and my chest stings and I vomit salty, salty tears of the sea.

I lie on the deck, too heavy to move. A meter or two away Moth is pressing Mirea's chest repeatedly with her hands. Mirea's head lies in a pool that is not just water. She is the colour of bone coral, and her chest is not heaving.

Octopus, who stands next to them, points at the hourglass. The final grains of sand drop to the bottom. Moth must have been trying to revive Mirea since they last turned it.

Moth's face is a darkening sky as she places Mirea's arms next to her sides and leaves them there. She closes Mirea's eyelids with her hand.

'Cover her with something,' Octopus says. 'We are leaving for the day.'

I hear another voice. My neck does not turn enough to see, but I recognize it as Stingray.

'There are still many hours of daylight left,' she says.

A short silence. Then, 'We are returning.'

It is Octopus. Her boots are heavy on the boards as she walks away.

The boat with blood-red branches resting in it is hauled to the deck and we are ordered down into the hold. Moth takes me into the cabin. At first I think it is to make me feel warmer. Then I realize it is because they want to isolate me from the rest of the prisoners. I already know that when we return to the House of the Tainted, I will not be taken to my cell, but somewhere colder and smaller.

I see Mirea's unmoving face before my eyes, and think of the images I drowned her with. I am ice and bitter water, and things that sting in dark crevices between stones.

I am taken out of the ship last, and when I walk along the deck, I see the horizon. The sea is smooth and almost without movement, and the shoreline is bare, like the waves are holding their breath. Everything is calm, like the dead are.

The only light in the cell comes from a glow-glass pipe above the door. It hovers on the walls, a blue-white flow that does not tell me if it is day or night. The floor is cold stone under my back. If I straighten my legs and place my arms over my head, I can touch the walls with my toes and fingers. There are no blankets or bunks here. In one corner there is a stinking hole in the floor. In another, a jug of water that tastes of mould, and a piece of bread with white stains growing on it.

Brine has dried on my skin, leaving it tight and itchy even where it is not covered in rash. I am still in my diving clothes. I think of Mirea, of her unmoving limbs and still face, and water and salt pour from my eyes again. My nose gets runny and blocked. I wipe it on the back of my hand. My chest is full of sharp stones. I wait for someone to come and ask about the rumours I have been spreading, the ones I really did start spreading, but longer ago than they realize: when we believed we had a plan. Before Valeria vanished, and I walked through the shadows.

No one comes.

A blue algae-mist floats in the glass pipe. I sleep for a moment or many. I dream of Valeria lying next to me, warming me. A singing medusa swims across the room and lands on my face, but instead of soothing, it stings. I wake up to the burning sensation on my brow and chill in my limbs. I scratch my forehead. Skin peels away in grainy patches that stick to my fingertips.

I do not know how long I have been here, when the flood bell begins to toll.

In a flash my mind-map of the House of the Tainted is before my eyes, and I am scanning it. The solitary confinement cells are not underground, but they are several flights of stairs below the other cells and dining halls. In any flood, they will be among the first to fill with water.

My legs tremble as I stand up. It is as if the very weight of the air is pressing me down, resting on my shoulders. I listen. Somewhere in the distance I hear people shouting and stomping, metal bars rattling. Footsteps run past, but they do not stop.

I begin to bang on the door.

'Help me!' I cry. 'Let me out!'

The noises above and far away continue, but none of them draw nearer. I hit the door until my fists hurt, then turn around and kick it with my heels. I scream until my throat aches and my voice is half-gone. I do not know how long the water will take to reach here. I have only ever seen floods from the hill of Webs, and from my parents' house. I slide to the floor, close my eyes and wait for the silence and depth of the sea to swallow me. I should have known it would not allow me an escape after taking Mirea.

A key turns in the lock.

I scramble to my feet as the door opens. Moth looks in. I take a step backwards. Breath tangles in my chest.

'Quick,' she says. She throws me a pair of boots, a pair of wide trousers and a brown, hooded jacket. 'Put those on, and then follow me.'

I stare at Moth's smooth, unreadable face, at her tall and angular frame. She has not approached me since the laundry. But I have caught hold of her eyes now and then in the dining hall, in the changing rooms, on the ship. I remember the strange demand in her voice when she asked me about the House of Webs.

Warily I grab the jacket, not turning my gaze from her.

'The flood will rush in soon,' Moth says, more than a tinge of impatience in the tone of her words. 'And then we'll have no way out.'

Whether it is a threat or warning, I cannot tell, but I do not doubt that it is true. I put the clothes on as fast as I can. At least they provide some warmth and coverage.

'This will be much easier if you come without resistance,' she says.

Staying here means a certain end. I step out. The corridor is dim and narrow, and locked by gates at both ends. We walk through the first gate and climb two flights of stairs. Moth stays a few steps behind me. Screams and footsteps are now closer, echoing off each other, twisting and turning in the deserted corridors. When we reach the top of the stairs, Moth stops me by grasping my arm. Her fingers are hard, her expression intent.

'Listen carefully,' she says. Her hand moves, and for a moment I think she is going to pull out her whip. Instead, she presses a key into my hand. 'This will open the gates you will need to pass through. Follow this corridor, turn right and open the small door hidden under a set of stairs. Follow the passage behind it until you come to a narrow spiral staircase, then climb as far up as the stairs will take you. At the top there will be three doors. Go through the left one. That is the safest route. Don't let anyone see you.'

My mind-map shifts its shape, expands: I see the corridors and stairs. They fit with what I already know about the house. I repeat the instructions in my mind, until I can see my path marked on the new map. Moth stares at me. I stare back, study her face. I try to see if her dark eyes are hiding things. I do not read insincerity in her, but I have been mistaken before.

'What about the other prisoners?' I ask.

'The house is being evacuated,' Moth says. 'This is not the first flood to strike here. Will you find your way?'

'I think so,' I respond. And because the only thing I understand is that I have been misreading her all along, I ask, 'Why are you helping me?'

Swift thoughts come and go on Moth's face. She almost smiles.

'I know who you are,' she says. Her face turns serious. 'I know what your house-elder did. You shouldn't be here.'

'But I carry the dream-plague,' I say.

'You and I both know that is not true,' Moth says. 'Go and find the one you came to find.'

'How do you know that is why I came?'

Moth's eyes flicker.

'I heard you talking about her in the laundry room,' she says. 'You said her name. She's not here. Go.'

Screeching, roaring sounds arise from below.

'Run,' she says. She seems ready to push me, if I do not go. 'Don't look back.'

I run.

The sounds grow into crashing, rumbling, bone-splitting tremors that haunt my footsteps. They follow me, so heavy that I am afraid I will be buried. It feels like the earth under the sea is going to smash the island to splinters and drown all who walk on it. The floor tilts and flees and ruptures, and once a great boulder falls from the ceiling behind me, so close I feel shards from it hit my skin. But not once do I look back.

I run, until my thighs ache and my lungs sting. Three times I need to stop to open doors or gates, but eventually the last one of them throws me onto a high landing on top of the wall. I barely have time to see how a new and greater wave carrying trees, people, furniture and entire houses on its edge approaches from the sea. I cling to the iron gate I have just walked through, take shelter at the mouth of the corridor and hope that the stone arc above me will hold.

Then the world turns into churning sea and hard-hitting pain and all-devouring darkness.

I stand amidst a landscape of water and sky and light. The houses are gone, and people. I feel the dream on my skin and know I could bring them back with my will, but I do not. This space and silence are all I need.

Before me falls a tapestry I recognize. Fine strands run from the edges towards the centre, shimmering like brightness bursting forth from the sun. In the middle there is a hole that is all blackness, shadow-painted, night sealed in the core of the earth. If I pushed my hand into it, it would claim me whole, and no trace of me would be left behind.

A figure stands on the other side of the tapestry, only visible as a shadow through the web of threads.

'Valeria,' I say.

The shadow turns around, but the tapestry is still between us and I cannot discern the features. The shadow walks further. I reach out my hand, but it nearly brushes the dark centre of the tapestry, and I pull it away quickly. I decide to rearrange the dream: I tell the tapestry to disappear, the figure to return.

The figure stops. Around it, behind the tapestry, the island looms as if I am looking at it from far above, its canals and streets and buildings blending with the patterns. I try to see the island more clearly, but the shadow approaches me now, it grows taller and wider and encloses the darkness. It steps through the hole in the tapestry, and the spell is on me once again. I am no longer standing. I am lying on the hard ground, and my body is held by invisible chains.

The night-maere rises over me. Its outline against the

light could be my own. It lowers its weight on me. The touch radiates into my whole body and with it, an unexpected power that tingles in my palms and glows in my veins. It fills me and quivers under my skin. The burn begins low in my belly, soft and sharp at once. I hear my own breathing as it turns ragged, and I feel every hair on my skin stand on end.

The power wells in me, making tall waves and seeking a way out, but the harder I struggle against the night-maere's grip, the more closely it binds me in place. The only movement I can make is with my eyes. I am water and waves inside, and yet air and light, bound to the rock I am lying on but floating where nothing holds me. I can feel the night-maere's mouth a mere finger-width away from mine, although I cannot see it. Its breath scorches my skin.

It whispers in words I can almost understand, sounds so close to sentences I can taste them on my tongue, and for the first time in my life I know the night-maere is trying to tell me something.

Something that is no longer just terror is pulled tight around me. I cannot move my body, so I focus my mind to tear myself free from it. I attempt to make words, but the inside of my mouth is unmoving stone and my face is still as glass.

The night-maere whispers again. The sounds swim and swirl, and are pulled away.

A raindrop falls on my forehead. The night-maere flees. My grasp of its words slips, and they are lost. My muscles twitch. Breath flows through me.

I have never been this surprised to be alive.

CHAPTER FOURTEEN

The wave has washed me onto a rocky landing. Rain
fizzles into the silent landscape. I listen to the ache swelling
and receding in my body. The pain throbs behind my eyes
as I force myself to sit up. I run my hands along my limbs,
feel my torso all over, and roll up my sleeves and trouser
legs. My skin is covered in bruises and contusions, but
nothing feels broken. Water drips to the ground and runs
away in vein-like rivulets as I wring it from my clothes. I
clamber to a low squat first, then to my feet. The ground
does not tilt and my bones do not crumble. I take a few
cautious steps.

I am alone on the landing.

Flood-borne jetsam is scattered around me: roof tiles,
shards of glass, pieces of wood, a battered pewter cup. A
shoe, no larger than a child's foot. I remember Mirea and
grief pulls at my guts. I push it away, somewhere it can
wait until I can let it come. I pick up the cup and put it
into my pocket. I will need to find water.

The return route to the House of the Tainted is cut
off. The doorway and the upper part of the staircase have

survived, but only slightly further down the roof has caved in. The edge of the sea has pushed straight over and through the tall wall, and in many places the structures have suffered damage. The other end of the house, which lies further from the sea and where the male prisoners live, remains standing. Silence hangs over everything. The heaps of stone rest still.

The sea is a landscape of grey and green, rolling closer and drawing away again. I walk along the wall enclosing the landing and see narrow slices of the city. Most houses are where they used to be, but some look like the island has tried to shake them off its back. At first glance the House of Webs looks undamaged in the distance, but then I see something has shifted. The change is small, nearly imperceptible. The wall meets the ground at an angle that is almost the same as before; the new shape of the hill could be only a whim of light and shadow. Yet every time I look again I am more certain that it is not.

The Tower stands tall as ever. The air gondola routes running to it and the House of Webs have collapsed, and at least three others too: the sky is devoid of the lattice of cables. I cannot see the streets from here, but I imagine the scenes taking place on them. People collecting the remnants of their possessions amid the devastation. Others crying, screaming or staring into the distance. Some lying still, perhaps, and even next to them you might not know if they are dead or alive.

I hold back a shiver and a sob. There is time for those later. I cannot stay here, and I can only think of one place to go.

Eventually I find a rusty iron ladder where the wall ends. Underneath is a vertical drop where the cliff runs into the sea. The ladder does not reach all the way down, but leads to another, narrower landing jutting out from the rock. It is clearly intended to be used only in extreme emergency or not at all. The rungs are far apart, covered by thick rust and the second one from top hangs loose.

I grab the wall, climb over it and drop myself onto the top rung.

I need to stop on each rung to draw deep breaths, but eventually I am on the landing below. My muscles tremble all over. I lie down on the cold rock, until I feel able to stand again. A steep, barely passable path leads away from the landing. I follow it. It winds down the side of the cliff and towards the small houses scattered along the slope. Some of them seem beaten by the flood, but here the water has receded.

Further down in the city the streets will have turned into tendrils of the sea. The water will have swallowed the pavements and ground floors, and buildings will stick out like teeth. Every opening between houses is a canal now. I consider my options. To get where I want to go I must cross a distance of twenty blocks at least, maybe more. I might be able to wade some of the journey, but the place itself lies on lower ground, closer to the sea.

I will need some kind of boat or raft.

This part of the island is so far from the city that it is almost like a tiny village. It does not take me long to find what stands for the village square, and there is what I am looking for. The deep-green water pump is decorated with a forged-iron sun. I pump the handle a few times. Water spurts out. It is clear, not muddled by the flood. I rinse the cup and drink until I am no longer thirsty.

The few houses stand dark and still. I do not hear words or footsteps. I begin to wonder if everyone has fled further up the hills, but a strong scent of burning seaweed wafts in the air. I scan the grey sky: smoke from a chimney paints a trail across it. The rain has stopped. Mud smacks under my boots as I cross puddles and streets barely wider than paths.

After a brief search I find the source of the smoke. There is a yard behind the house, a mess of piled stones and crooked bushes and weary wild herbs. There is also a boat.

It is small and the paint has peeled off, and the wood used to construct it was probably felled long before my parents were born. But it is still a boat, and it is mounted on a skewed cart on wheels. It would be easy to move to the edge of the water.

The back door of the house is open. White steam puffs forth from the inside. I hear clattering of dishes. I smell boiled seaweed and grains, and realize I am extremely hungry. I crack the side gate open and step into the yard.

A short man emerges, bony and olive-skinned. A bald spot grows on the crown of his head, his boots are in need of repair and he is carrying a steaming bowl in his hands. He stops in his tracks when he sees me.

'Excuse me, sir,' I say. 'Could I possibly borrow your boat, please? I promise I will return it as soon as I can. I will even pay for it.'

It is not too big a lie. I intend to bring the boat back with some compensation.

The man stares at me and says nothing. I take a step towards him. He hurls the bowl at me, but misses. It lands next to me on its side. Cooked grains and seaweed broth pour out.

I take another step, trying to look as friendly as I can. The man recedes towards the door, then turns, runs back in and slams the door shut. I hear the sound of a key being turned in the lock.

I look at the food remaining in the bowl. I wipe my hand on my trousers and ladle the rest of the grains into my mouth with bare fingers. Only a handful remains. I carry the bowl onto the doorstep.

My knuckles hurt as I knock on the door.

'I would just like to borrow your boat,' I say. 'Please.'

'Go away,' the man says from the inside.

I see a curtain part slightly on the small window next to the door. I try to peer in. It is hard to see anything. There is no light inside the house. The window glass reflects a white-and-grey sky, and the rocky hill behind. And my own face.

That is when I understand.

The tattoo is clearly defined on my forehead, the skin around the mark red and swollen.

'Take your plague elsewhere,' the man says. His voice is caught in the rigid old stone-and-wood structures, warped by them.

I look at the boat. I look at the locked door. I look at the boat again.

It is not smooth gliding. The vessel is barely even a skiff. It rocks and tilts and rotates, and one of the oars is missing. I use the remaining one for punting the boat along, although it is a mere stub compared with a proper pole. For a moment something underwater scratches the bottom, and I wait to see if water will come seeping through. But despite its infuriating shape and tiny size, the skiff seems well enough put together, and my feet do not get wetter than they already are.

Staying away from the busy neighbourhoods is not

difficult. Few people wish to live near the House of the Tainted, and in this area the northern shoreline of the island – considerably changed after the flood – is all but abandoned by former inhabitants because few tolerate the stench and fumes from the Ink Quarters. Just in case, I pull my hood down to cover my forehead.

The angle of the light behind the clouds has changed by the time I eventually reach the abandoned house where Janos, Valeria and I used to meet before we talked to Irena. As I expected, the ground floor is underwater. I paddle clumsily around the building with my one oar and find the same thorny vines that cover the door we used before, now half-drowned. I push them aside with my oar. There is a window behind: it looks barely large enough for me to climb through. I tear a piece off my trouser bottom and use it to tie the skiff to a hook rusting in the wall. The ancient wood of the window frame is swollen shut, and eventually I have to break the window with the oar to be able to get in. I arrange the vine to cover the boat: it may not fool anyone who comes close, but from a distance, at least, it will conceal my vessel and my way in.

Everything smells of dampness, and the planks feel fragile under my feet. I stay at the edges of the room. I try to find a place where I will not need to move too much. At the centre opens a hole where the steps began once upon a time. If I dared to go closer, I might see the lowest steps of the wide staircase underwater, leading nowhere. I might see the pages of abandoned books floating in the weightlessness of water.

My body is heavy. I curl down on the floor and place the oar next to me. The corners of the room are growing darker. I have nothing to give me light. My forehead stings.

My throat is sticky with thirst. I wonder if I should go out in search of food and water before nightfall, or wait until dawn. I do not dare go. I may not find my way back in the dark. I stay.

Someone cries out in the distance, a bird or human, I cannot tell. Shadows spin closer. I hold onto myself and onto what is left of the world I know.

Darkness has rested in the room for some time, when there is a knock on the window pane. I grab the oar and get to my trembling feet. A hood-covered figure pushes its head through the window, halts for a moment and vanishes. A leg appears, then a whole body. I stay in my silent corner and raise the oar. The figure that has entered the room reaches a hand out through the window. A lantern floats into sight, bright orange and holding a live fire.

'Eliana?' a voice says.

I think I recognize it. The figure steps closer, steps back when the floorboards give a little, then steps closer again with more caution. It places the lantern on the floor and removes the hood.

I lower the oar.

'Some people might consider showing their faces before approaching terrified runaway criminals in abandoned buildings,' I say.

'And some people might be happy that they've been found at all,' my brother replies.

Shriek-like laughter pours from me and draws tears with it.

'They are,' I say. 'Very happy.'

Janos takes another wary step nearer and I close the distance. He pulls me into a wide hug. He smells of ink and soap, and just a little of sweat.

'Are you hurt?' he asks and steps back. I feel his eyes skim over my forehead. They make an attempt to look away but return to the mark.

I remember Mirea's downturned face, her fingers scratching the rash on her instep. I see her swimming away from me, turning herself into a story I will be able to tell one day, but not yet.

'Mostly just bruised and starved,' I say. 'Do you have any water?'

Janos takes a skin from his belt and hands it to me. I drink.

'There's more in the boat,' he says. 'Finish it, if you need to.' He pushes a hand into his pocket and gives me a piece of bread wrapped in cloth. 'And eat this.'

I do. The bread is soft and crusty, no older than from this morning. I could choke on it and die content. Janos watches me.

'There will be food where we are going,' he says. I hear a smile buried behind his concern.

I hand the skin back and wipe my mouth with the back of my hand. Janos studies my face.

'So that's where they kept you,' Janos says, and I feel his gaze on the tattoo of the Tainted. 'I suspected as much.' His fingers brush my forehead. I start. The touch is light, but it burns the raw skin like a firebrand.

'How did you find me?' I ask.

'A message was delivered an hour ago,' he says. 'The House of Words is mostly intact, but we've been moving scriptures all day long, building a makeshift library on the roof. The messenger looked like he had journeyed to the continent and back in search of me.'

'What did the message say?'

'Only that you were alive and had escaped the House

of the Tainted. I couldn't think of anywhere else to look for you.'

'Where did the message come from?'

'I don't know,' Janos says. 'There was nothing else in it. But I doubt it was sent from the House of Webs. Its foundations were damaged in the flood, and the City Guard are moving the weavers away. There is probably no one left there.'

I remember the strangely tilted silhouette of the house on the hill, a crack in the landscape.

Moth had said she knew who I was. Could she have been working with the Dreamers without me knowing it? But if that were true, why did she not help me sooner?

'How long was I gone?' I ask.

'Two and a half months.'

That corresponds with the rough track of days I have been keeping. All that sky-gazing, every memorized moon phase was not wasted, after all.

One question has been scorching my throat since Janos removed his hood. I have to ask.

'Have you found Valeria?'

A shadow deepens on Janos's face, then dissolves into light again. I cannot tell if it is the lantern-flame growing fainter and brighter, or something else.

'We still don't know what happened to her,' he says. 'I'm sorry.'

The words are slow, deliberate. He must have known I would ask. I breathe in the meaning.

Valeria has been missing for two and a half months.

'I spoke to your house-elder after you disappeared. After I received your note.' Janos's voice is calm, calmer than I would like it to be. 'She claimed to know nothing. That you had simply left.'

'Weaver?' Anger rises in me, bitter as bile. 'She's lying. She showed me a way out of the House of Webs, knowing it would take me to the House of the Tainted. I'm certain she had something to do with Valeria's disappearance.'

Two vertical lines appear between Janos's eyebrows.

'Don't you believe me?' I ask.

'I do,' he says. 'But why would she have done it?'

'The Council must have pressured her into it somehow,' I say. 'I just don't know why.'

We stare at each other without answers.

'Are you certain Valeria was not in the House of the Tainted too?' Janos asks.

Moth's words surface from my memory. *She's not here.* But she could have been lying.

'I didn't see her there the whole time,' I say.

My mind wants to create a way out for Valeria, a hundred ways out. I see her flee the House of Webs and hide in an abandoned building, stealing her food from the market. I see Valeria assume a different identity, take on another name and find work as a weaver, or perhaps a net maker. I see her buy a place on a trading ship some-how and leave the island. I believe in all these scenarios, and any others that will help her survive. Yet under them lies another possibility I cannot deny.

'Do you think she's alive?' I ask. I have thought the sentence many times, but speaking it aloud wrenches my heart.

Someone shouts in the distance. Janos turns his head and looks towards the window.

'We should go,' he says. 'It's getting late. The city may be restless tonight, with looters coming for the broken buildings.'

'Where are we going?'

'Somewhere safe,' Janos says and picks up the lantern from the floor.

I note that he did not answer my question.

After long, quiet canals and distant lights moving in the thickening dark, we stand in a sheltered and shadow-filled space, and Janos opens a door into a shaft. It is wide, made for something larger than humans, and iron rungs descend into its deep maw.

'You'll need to climb down,' he says. 'Do you feel strong enough?'

I do not.

'Yes,' I say.

But the drop is long, and we are going underground. I imagine water, flood. Entrapment. Some of it must show on my face, because Janos says, 'This place is entirely flood-proof, if that's what you're thinking about. Place your hand on the wall.'

I do. Its murky surface is not cold enough to be metal and not warm enough to be wood. It is not coarse enough to be stone, and it resembles something I recognize, something like . . .

'Glass,' I say. 'Why are the walls made of glass?'

'To keep the water out,' Janos says. 'This is one of the two entrances, which are both higher than floods have ever reached. The space we are about to enter is enclosed in a thick shell of glass. There is no crack for the water to seep in.'

I turn to look at him.

'Who built this?' I ask.

'We don't know,' Janos replies. 'We think it may have been the Web-folk.' He nods towards the rungs. 'Do you want to go first?'

I say nothing, but he sees my face.

'I'll go first,' he says.

The lantern light hovers on the walls, shifting and swinging with Janos's movements. He climbs down much faster than I do. His boots hit the rungs below me. I squeeze the ladder with tight fingers, and my breath dangles dense and thorny in my throat. Eventually my feet meet the floor. I kneel to brush it with my hand: it really is made of glass. It is scratched and dusty and has lost whatever polish it may once have had, but it is beautiful nevertheless, the colour of dark seawater and stones slickened by it. I think of the Glass Grove, of the few traces left behind by the Web-folk. What did they wish to hide from when they built this?

Janos leads me to a thick metal door with a heavy knocker on it. At first I mistake the shape for the sun of the Council. But as I look closer, I see it is slightly different, and the rays are surrounded by an oblong outline. Janos knocks five times. A similar knock responds from the other side. Janos repeats the knocking once more.

'Don't be scared of what happens next,' he tells me. 'You're safe here.'

A peephole opens in the door.

'Identify yourselves,' a voice says from within.

Janos places his palm into the peephole.

'Approved,' the voice says after a short moment. 'What about the other one?'

'I will guarantee her,' Janos says. 'She's my sister.'

Slowly the door opens. Janos looks at me and steps in, carrying his lantern. I follow.

It is almost entirely dark in the room. I see a pale woman holding a glow-glass, a sphere of dim speckled-blue light. At the edges of the room I sense human shapes, unmoving, watching. The gatekeeper swings the glass back and forth. The pendulum movement wakes the algae, and slowly the light spills wider around her. In the dark the marks begin to glow white-bright, forging a chain around the space. Janos turns his palm upwards, and I see the mark shining on it, too.

An eye with the sun in the centre. The invisible tattoo of Dreamers.

The tattoos glow like eyes turned towards me. A flame bursts to life in the room, catches the core of a torch and grows. Hands move to light more fires. A tall, dark-skinned man carrying a torch steps forth towards us. Behind him, I notice a short woman with a birthmark on her face watching us intently.

'This is your sister, then?' the man asks.

'Yes, this is Eliana,' Janos replies.

The man steps closer and lowers the torch towards my face. I feel the heat from the fire. I have been cold so long that its ripple on my skin is pleasant until it turns scorching.

'I'm Askari,' the tall man says. He nods at my forehead. 'You'll need something for that.'

I raise my fingers to my brow. The stinging has grown into an aching burn.

'It's best if you don't touch it,' a familiar voice says. 'Leave it to a professional.'

Between two torches the shadows part and Alva walks towards me. She has changed her white coat for a brown jacket, and my eyes catch the tattoo on her palm before her fingers fold around it. She stops before me and regards me.

'You will need a bath,' she says. 'And a hot drink. Eimar, is there any soup left?' Alva shouts over her shoulder to a robust red-bearded man.

'I'll go and have a look,' the man says and walks away, presumably in the direction of the kitchen.

Askari stares at me, then turns to whisper something to the woman with a birthmark. She gives me a look and nods. Askari straightens his back and speaks again.

'Are we to understand,' he says, 'that you have been to the House of the Tainted and escaped?'

'Only because one of the guards helped me,' I say.

Askari and the woman glance at each other.

'Unusual,' the woman says. 'We would like to hear more about it.'

Alva places a hand on my shoulder. Askari stands silent for a moment, as if considering what to do. Then he says, 'I believe Eliana will better be able to tell us the whole story once she's had some food and sleep.'

The room is still. Everyone waits. The woman watches me in silence. Eventually she nods. Alva gives a slight nod back to the woman and Askari.

'Come with me,' she says. 'Let's see about that bath and the soup.'

I follow her along narrow corridors that every now and then open into circular rooms in different sizes. In one of the rooms through which we walk, three Dreamers sit at a table. One of them is turning his hand in the light of a bright glow-glass. No tattoo is visible on his palm. Another one dips a sponge into a glass bowl with a jelly-like substance in it, and the third is brushing jelly on his palm. The tattoo of the Dreamers begins to fade as the jelly touches it. The man holding the sponge looks up as we pass them, and I recognize his face. The memory becomes clear: the man I saw at the Museum of Pure Sleep on the day of the Ink-marking, the tattoo that disappeared.

He turns to say something to the other man, who is

waiting for the jelly to dry on his skin. His face is familiar too. It takes a little longer for it to take a place as part of the memory.

The guard who stopped the scar-handed man in the museum.

My thoughts fill the holes in the scene, the hidden spaces I did not see at the time. The scar-handed man, perhaps taking an urgent message to the museum guard who secretly worked with the Dreamers already back then. The museum guard who noticed the Scar-handed had forgotten to cover his palm tattoo. Perhaps the guard had some jelly with him just in case; perhaps the Scar-handed gilded his palm with it in the empty moment between the visitors before the next group stepped into the room, led by the guide.

I glance behind me as we walk out of the door. I see the Scar-handed look at me, and I wonder if he has recognized me too. Alva notices my gaze.

'The palm is a tricky place because the solution covering the tattoo wears off quickly,' she says. 'I have tried to improve it to make it waterproof, but the raw materials are difficult to get.'

She opens a door to a dim room where bathtubs are lined up against the wall.

'I will arrange some hot water for you,' she says.

I collapse on the floor and close my eyes.

I sit on a stool wearing garments that are too big but clean. My limbs rest languid and the long soak in the hot water has left my head foggy. The space is more a cupboard converted into an emergency room than an actual room. The shelves are as tall as the wall and stacked to the ceiling with glass jars and small sachets that emit a faint scent of herbs. Alva dips the corner of a towel into a steaming pot of strong-smelling brew and begins to gently pat my brow with it. I start with pain, when the cleansing brew touches my skin. Alva pulls back and hits her elbow on the edge of a shelf.

'I do miss my old working space, I must admit,' she says, rubbing her elbow. 'You've allowed that to get bad. Don't touch it!' She brings the towel to my brow again. I squeeze my hand into a fist and feel my nails bite into the skin of my palm.

'How long have you been here?' I ask.

'I left the House of Webs over a month ago,' Alva says. 'I reckon they will have found someone to replace me by now.'

'Why did you leave?'

I watch Alva. Her eyes move quickly, her mouth looks for the words.

'After you disappeared, your brother got in touch,' she says. 'He . . . convinced me. That I would be more use here.'

There is a little more colour on her face. It might be just the steam from the pot. I decide not to draw any conclusions yet.

'So you don't know what's happening in the House of Webs?'

'Not since I left,' Alva says. She presses my forehead lightly with the dry end of the towel. 'Dreamers have people in many places on the island, but no one in the House of Webs.'

'Do they get caught often?' I ask. I remember how the number of prisoners grew in the House of the Tainted over the past weeks.

'More often after the City Guard understood the connection between the algae-light and Dreamer tattoos,'

Alva says. 'There's been an increase in places that have glow-glasses.'

Yet another thing clicks in place. I remember the taverns we visited in disguise with Janos and Valeria, and my wonderment over how many new glow-glasses had appeared in the city.

'Aren't you afraid that someone who has been caught will reveal this place to the City Guard?' I ask.

'Every day,' Alva says. 'The base has already moved several times. We will have to do so again soon.'

The thought of Valeria has remained as a spark inside me. Alva folds the towel over the lip of the pot and places the pot on the floor. She reaches for a jar on a high shelf.

'Janos told me that you still don't know what happened to Valeria,' I say. My voice feels bruised when I speak her name.

Alva's arm continues its movement, but her back freezes for a short moment. I cannot see her face. Then she moves again, turns to me with a dark glass jar in her hand.

'That's true,' she says. 'We don't. I'm sorry.'

She opens the jar. I recognize the scent rising from it.

'You haven't given up on looking for her, have you?' I ask.

Alva's eyes follow her hand into the jar.

'Of course not,' she says.

My arm prickles. I pull my sleeve up and scratch my skin.

Alva raises her gaze and freezes.

'Pull your sleeve back up,' she says.

I do. Alva wipes the ointment on the edge of the glass jar, places the jar down and leans closer. She looks at my arm and turns it in such a way that the light of the glow-glass falls on it.

'Have you had this for a long time?' she asks and points at the blotch of rash on the crook of my arm.

'It appeared after a couple of weeks in the House of the Tainted,' I say.

Alva takes a magnifying glass from her pocket which she brings close to my arm. The edges of the lens distort the rash, turning it convex, but the centre shows it more clearly: it is formed of small purple dots.

'Do you have rash elsewhere?' she asks.

'On my legs and ankles.'

'May I have a look?'

I roll the trouser bottoms up. Alva studies my ankles through the magnifying glass.

'Did many in the House of the Tainted have rash?' she asks.

'Everyone,' I say.

'Where did the water used for washing come from?'

'We didn't wash often,' I say. 'But we spent a lot of time in the sea. The prisoners are used for collecting blood coral.'

Alva lowers the magnifying glass and pushes it back into her pocket. I can almost see her shaping sentences in her mind to write them in her notebook.

'Did you see anything unusual in the sea?'

'Mud. A few dead fish.' Then I remember. 'A rust-coloured sediment floated around the coral reefs. Not everywhere, but especially in the shallows where we would dive.'

Alva's expression turns more alert.

'How far from the island?' she asks.

'I don't know exactly,' I say. I try to tell apart the days that have blurred and faded into one in my memory. 'Sometimes hours away. Why?'

Dark worry visits Alva's face. Yet she pushes it away and grabs the ointment jar again.

'Let's talk about that later,' she says. 'Now you must rest.'

She is right; sleep is already brushing my eyes, and my thoughts are drifting apart like mist over the sea.

'Do Dreamers have someone working in the House of the Tainted?' I ask.

Alva looks at me, surprised.

'I don't think so,' she says. 'The security is too tight. We know very little about what happens in there. That's why Askari and Tirra wish to speak to you.' She begins to rub the ointment on my forehead. It soothes the hot stinging on my skin. 'Why do you ask?'

I remember Moth pressing the key into my hand, showing me the way. Telling me Valeria was not imprisoned in the House of the Tainted. The stare, the sincerity of which I did not dare to be certain.

'I simply wondered,' I say.

Alva closes the ointment jar and hands it to me.

'Use this for a few days,' she says. 'There may be others who need it, but your brow is currently in a worse state than anyone else's tattoos.'

I accept the jar gratefully and push it into the pocket of the too-large jacket. We sit in silence for a while, I on the stool, Alva on the floor leaning her back against the wall.

'I still mean to find her,' I say quietly.

Alva's mouth tightens, as if to seal something within, and softens again. She does not seem to have noticed the shift in her expression, but it remains as a ghost in my mind.

'I've arranged a hammock for you in the women's dormitory,' she says. 'There is also a spare blanket. I'll come and show you.'

As I press my head down on the pillow and wrap the blankets around me, I wonder if there is something they are not telling me, but sleep comes soft like warm water and all thoughts drift away.

The round room is lit by dim glow-glasses, and four tattoos stare at me from chairs arranged in a circle. Above them I watch the shifts on the faces of Alva, Janos, Askari and the woman with the birthmark, who introduced herself as Tirra. I tell them about the day I left the House of Webs, about Weaver and Lazaro and Biros. I say nothing about Spinner, or the underground grotto where her ancestors sleep in their amber shells, because that cannot be of importance to them, and I wish to keep it as mine alone. I tell them about the House of the Tainted: the tattoos, the guards, the ships and the coral. I can see that only some of it is news to them. As I speak, I begin to feel as if my words are rain against a glass wall. They shatter and pour down to the floor without making a mark.

When I have finished, they are all silent.

'You've been through a lot,' Tirra says eventually. 'Thank you.'

'Is there,' I begin, and stop. This room is strange to me, and there is something behind their silence that is tall and wide and heavy. 'I mean to say, could I ask what has happened while I was away?'

Alva's eyes move. She does not quite give a quick sideways glance at Janos, and Janos does not quite respond to it.

'Is there anything else I can do or help with?' I continue.

'Not for the time being,' Askari says. 'But I think it would be fair to give you an update.' He pauses and looks at Tirra, whose mouth grows taut, then softens. She gives a slow nod.

Askari turns back to me.

'Dreamers working in the Ink Quarters have begun to alter the composition of the tattoo ink according to directions from Alva and Irena.'

I notice Janos looking at Alva. He is probably unaware of the smile that lifts his face for a moment. There is admiration in it, and more.

'But it will probably still be months until enough people will begin to get their dreams back,' Askari continues.

I remember the original plans we had for the timing when we first began to talk about the possibilities with Janos, Valeria and Irena.

'Are you aiming for the next Word-incineration?' I ask.

'We were,' Janos says, 'but we are getting worried about how much longer we can wait. Yesterday's flood caused a lot of damage on the island.'

Their faces are serious and weary. I have thought about the same thing. The island may not be able to take another flood.

'We still wish to use the contents of the codex to convince people to leave,' Askari says. 'But we may have to proceed faster than intended.'

'Leave, you say,' I reply. 'It would take a lot of ships to carry everyone. How would you do that?'

'There are enough ships on the island,' Askari says. 'It's a matter of getting people on those ships, and getting the ships' crews to work for us. We are almost ready. Our work didn't begin three months ago, or even a year ago.'

Tirra places her hand on Askari's, and he quiets. I wait until I am certain he will not say more.

It is a strange realization, and one that brings a faint

wave of shame with the understanding. Valeria, Janos and I may have come across the codex, but we are pebbles on a wide and far-stretching shore, not the moon that will turn the tide. Without us and the codex, Dreamers would have found another way to proceed. They may have been dreaming of a new future for the island when we were not even babies in our cots yet. And they have known me for less than a day; there is no reason why they should trust me with their most important plans.

'I understand,' I say. 'But I want to continue looking for Valeria. How long do I have?'

'It is time,' Tirra says, not to anyone in particular.

Askari turns to look at Alva and Janos. Janos shifts on his seat and I see two lines appear on his brow. Alva takes a deep breath.

'Time for what?' I ask. A tight knot is forming inside me, pressing at me like a fist from within.

'Eliana, after you disappeared, we looked for both of you everywhere,' Alva says. 'Dreamers all over the island, in the City Guard, in places where they would hear things. Nobody knew anything.' She pauses to take another deep breath and glances at Janos, who places his hand on her arm. 'Then, three weeks ago, a woman was found in Halfway Canal. She had been in the water for some time.'

The fist inside me clenches tighter. Its knuckles are sharp, like broken glass. I cannot hear this.

Janos gives Alva's arm a quick squeeze.

'She was Valeria's age and size. She had red hair and pale skin.'

'There are other red-haired women her age on the island,' I say. My voice is hollow, made of shards that will fall apart at any moment.

Alva looks at me and there are tears in her eyes.

'I went to see her. It was her.'

'How can you be certain?' I ask. The words break, they fall into the wind and are swept into the sea with everything else.

'She'd been in the water for a long time,' Alva says. 'But I saw her tattoos. She had your name tattooed on her palm. Eliana, Valeria is dead.'

CHAPTER FIFTEEN

The world stands still around me. The tattoo-eyes stare, unblinking. Somewhere outside and above there are canals and houses, but no one moves in them. The clouds in the sky have stopped, the waves stalled as if their crests are carved in ice. Sand in hourglasses has ceased to flow. I seek within me the certainty that this is a dream, fumble for it with desperate hands, and clutch only the understanding that I am awake.

I stand up. The chair scratches the floor behind me: a long, rending sound, sharp as a scream.

Alva gets up, walks around the table and pulls me into a hug. I stand straight. Perhaps my arms move to wrap around her. Perhaps they do not. She is saying something, soft words that fall into a repetitive rhythm, sorry, so sorry, so sorry. Like a bird's wings brushing against a confined space.

No one should be able to move or speak in this moment that has fallen outside of time, but Janos and Alva do, and Tirra and Askari. I watch them as if they are behind a thick crust of glass that suffocates all sound and warps every gesture. They belong in some other world where the language is strange and the shape of living things unknown to me. I turn and walk away, along corridors where glow-glasses pick up white-shining eyes floating past me. Fingers grasp my arm, but I yank it away. Finally I find my hammock and climb into it and close my eyes.

Someone stands next to me for a long while. I hear her breathing. I imagine that when I turn and see her face, it will be Valeria. I think of this as a dream-room, where I can make her Valeria. I do not open my eyes because as long as I keep them closed, Valeria is standing next to me.

Eventually I hear her sigh and walk away.

I think about the last time I saw Valeria. I think about the first time, and every time. The way her mouth turned to a smile and dropped it again, the way light fell across her face, and shadow. I speak to her, because there is no one else I want to speak to.

Valeria, I say. Somewhere is another island where we walk, with sand shifting under our footsteps, and a rock we climb up together, still warm to touch with the day's glow. There, on the blazing late-summer shore, we sit side by side, our shoulders brushing each other. Light-coloured leaves float in the water-space, and when wind folds it, they move away from us, towards winter. There is nothing between us but peace, and we rest in this moment, a premonition of the coming autumn on our skin. It is not harsh, but translucent instead, and bright as the wing of a dragonfly spreading to take flight. On tree-branches years will curl into buds and shrivel up only to grow again, and beyond them the sky is calm and unbroken. If I place my hand on your arm, you will let it stay there, and if I do not, the moment will not be any less full for it. The water is quiet, and moves, and is still again.

I listen, but Valeria is silent. I am silent too.

Tears come and go.

Footsteps come and go.

The smell of food wafts into the room.

It may be night or day.

It may be full moon or new.

Eventually I get up with limbs as stiff as if their flesh has been parted from the bones, buried, turned to dust and put together again. My throat is just as dry. I find a bowl of cold herbal brew on the floor next to the hammock. I sit cross-legged and drink in big gulps.

A noise like long and hollow metal wands being beaten together pierces the room. I stare at the air, expecting to see the source of the sound appear before my eyes until I realize it will not. There is no one else in the dormitory, but I hear running and talking outside.

The noise stops.

After a while, the door opens and Alva peers in.

'Are you awake?' she asks.

I nod.

'The alarm went off because one of ours sent a fore-warning that she was bringing visitors,' Alva says. She looks at me, up and down. There is concern on her face. 'They wish to speak to you. They say it's urgent. Do you think you are well enough?'

I do not. I nod. Alva extends a hand to me, and I take it. She gives my fingers a light squeeze.

We step into the round room with chairs around the edges. There is more light this time: live fires enclosed in lanterns blend with the blue spheres of glow-glasses. Tirra sits on a chair with Askari standing by her side. Janos is there too, and three other people. I recognize two of them immediately. Irena turns her head as we walk in, and grief is raw on her face. Next to her I see Moth, the short-haired guard who helped me escape the House of the Tainted. The third person stands in silence, head covered by a hood. Alva points at a chair, and I sit down.

The third person turns around and pulls back her hood, revealing a dark face I know.

I stand up.

'I won't listen to anything she has to say,' I say.

Tirra watches me. Her voice is calm when she speaks, without a rift.

'That is your choice,' she says. 'But before you take your leave, you may wish to know your house-elder has offered herself as a hostage in exchange for the opportunity to speak to you.'

Weaver's gaze holds mine, black and steady.

'I am glad to see you are alive, Eliana,' she says quietly.

I search for any shift, a blotched outline that would reveal unease, and do not see it.

'You sent me to the House of the Tainted,' I say.

And there it is: Weaver's eyes drift, stop on Moth for a brief while, and turn back.

'I had no choice,' she says.

The others are watching us. I could easily have gone to the kitchen and taken a knife from there. Now I wish I had. If I used my nails and teeth, bit Weaver and clawed bloody scratches on her, how much damage could I do before they pulled me away?

'I don't believe you,' I say.

Moth does something strange: she steps closer to Weaver and takes her hand.

'I believe you met someone in the House of the Tainted,'

Weaver says. 'Your brother might not have found you, had it not been for his message.'

I stare at them, standing side by side. The world around me is still the glass-enclosed world I do not recognize, its creatures still strangers speaking a strange language.

'I apologize for my mother,' Moth says. 'She acted without my approval.'

I only see it then. The similar face shape, the bearing that is the same despite the different build. The same arc of the head under the short, curly hair. I look from Weaver to Moth and back.

'Is she your daughter?' I ask Weaver.

Weaver's expression shifts, but Moth speaks first.

'Not her daughter,' she says. 'Her son.' She pauses for a moment. 'My name is Ila.'

And I understand, or believe I do. Her low voice and angular shape that is not without softness. His shape, I correct in my mind. Not hers. But simultaneously, as the image finds its form, a feeling bothers me that it is not whole. There is something I cannot place.

It is entirely quiet in the room. Tirra shifts in her chair. The rustling fills the space.

'But you lived with the female prisoners and guards,' I say.

Weaver and Ila look at each other, a slow look that has been exchanged before. Weaver's mouth opens. Ila moves his head very slightly. Weaver closes her mouth again.

'When you look at me,' Ila says, 'what do you see?'

The mark on his forehead is clear, but my eyes slide down, trying to understand the meaning of his words. I feel strange and rude about looking, as if I am intruding on something private. His hips are narrow, his shoulders wide, and there is a nearly invisible swell of breasts under the jacket. His face has no sign of a stubble, and his upper lip has no more hair than my own.

'I don't know,' I say.

'Neither did the midwife who helped deliver me,' Ila says. 'Do you know what is done on the island to newborn babies whose bodies cannot be named male or female at once?'

I do not respond. I have never thought about it. I did not even know it was possible.

'If you haven't seen others like me before, it is not because my kind are not born into this world,' Ila says. 'It is because we are not allowed to live.'

'But you live,' I say.

'Only because of my mother's courage,' Ila says.

He turns to Weaver and lowers his chin in a nod. Weaver looks at her son and responds to the nod with a similar gesture, and for a brief moment their resemblance is so striking I am surprised I did not see it before. I have never seen Weaver's face like this, soft with unspoken things.

'When my son was born,' Weaver says, 'the midwife intended to kill him. She said it would be more merciful. But I didn't let her.' The words exit her mouth weighty, yet without hesitation. 'I hid him in the only place on the island where I believed he would be safe.'

I finally understand Moth's questions, why he wanted to know things about the House of Webs. I see the years he has spent in the House of the Tainted, imagine the childhood that was even more hidden than my own. I imagine the loneliness: reaching in all directions, the few and secret moments when a stranger who called herself his mother visited. The pieces move and come together, settle into an image where it all finally fits.

'But the Council learned about him,' I say. 'Is that it?'

All softness falls off Weaver's face, and for a moment it is a wide-open wound.

'Yes,' she says. 'They could crush him like an insect. And that would be my end, too.'

'You bought his life with mine and Valeria's,' I say. My voice is cold and hollow. Irena stands like a spectre behind Weaver. Orange and blue light flickers across her skin and clothes, tugging them in two different directions.

'I didn't know,' Ila says. 'I wouldn't have agreed to it.'

'He speaks the truth,' Weaver says. 'I'm only here because he eventually learned what happened and demanded that I come.'

I turn to Ila.

'You helped me,' I say. 'And I'm grateful for that. But Weaver betrayed us.' It is almost a cry.

A voice speaks from the edge of the room.

'Would you not do the same?'

It is Tirra. I turn my head.

'I ask you,' she continues, 'would you not save the life that matters to you most, if you were faced with a similar choice?'

She is right. I would sacrifice Weaver in an instant, if it brought Valeria back. I might sacrifice everyone in this room. The realization is an unfamiliar and chilly undercurrent, yet impossible to deny.

'I don't know,' I say.

Tirra gazes at me across the room, then turns her face to Weaver. She turns up the palm of her hand, bends her fingers to invite more words. The eye on her skin stares.

'In any case, you are mistaken,' Weaver says. 'Valeria is alive.'

Hope flares so white-hot it hurts and is gone just as

swiftly. Irena's eyes widen and her face sharpens. She stands straighter.

'I'm tired of listening to your lies,' I say.

'It's true,' Ila says.

'Where is she?' Irena asks.

'In the House of Webs,' Weaver says. 'She has been there all this time. The City Guard wanted to take her away. I managed to persuade them to let me keep her captive in the House of Webs without anyone knowing. I was trying to protect her.'

'But you sent me to a trap,' I say.

'It was the only way I could protect you and the House of Webs,' Weaver said. 'The two of you had to be separated. Otherwise they would have killed you both.'

Alva has been standing behind me and takes a step forward, to my side.

'We saw Valeria's body,' Alva says. 'She had the same tattoos. Even the invisible one on her palm.'

'It is not difficult to find a dead body in this city,' Weaver says. 'Or copy those tattoos. I staged her death, because I knew the City Guard would eventually demand to have her.'

I think about it. I want it to be true. Time begins to flow again, clouds move across the sky and shift their shapes, grains of sand fall in hourglasses and sea breaks free from its frozen spell.

'If that is true,' I say, 'why did you leave her in the House of Webs?'

'The house was evacuated with help from the City Guard. They would have seen her. I intended to go back for her later.'

'Someone must go to the House of Webs immediately,' Irena says.

A cold current rushes through me.

'Not someone,' I say. 'I. I must go.'

'Too dangerous,' Alva says.

'I cannot let you,' Janos says.

I turn to look at him.

'It's not your choice,' I say. 'I'm the only one who knows the way through the web-maze. All other routes are cut off.'

Janos stares at me.

'Weaver knows the way,' he says. 'We could send her.'

'Do you trust her well enough to bring Valeria back unhurt?' It is Irena.

A silence encloses the room. Eventually Alva says, 'Eliana is right.'

I look at Tirra and Askari, who are whispering to each other. Askari straightens his back.

'The choice is yours,' he says. 'We wish you the best of luck.'

I wait for Tirra's words, but there are none. Janos says something to Alva, who nods. He walks to me and says, 'I need to talk to you alone.' His expression is tense, all taut jawline and dark eyes. I nod at Tirra and Askari and follow Janos out of the round room.

There are few places at the base that offer any privacy. Janos walks me into Alva's makeshift emergency cupboard and pulls the door closed behind us.

'It is not safe for you to go,' he says.

'Would you not go?' I ask. 'If it was me. Or Alva?'

Janos looks away, then lowers his gaze. His mouth is a tight line.

'I would,' he says. 'But you don't understand. Tirra and Askari will not stop you, but they won't let anyone go with you, either.'

'Why not?'

274

Janos takes a deep breath.

'Everything they – we – have been working for is ready now,' he says. 'Every gear of the plan will be in motion soon. They are just waiting for the right moment. It could be tomorrow. It could be today. They will not be able to spare anyone. We all have our part to play.'

'All except me,' I say.

Janos stares at me. His mouth turns, makes a movement like he is swallowing something unpleasant.

'You were gone for nearly three months,' he says. 'We didn't know if we would see you again.'

'I know,' I say. 'It's not your fault. But it means I'm the only one whose life counts little enough.' There are thick strands in my voice, jagged and bitter. 'Besides Valeria's.'

'That's not true,' Janos says.

'And yet it is,' I say. 'Dreamers would leave her to die.'

'You don't even know if she is alive,' Janos says quietly. 'Weaver may well be lying.'

'I know.' I look him in the eye. 'But I cannot turn my back without finding out.'

Janos wears the two vertical lines between his eyebrows again. For an instant I can see how he will look in twenty or thirty years' time. He gives a nod, another.

'Be careful,' he says. 'And if you hear the flood bell clang briefly, then hear it pause, then hear it again, don't head back here. Go to the trading harbours instead.'

'I will.'

I hug him, then force myself to smile.

'Take good care of Alva,' I say.

Janos smiles back, but not without a shadow on his face.

When I walk past the round room, I see Weaver still sitting there. Irena is with her, and there is a live-fire lantern at her feet.

'Wait.' It is Weaver's voice.

I take a few steps back. Weaver picks up the orange-burning lantern from the floor and offers it to me.

'Take this,' she says. 'You will need it.'

I take the lantern.

'I hope you find her,' Weaver says.

So do I, I think, but I remain silent and turn back to the corridor. Irena gets up and walks to the door to close it.

The last thing I see is Weaver's face and her expression, which I cannot read.

I drag the skiff a short way up the hill, to where the web-maze begins. I hide it in a side alley where I tie it to a stone gatepost. A silence of empty houses and streets is caught in the webs, it sways slowly in the passing breezes. Weaver was right: the lantern will help. The weight of early evening is already upon the day, and most of the glow-glasses in the maze have lost their light. All algae on the island is dying.

The web encloses me, wraps itself into gauzy layers that protect me against everything, yet nothing. I climb towards the house. It is strange to think that this will be the last time I walk up the hill. For many years, the House of Webs has been the only home I have known. Now it is a cluster of dark dead alleys and buildings, bone-smooth floors and grave-cold rooms where only the slow stirrings of sea and earth and air make sounds.

Something beyond my own ragged breathing and footsteps falling on stones catches my ear. I listen.

Ta-tap, ta-tap, ta-tap.

Someone else is moving in the web-maze, not far away from me.

I stop. The footsteps proceed almost exactly in the precise

rhythm of my own. As an experiment, I take a few more steps. Like an echo of mine, the movement proceeds, *ta-tap ta-tap ta-tap*, soft-soled shoes on the humid stones. Their sound is strangely two-phased, like a heartbeat.

I stop again. The other footsteps do the same.

The movement begins to roll in the wall-webs like a wave: it billows one wall first, then another, something denser than wind and air. A body swaying under a sheet. Someone is looking for me, trying to reach towards where I stand.

'Valeria?' I say.

Everything goes completely quiet. The movement in the webs undulates to an end. At some distance I see a small flame through the layers of webs: another lantern. Then I hear approaching running steps and see the outline of a body crash onto a web, harsh and violent. The wall-web holds; its fragile and veil-like appearance is woven to mislead. The bottom edge is knotted to metal rings on the ground with multi-layered threads, so you cannot crawl under it. It is hard to climb over, because the fabric offers little foothold. In the light of my lantern I see how a burnished blade thrusts through the web, begins to pick apart the threads and pierce a hole into the surface.

I realize I have made a mistake.

I am not far from the house any more. I blow out my lantern and cannot help but wonder: did Weaver give it to me so I could be more easily seen in the maze? For an instant, doubt drowns me like sudden deep water. Maybe Valeria is not alive. Maybe this is simply another trap laid out for me. But if ever there was a moment to turn back, it is lost now. I abandon the lantern along the way and begin to run up the hill along a route I would find in pitch-dark. I hear the sound of tearing webs behind me and accelerate my pace.

My feet find the way easily. I take caution not to touch the wall-webs so as not to give any other sign of myself apart from the footsteps. I know from experience that the threads muffle sound and make it more difficult to perceive its direction. The other lantern burns further and further away and moves sideways, not drawing closer. Whoever carries it has lost direction. Or so I hope. But the webs will not hold the sharp knife forever.

The stone buildings rise before me as dark figures against the evening sky. The shortest way to Weaver's study is across the square, but inside the buildings I will be better hidden if my follower reaches the house. On the other hand, I will not see if he finds his way to the square.

I choose the fastest route. The pool in the middle is a dead, dark eye, without a trace of glow left. The contours of the buildings are already melting into the deepening dusk. Soon it will be impossible to see anything.

The outermost folding door of the Halls of Weaving is slightly open. I enter through it and glance behind me: no light or movement anywhere. I pull the door closed quietly. I fumble my way between the looms and hit my knee against the corner of a wooden frame. Something clatters to the floor and pain bursts along my leg. I stop to listen. It is quiet.

I reach the door that opens to the corridor and slip through it. Weaver's study is only twenty steps away. Its tall door opens easily and without sound.

There is barely any light in the room. A narrow waxing moon is floating upwards in the sky outside the corner window. The watergraph gleams as a tall, mute statue.

'Valeria?' I whisper into the air of the study.

A faint wave moves from one tapestry to the next on the walls. It may be just air flowing through the open door. It may be just imagination. I listen to my own breathing.

'Valeria?'

The word fades into the space of the room.

I hear a sound, brief, wordless. I walk towards it, taking short, wary steps. I stop before a tapestry falling all the way to the floor near the corner where Weaver keeps her medical store. Our Lady of Weaving stands in front of me, covered in layers of web, face and limbs half invisible. Behind the tapestry I sense a slow and faint breathing, forced into silence. I grasp the tapestry and push it slightly to the side.

I see movement in the dark. I hear water slosh inside a glass. A frail, blue light as thin as a singing medusa's tentacle begins to grow. The space is a simple alcove with a bench embedded in the wall, a blanket fallen into a heap and a jug of water. Valeria gets up from the bench. Her eyes are big and full of dusk when she steps to me and pulls me against herself. I stay there for many moments, listening to the rhythm of her breathing, always faster than mine, and I let her warmth absorb into me. Each curve, rise and dent of her body fits in with mine.

'Are you well?' I ask.

Valeria pulls away from me and nods. Her gaze is serious. It falls upon my brow. She raises a hand to my face and strokes the still-stinging tattoo with her fingertips, a touch light as air. Then she clasps my hand and places it on her chest. We must run and hide, but her face is close to mine and I do not wish to move away from under her touch. The night coils further, the killer's footsteps draw closer and the world will not stop turning, the sea rolling its wrap over the island.

'We must go,' I say eventually.

Valeria picks something from the bench. I recognize it as a piece of charcoal when she begins to write on the wall with it. I notice now the walls are full of faint writing. I discern words among them: *Father. Mother. Weaver. Council. Eliana.*

Weaver told me to wait, Valeria writes. Something overflows within me. I realize she has continued to learn to read during her imprisonment. I want to ask her to write everything she has wished to say and could not, but time is running out, light is running out, and we must get away.

'I know,' I say. 'But someone followed me here.'

Valeria's eyes widen and her mouth settles into a line. She nods, takes my hand and picks up the glow-glass. I listen. I hear no movement. We step out from behind the tapestry and walk across the study to the door.

'We must make it to the maze,' I say. 'Other routes are cut off.'

The corridor throws echoes of our footsteps at us as we walk along it towards the Halls of Weaving. The looms stand tall and silent in the dark. We are careful not to touch them. I do not wish to cross the square again, but we must walk the short distance between the Halls of Weaving and the dormitory building outside. After we have passed the dormitories we can turn and exit through the door that will take us nearest to the web-maze.

I open the folding door slightly and peek out to the square. Darkness rests mute against the stones. I am about to start towards the door at the end of the dormitory building, when Valeria clutches my arm.

'What is it?' I whisper.

She points towards the dormitories. At first I see nothing. Most of the windows that side of the square are the empty, black windows of the dormitories, hollow and quiet. Yet above them runs another, sparser row, built to bring light to the corridor. At first I think it is some kind of reflection, but as I follow it, I see clearly how the orange-glowing light moves from one window to the next.

Someone is moving towards us along the corridor.

Valeria pulls me back into the Halls of Weaving and closes the door soundlessly. She begins to drag me with her. We cannot stay in the halls. There is nowhere to hide in here. With his lantern, the killer will see us from the doorway. There is no exit at the end of the Tapestry Rooms. We have barely made it into the corridor when I hear footsteps outside, the same two-phased beat as before: *ta-tap ta-tap ta-tap*. The folding door on the side of the square opens, the same by which we stood mere moments before.

'Weaver's study,' I whisper to Valeria.

We run.

The key to the tall wooden door is gone. I cannot lock it from within. We must simply leave it closed. There is one hiding place in the room, one possible way out.

'The corner,' I whisper.

I pull Valeria by the hand behind the tapestries. Our Lady of Weaving looks the other way, does not know her face will conceal or reveal us.

There are footsteps in the corridor. An orange glow draws a line under the door, a sharp-edged cut in the dark. The door begins to open.

I push the worn wooden surface and wish.

The low door lets us into the darkness and closes behind us without sound. Valeria stiffens against me.

'Don't be afraid,' I whisper very close into her ear. 'I've been here before.'

281

But the truth is I am afraid, too. Not just of the killer on the other side of the door, but also of the creature in the dark. There is no sound at the other end of the room. I wonder if Spinner has already left the house, perhaps the island. Perhaps the world itself. For what do I know about her in the end, except that she is older than time and history, at least the time and history I am able to comprehend? Maybe Spinner is climbing the Web of Worlds at this very moment, seeking other skies, other lands in which to settle and spin her webs. Other spaces inhabited by people wiser than us.

Webs undulate around us, translucent and persistent.

We must move away from near the door.

I begin to thread through the webs towards the dark end of the room. Valeria follows. I lead her as best I can, although I am about to get tangled in the webs myself. They grab me like greedy hands reaching for prey. Estimating the distance turns difficult in the dark; I half-expect my extended arm to meet the large body of Spinner, a part I may not recognize at first touch. I do not know which thought is more frightening: that it will move, or that it will not.

Yet there is nothing ahead but webs. We make it to the end of the room, where it is empty and quiet. I begin to feel the wall. At the same moment when I feel the seams of the door under my fingers, a wedge of light cuts into the room behind us.

I pull at the door. It opens slowly. The stone scratches my fingertips and cleaves my nails. Together with Valeria I drag the door open. I push her into the tunnel ahead of me.

'Down the stairs,' I say.

The glow-glass slips from Valeria's hand. It does not break, but begins to roll down the stairs. I hear it knock against the stones further away. Its echo climbs the walls. Then I hear a splash. I grab Valeria's hand.

I knew, and yet I hoped. The tunnel has flooded.

At the top of the stairs a wide figure holding a lantern steps to the doorway. Behind him follows another, like a shadow.

Orange light glistens on the long blade of the knife with thin shreds of webs caught on it, reveals *the tale still told on the island.*

This is how it goes:

Our Lady of Weaving started with the sky.

She stretched the space with her limbs until the jewels of the Web of Worlds shone through. In their light, under the stars she sighed life into the air, and far below she drew the dark ends of the earth.

Between the sky and earth she made warps of sunlight and rain, tall and taut bones of the world.

Then she began to dream.

From her sleep rose those who walked on four feet, and those who walked on two, and those who did not walk at all. She dreamed oceans and islands and trees. As she dreamed, silk spun from her many fingertips and began to weft its way through the warp binding heaven and earth together. Her dreams wove the thoughts and desires of those who walked under the stars, their gaze and their blindness, for them a will they could follow. And her dreams wove what they began to call a soul.

This is the world she made. This is the world she shelters with her limbs. One day, when she grows weary of those she brought to life, she will pluck a thread and pull, and all will unravel the moment when

CHAPTER SIXTEEN

Biros's face is a landscape of light and shadow. He places the lantern on top of the staircase. Lazaro stands behind him, unmoving. The knife in Biros's hand is long and strong-bladed, like a sabre. The kind butchers use to cut the throats of goats. He takes two steps downwards.

'Too bad,' Biros says, 'that it has come to this.'

I look in him for any trace of something to seize. Hesitation; indifference that might make him turn away and take the knife with him. Or caring. Maybe he has a family that knows a different side of him: a wife, children, perhaps elderly parents.

Nothing breaks in his posture. Nothing stirs in his expression. The lantern burns behind his outline, and his eyes are two black wells that do not reflect light.

'The island is in chaos,' I say. My voice trembles, although I try to keep it smooth. 'No one would know if you let us go.'

Biros does not reply. Lazaro shifts on top of the staircase. The gleam of the fire makes his features even more angular. I try to imagine him holding a child in his arms, or writing in his notebook late at night in the light of a candle, wearing small nose glasses. I notice it is not difficult.

I intend to direct my next words at him, but he speaks first.

'We would,' Lazaro says. His low voice echoes in the walls of the staircase.

I understand I do not have a chance to reach behind their masks. Whatever there is, they have closed it out of reach, for other times and places. Right now the face they wear is their only one. I recognize it, because I too have lived like this. And while I never wish to do so again, I see I cannot change their minds.

Valeria clings to me. We do not move. I hear her ragged, panicked breathing, and the beating of my own heart.

'Did Weaver send you?' I ask. My voice is a mere whisper at the heart of a storm, shattered by the surrounding breeze even before it leaves my lips.

'Does it matter?' Biros says.

'Why?' I ask.

Biros does not reply. For a moment nothing moves. Then Lazaro snaps his gloved fingers. The sound is soft and muffled, without an echo. Biros does not turn to look. They both take a step towards us. Their shadows grow taller on the walls.

I begin to back down. Valeria follows. I do not know which one of us trembles more. We could try to attack them. But they are armed, soldiers. I have never held a sharp weapon larger than scissors.

Without looking at Valeria I clutch the hem of her coat and tug. The movement remains hidden from Biros's and Lazaro's eyes. So I hope, at least. Valeria understands and nods so slowly that it could just be an arbitrary movement of her head. I cannot be certain she has understood my meaning, but I must trust it. We stop. Biros and Lazaro continue to move closer.

'We should have got rid of you to begin with,' Biros says.

I am not certain if he is talking to me or Valeria.

'Do you wish to know what we did with your tongue?' Lazaro asks.

I catch a glimpse of nausea on Valeria's pale face. I tighten my grip on the hem of her coat. My fingers count against her side with small, small movements. *One, two, three.*

I tug hard at Valeria's coat: *now*. We rush towards them. Biros moves so fast I understand he has been expecting the attack all this time. He steps forward and gives my shoulder a painful kick while Lazaro simultaneously grabs Valeria's arms. I stagger backwards and lose my balance. I have time to see Lazaro twisting Valeria's arms behind her back and forcing her onto her knees in the staircase while Biros lowers his knife to Valeria's throat. I fall down several steps and the back of my head hits the wall. Darkness pulls me into its embrace.

The House of Webs is here, yet gone. Water gathers into pools around me, and lakes and oceans, and columns of mist that grow all the way to skies and stars. The Web of Worlds supports me. I am a pebble cast into water: expanding circles emerge from me, reaching in all directions. They grow ever wider, join other circles far beyond me, but they do not disappear. They hold everything together. The city is empty, and the sea and the sky. It is cold and completely quiet.

A shadow approaches across the water. Its grasp binds me in place already, even though it is still a distance away.

My hands do not move. My feet do not move. My breathing withers and grows thinner.

The night-maere interlaces its dark, icy fingers with mine and climbs onto my chest. Its thighs squeeze me from both sides and its weight crushes my lungs, but with its touch a tingling power floods into me again. It unravels from my palms and mouth and eyes, flows from me as glowing strands that stitch me to the weave of the world.

The night-maere brushes my ear with its burning lips and talks to me, says what it has been attempting to say for a long while, when I was not ready to listen. This time is different: I can finally discern the words, each and every one, and I understand. I stop fighting back. I let the sensations, the fire-glowing gleam and the hum of the words wash over me. Slowly the fear flows away in soft trickles, disappears into the cracks of the street, the stony pores of the city. I breathe, still not freely, but now ready to receive what the night-maere wishes to give me. Strength settles in me, becomes part of every shift of blood in my veins. All threads twine together and the pattern grows dense and recognizable, an image that has been before my eyes all along. I listen to the message of the creature, and there is nothing in it that I do not already know.

When the night-maere has told me what it has to say, it presses its forehead against mine. My heart opens, bare and susceptible, and the creature begins to be absorbed into me like water swirling into a hole in the ground. Slowly the weight withdraws from my chest, the creature fades until it is gauze-like and lighter than smoke, and eventually the final remnants of the night-maere disappear into me, within my limits and outlines. The chasm on top of my heart seals itself.

I draw a deep breath and my limbs move again, and I am finally whole.

The stone steps dig painfully into my back. My arm is bent under me, and the back of my head aches. Time has not moved. Valeria is on her knees in the staircase, Lazaro's fingers squeeze her arms and Biros's knife has stopped on her throat. Something vibrates in my field of sight, like a ray of light, or a shred of web-yarn lighter than air. I try to brush it away, but my hand slips through it and it grows brighter.

At the height of my chest a thin, white-glowing strand runs from me to Valeria. I think about the knife on her throat, and how a small movement by Biros could take her away from me. I feel a tug in my heart. It sends a vibration towards Valeria along the shining strand. The vibration sinks into her chest like a shooting star swimming through the night. She remains still, but the air around her stirs and settles again.

I begin to crawl up the staircase towards Valeria. My knees and palms sting. The stone sucks the dark stains I leave on it. Biros hears a sound that my body emits, a sob or perhaps a snarl. I do not recognize it myself. Time begins again. Lazaro remains still. Biros's head turns slowly, as if the movement is muffled by water. Shadows paint visible his skull, the black eye sockets, the deeps of his cheeks, the mouth which opens to show the teeth and the void behind them.

The hand presses the handle of the knife; the blade moves along the skin. The white-glowing strand between Valeria and me tenses and shines brighter. It gathers as a tingling under my skin, lights up the flight of stairs, the whole surrounding darkness, and shifts the shape of everything. I look at the reality, but all is like in the dreams where I know I am dreaming and where the dream is mine to control. The walls of stone around me are dream-walls, which I can crush by raising my hand. The dark water below is dream-water, which I can harness against my enemy by whispering an invitation. If my body dies, it will be mended again, because dream-death does not reach beyond the borders of waking.

And because the dream around me is mine to mould and command, I command.

Stop, I say without words. *Let Valeria go.*

Biros's hand freezes. He turns his gaze to me, and Lazaro does the same. Something appears on their faces that I have not seen on them before. Biros's arm shakes with strain, but the knife does not move.

Let go, I say. *Of the knife and Valeria.*

One by one Lazaro's fingers loosen their grip of Valeria. The knife clatters to the stones from Biros's hand, rolls down the steps, past me. I let it go. I will not need it.

Biros steps away from Valeria, further up, towards the doorway. He stares at me. Lazaro follows him.

'What did you do?' he says in a voice that is like an animal caught in his throat.

Go, I say. *Run.*

Biros tries to reach for Valeria again. I command reality like I would a dream. Air turns into a wall he cannot penetrate, and he is thrown backwards, to the doorway. He doubles over as if he has been struck hard around the middle. Lazaro takes a slow step away from Valeria and me.

Things happen quickly. I have time to sense a presence that is entirely different from Biros, Lazaro and Valeria. It makes a rift in the reality beyond which there is no void, but a strange intelligence, unlike a human's. It approaches, seeks. It stops to probe. It surges forward.

The empty space behind Biros fills. A black limb covered by bristles darts into it, and another. Flames are reflected in eyes that shimmer dim like stars hidden beyond space. The arched spikes of the jaws bite into bare skin. Biros flounders in Spinner's jaws until his body grows weary. His limbs twitch once, twice. Eventually the final spasm is over. Spinner pulls away from the door. Lazaro stares, frozen in place, then begins to crawl through the doorway. His feet disappear from sight.

I hear a short howl from the chamber. Then comes silence.

Valeria sits hunched against the wall, her face pale and bare. Her chest rises and falls faster than my heart beats. I reach my hand out to her. She takes it. I squeeze her fingers. They shake between mine. Or so I think until I realize my own hand is shaking against hers. We make no sound. A tremor runs through me, bringing with it a distant, unfamiliar twinge of pain and a wave of weakness, as if I have put a strain on a muscle I did not even know I had in my body.

Valeria's face breaks into relief. She pulls me closer and our foreheads rest against each other, my dark tattoo against her pale and unmarked skin. Her lips are soft and salty when they press to mine, and I still feel their touch when she withdraws. I run my hand down her cheek. She lives and breathes by my side, and this is my dream, and this is my reality.

'Let's go,' I say and get up. Valeria stands up after me. She does not let go of my hand.

With trembling legs we begin to climb the stairs. I notice a thin streak of blood on Valeria's neck. I nearly think it away, but I stop myself. I do not wish to change anything about her. If something leaves a scar, I want to feel it, as part of her. Just as she accepted my dreams and my night-maere

292

and my mark. Her arm settles tightly to support my back. The lantern still burns on top of the stairs where Biros left it. Spinner's aim was sharp, with no room for stray movement. I pick the lantern up.

The chamber is dusky and quiet, but there is a slight rustling and whizzing sound from above. I raise my eyes. The light of the lantern catches in the shimmering webs crossing the ceiling. Spinner is crouched in the web. Her two front limbs are wrapping a human-shaped bundle in silk. I discern a hand balled into a fist, a twitching knee. Further up I see another, unmoving bundle. A draught blows across the floor, swaying the webs. We begin to walk towards the other end and the door which is ajar. The webs brush our bodies and the lantern paints slow-floating patterns on the walls. Valeria accelerates her footsteps. Her hand is already on the door handle, when a voice speaks from the shadows.

'I see the power of Dreamers is not dead, after all,' Spinner says.

I freeze in place. Valeria pulls the door open and her face urges me to follow. But Spinner's words hold me, will not let me leave yet.

I turn to face the room.

'What do you mean?' I ask.

The silence stretches. Eventually a distant wind and space-dust creep into it, a rustling that is the movement of sand and bones turned to earth.

'What do you know of the world?' Spinner says.

Her voice is supple as a vine entwining around a tree-trunk. The question feels like a slab of stone Spinner is laying at my feet, paving an unknown path. I do not see where it will lead me, but I cannot turn away.

Valeria steps next to me and takes my hand.

'There is a lot of water and little land,' I say. 'Some seas are too wide for ships to cross.'

'Is that all?'

A silence gathers around Spinner while she waits.

'Not everywhere is the same as on the island. There are places where people are allowed to dream freely.'

The silence shifts. A limb makes a small movement. In a human I would interpret it as impatience.

'What do you know of the past?' Spinner says.

'The island did not always belong to humans,' I say. 'A long time ago it belonged to the Web-folk. They left their traces on the landscape, but they no longer exist.'

Spinner lets out a crackling noise that drags back and forth. It takes me a while to realize she is laughing. Valeria's breaths have turned taut and short.

'Imagine,' she says, 'that once, a long time ago, the entire island was covered in webs. Not man-made, picture-patterned and easy-fading, but wider, more persistent. And imagine a ship, aboard it people who had not set a foot on steady ground for months. One calm morning the island loomed on the horizon, and they saw it across the glistening surface of the sea. The radiant halo of the web-gauze reached from treetop to treetop, hill to hill. The strands of the sun caught on the threads and burst along the night-born drops of moisture, glowing bright enough to burn their eyes and tug at their spirits. They could not help but reach for the glimmer. Your people have always looked far, and yet only seen what is near.'

Spinner quiets. Her eyes stare at emptiness, and yet at me.

And I remember. The amber walls, the creatures frozen within. Her kin.

'You are of the Web-folk,' I say.

I feel a shiver run through Valeria by my side.

'Yes, you have seen them,' Spinner says quietly. 'A shard of the past your people buried. Those frozen under the sea have been there for longer than anyone knows. They were already ancient when my kin inhabited the island. We recognized them as ours and made the tunnel so we could visit them.'

'Why did you send me there?' I ask. 'You knew it was a trap.'

The lantern flickers small and weak against the wall of shadows around us. Spinner's voice adds another step to the path, inviting me closer.

'Sometimes it is necessary to step into darkness alone and find your way back,' Spinner says. 'To carry something with you into light you could not have found anywhere else.'

The patterns of the underground walls glow in my memory. Long-forgotten words in a language none on the island speaks now. The sun that was Our Lady of Weaving, twining together the threads of life. Small humans at her fingertips: Dreamers shaping their reality like it was a dream.

'Those you are descended from built the sanctuary through which you walked,' Spinner continues. 'A sanctuary for words, weaving and dreams, when they were still one and had not yet been forced apart.'

I swallow the lump in my throat, but it does not disappear. Valeria twitches. I realize I have been squeezing her hand too hard. My voice is thinner than a whisper.

'Dreams?'

'The Web-folk conversed through dreams before humans came,' Spinner says. 'And for a long time after. Among your people those whose gift for dreaming was strongest were the first to find a connection with us. We opened our world to them, because they listened to what we had to say. They saw what we wished to show them. With their help we taught your people the skill of weaving. We gave them our silk, and they learned to make tapestries from it. Together we wove fabrics unlike anything the world had seen before. And so humans built the House of Dreams, the first house on the island.' She takes a short pause. 'You know it as the House of the Tainted.'

I think about the pictures on the walls of the Museum of Pure Sleep, of my mother's words: *never tell anyone*. Dreamers standing on the dais at the Ink-marking and pulling sticks from the bowl. Every night I have stayed awake in fear of dreams, or the night-maere.

'What happened?' I ask.

'Dreamers' skill of communicating with the Web-folk gave them power,' Spinner says. 'That did not please everyone. And when some of them discovered at the core of their dreams the power that had always lived there, everything changed.'

The path grows longer. One stone, another. We are drawing closer to where she wants to lead me.

'The power of Dreamers,' I say. 'What is it?'

Even as I ask, I sense the strange tingling again, in my hands and in my thoughts and in my body. The shimmering threads I saw after the night-maere came to me are within my reach.

'You know,' Spinner says. 'You have already used it. You can do it again.'

I wish to see her better, and Valeria. The room around us is still a dream-room, mine to command. I look at the threads above our heads and think to them, *shine*. The thought is not heavy or forced. It merely brushes through me, floats for a moment and is gone.

The silk of the webs begins to emit a soft light. Valeria shudders.

'How does it work?' I ask.

Spinner's form is clearly visible now. The long limbs support the rounded body, and the eyes are dim mirrors, reflecting a place I cannot yet see.

'You moved the threads of the Web of Worlds, like ancient Dreamers did,' she says. 'Even among them, it was a rare skill. That is why few could use the power, and that is why so many feared it.'

I think about all the times I have wished to change something and could not.

'Why can I do this now?' I ask. 'Why not before?'

Spinner is quiet for a while. When she speaks again, the words are slow, as if she is dragging them to light from dark corners of ancient memories.

'The Dream-power is not born of nothing,' Spinner says. 'It is born of everything that has made you who you are. Of each day when you have breathed in the scent of the sea in the chill of the morning and ran the shuttle through the warp with weary fingers. Of each moment when you have loved or desired or lost. Of each time you have looked away from yourself, and become aware that something in you has shifted irrevocably. Of each dream you have dreamed, and each step you have taken.'

Spinner pauses briefly.

'Do you see now why it was necessary for you to walk through the darkness?' she continues.

I do not reply. The world is a white-hot globe of molten glass, ready to assume any shape I wish to give it. My whole body aches like it is filled with light trying to burst through my skin, sparks with an urge to move the reality out of place and bring about a new one where all obeys my will. And yet I sense another ache underneath: like a muscle sore from too much strain, a phantom limb weary from exertion. It is familiar from every dream I have bent to my will, from every waking afterwards.

The glass freezes into shape and shatters, and I know the answer before I ask.

'But the power is not without limit,' I say.

Spinner is silent. I sense a soft brush of thought across my mind, seeking, withdrawing.

'No power is without limit,' she says. 'And a power that can shift the shape of reality has a higher price than many others. Every time you use it, it will make a rift in you. Rearranging the fabric of the universe is not easy or without danger. Sometimes the limits of the body give in and your spirit goes astray, and the threads come loose from your grip.'

'What if I don't want this power?' I say. My voice drifts across the room and shatters against the wall. Valeria's fingers tighten around mine.

'It is a part of you, whether you wish it or not,' Spinner says. 'No one gave it to you, and no one can take it away.'

Just then, a bell begins to clang in the distance. After only a brief moment, the sound collapses into silence. After a few breaths, it begins again. This time the clanging continues for longer, until it is followed by another silence.

The evacuation signal of the Dreamers.

I turn to look at Valeria.

'We must go,' I say.

'Yes,' Spinner says into the dusk behind her many eyes. 'It has begun. The ships await, ready to be claimed, and Dreamers hope for a wind that will billow the sails at dawn.'

She goes quiet. Valeria takes a step back, another. She pulls me by the hand to go with her.

'But they will not make it far,' Spinner says.

I know then that we have finally come to the place where she has been leading me all along. This is the end of the path, the hidden heart behind all her words. I am afraid to see it, and yet I cannot turn away.

'Why?' I ask. My words float in the room like speckles of dead dust.

'The earth under the sea is readying itself to move,' Spinner says. 'Soon it will shake the foundations of the island, and every stone your people have placed on top of another will crack and fall. Your traces will soon be gone, and you will no longer be here to mend what is broken.'

Valeria shivers, but stays next to me.

'Are you certain?' I ask Spinner.

'I have seen it,' she says. 'I have felt it.'

I ask the question to which I dread to hear the answer.

'Can you stop it?'

A low hum rises from Spinner, song-like, and fades.

'Yes, I can,' she says. 'But I will not.'

I draw a deep breath.

'Why?'

'I will show you,' she says. 'If you come closer.'

Alarm ripples on Valeria's face. I look at her and loosen my grip of her hand. I take a step forward.

I stand there, in the soft glow of the webs. One of Spinner's limbs reaches out and settles on my forehead. I feel a light prickling where my skin has not yet healed completely. And then

I see with her eyes and she sees with mine.

I see a time of peace turn into a time of war, when some men grow restless at Dreamers doing things they

themselves are not capable of. They believe the Dream-power comes from the Web-folk, and they turn against us. At first they build their houses where the Web-folk have always lived, and make fields for their crops where the Web-folk have always fed. When that does not push away those to whom the island belonged before the ships arrived, men take their torches and blades to the web-forests of the island. The fires are slow to die and the screams of pain last long.

A long time, long. Years bundled together and pushed further and further away, like barely visible stars, their jewels ever dimmer in the outstretched Web of Worlds. No one else left now. No one else to tell the story. And age, it gnaws and corrodes, slowly crumbles every limb, adds weight to every movement: even the longest life is a vanishing flicker against the silence that surrounds all lives, a space so deep it will eventually drown everyone. Must find someone to carry the story forward. Must not let it vanish into the void that draws nearer every moment. Must not let the lost people be forgotten.

Waiting in the dark, and then there is no more time left to wait. Must call whoever will hear even a faint echo of the call, and will come. She is too scared. Too used to hiding. But there is no one else. No others to hear, no one with Dream-power. And I am showing her this so she can take it with her and see through my eyes, if she lives,

Spinner says without any words.

My knees hit the floor and pain surges through me. My teeth clatter together. Tears are running down my face.

'I didn't know,' I tell Spinner. A weight greater than a night-maere's grows in my chest. 'I'm so sorry. I didn't know.'

The forests still burn before my eyes and somewhere in

the shroud of the past, in a moment that has never come to an end, the Web-folk are being torn apart, limb by limb, and I do not believe I will ever stop hearing their screams.

'I will take your story with me and tell it again and again,' I whisper. 'If you let us go.'

'You are free to go,' Spinner says. 'Save yourself and this girl you love.' Valeria's arm twines around my waist. 'Find a boat. Leave. You may make it to the continent, if you use your power sparingly. There is nothing you can do for the rest of your people. Leave them.'

I see the ships and Dreamers in my eyes. I think about everyone who has hidden their dreams as I have, and those who have been deprived of their dreams unknowingly. People who wake up in the morning and collect seaweed for their food, raise chickens, comb their children's hair and fix their leaking roofs. I think of their fear when they look at those who carry the mark on their foreheads, and of their weariness, which makes it easier to take orders from the Council than to imagine how something could be different. Of their hopes, and their ability to change, or the lack thereof.

'I cannot,' I say.

'Why help them?' Spinner asks. Her voice is a soft hiss, sizzling of water against hot metal. 'Your people have drowned the world over and over, and forgotten, and then done it again.'

'Because they have also rebuilt the world over and over, time and again finding hope where none once existed,' I say. 'Does that mean nothing?'

I look at everything through dream, and the Web of Worlds is at my reach. I feel its threads at my fingertips. I see their routes: shimmering through space, endlessly intertwined, never-ending. I follow the threads to the island, into this room, into this moment and deep under the sea. I see movement that is ready to proceed, to tear down the ground beneath our feet.

I press my hand onto the bones of the earth and stop the movement.

'Your power will not hold it,' Spinner says. 'The wrath of the earth is stronger than your spirit. It will make a rift in you that will not heal.'

Valeria turns to me. I see distress on her face.

'Someone died in the House of the Tainted because of me,' I say. 'If I can rescue even some of the people of the island, I must do it.'

Spinner makes a quick dash towards me. Her limbs patter the floor. I start when one of them reaches out and tears the burning lantern from my hand. Spinner takes a few backward steps as fast as she moved forward. I cannot think the lantern back from her, because all my powers are underground, holding others that wish to break through. The lantern swings at the end of Spinner's limb. She is quiet. We wait. Somewhere the earth is ready to turn, the sea to move, and it is time for people to board the ships.

'So be it,' Spinner says. 'You may remain where you are and die. Or you may run through fire and perhaps live.'

Her limb surges through the air. The lantern shatters into pieces and there is a searing ripple, as fire devours silken webs. Flames run along the threads, drawing a scintillating lattice above us, which begins to scorch into ashes before our eyes. I am petrified, but Valeria takes a step back and pulls me with her. Finally I move. We run out of Spinner's chamber and across Weaver's room.

Deep inside the earth the stones wish to turn, and there is nothing to hold them but my dream.

CHAPTER SEVENTEEN

The web-maze is torn and tattered, turned strange and almost impassable. I still know the way, but the path is blocked by downfallen wall-webs, broken threads, slashed streets and buildings. Valeria has picked up a dim glow-glass somewhere along the way, but it is dying and does not show every pile of yarn ahead. She stumbles, almost falls.

'Wait,' I say.

I stop and turn towards the House of Webs. The wind blows this way, carrying the scent of smoke.

The sphere of the fire blazes above the buildings. I try to conjure the time that is diminishing for us, attempt to see the route of the flames in my mind. The threads of the tapestries in Weaver's study are dry and brittle; they will cling to the fire greedily. The wooden furniture will feed the blaze further. From Weaver's room the fire will spread to the Halls of Weaving and into the Tapestry Room, where silkweed sparkles in all colours. I do not know if it will emit a sweet or salty scent as it burns. Then the fire will reach the linen in the cells and dormitories, if there is any left, and the oils in the kitchen and sick bay, and the liqueurs and medicinal supplies. When the solid buildings crackle in the wrap of flames, it will be the turn of the web-maze.

The fire is dream-fire, and I demand it to tame and stall. Nothing happens. The glow continues to swell.

I command the fire again. The Web of Worlds hovers nearly within my reach, and I grasp for it, but I can merely brush it before it yields. I reach closer, raise my hand against the flames.

The knot that binds the waking of the earth stirs.

The tremor is no stronger than a common shudder as it passes through me. But when I look at Valeria, I see she has felt it too.

'I cannot,' I say. 'I won't have the strength to hold together the foundations of the island if I stop the fire.' And I may not want to; there are constructions for which the time has come to crumble.

Valeria steps to me, takes my hand and pulls me into a run.

Clouds of smoke push past us. My eyes and throat begin to sting. I do not think of all corridors and corners of the maze, of every forking path, but only of the next turn: to the right after the third alley, past five openings and to the left, across the clearing and a tight turn in the opposite direction. The orange light grows in the direction of the house, and the heat. The air was still cold when we left the house, but sweat pours down my cheeks and between my breasts, dampens my forehead and eyebrows and upper lip. And underneath everything a slow ache throbs. I push it away.

We find the skiff and pull it down the slope into water, when the first flames burst into view. The threads wither and blacken and crumble into ash that scatters into wind, colourless. We begin to punt along the canal that has burst its banks. The streets are near-deserted here. At the doorway of one house stands a man, maybe the age my father would be if he were alive. I glance at Valeria. The skiff is tiny, but it may just carry another person. She nods.

'We are headed for the harbours,' I yell at the man. 'The island cannot take another flood.'

The man stares at me.

'I'll be damned if I get on the same boat with a Dreamer,' he says. 'Or believe what your kind says.'

The tangle inside me tugs. At first, holding it was like tensing a muscle somewhere in my body: I felt it, but was able to push the sensation aside and do other things. Now I am more aware of it every moment.

The man spits towards us. The saliva makes a circle in the black water.

The tremor is like a shiver of cold, slight and soon over. I think it must have come from within myself. For a moment everything is quiet and still. Then there is a great roar in the distance, like something huge slipping out of joint deep under the island. A shooting pain cuts through my innards. It is gone quickly, but leaves behind a hollow feeling, as if my blood runs thinner.

The man at the door starts, glares at me and throws the door shut.

The sound of the seashell horn carries along the water and stones. *Go to the trading harbours,* Janos said; he must have thought it was safer. But if the Council has called a citizens' meeting, he will be at the square, and we must warn the Dreamers, warn everyone.

'There isn't much time,' I tell Valeria.

305

She takes the oar from my hands and pushes the skiff forward.

The Tower still stands smooth and unbroken, a blade slicing the sky. Yet its surroundings have turned into a churning vortex of people. The call of the seashell horn splits the air again. People are streaming in from all directions, like into a tightening net, which pulls them towards the same centre. They come wading through the streets and along canals, along rope bridges running between rooftops and on the walls of buildings. We guide the skiff among other boats as far as we can. Eventually we hit a jam we cannot pass.

More boats are arriving behind us, and we cannot turn back. At the edge of the canal the water has receded enough to leave only a shallow layer on the pavement. Valeria stands up in the skiff. It sways furiously as I do the same. Valeria steps onto the nearest boat. The family sitting in it barely has time to move, before we have already crossed over them from one side to the other. The father shouts curses behind us. On the next boat, two disgruntled-looking old women stare as we use their vessel as a stepping stone.

'I'm sorry,' I say to them.

'Some manners, if I may make such a bold request, young lady,' one of the women says and squints her eyes.

The other one, whose face is more wrinkled, sniffles and takes a more comfortable position on the seat.

'Don't mind her,' she says.

'The Council had better replace my loom,' the other one adds. 'Quality wood from the continent. Swollen as a drowned man's tongue.'

'Don't mind her,' the wrinklier one repeats.

I jump to the edge of the canal, where the water splashes in all directions and then settles at the level of my ankles. I glance at the Tower. Sounds, talk and words carry from the square that I cannot make out. Further ahead, Valeria has stopped to wait. When she catches my gaze, she begins to wade towards the square.

I catch up with her and seize her hand. There are too many people here, and I do not want to lose her. The voices from the square are clearer now and louder, their words assuming recognizable forms. We thread our way through the crowd and pass through the arched stone gate. The sharp point of the Tower pricks the clouds. On the other side of the square, beyond the waves of people, the skeleton of the Museum of Pure Sleep has been worn even barer.

In front of it, a group of Dreamers stands in the auditorium, which rises from the water like the back of a large animal. I see Askari, Irena and Janos. I recognize Ila. I do not see Alva or Tirra. There are also others whose names I do not know, maybe fifty of them. They look barely a handful compared with the crowd, a scant scattering of sunlight on a mass of dark waves. One of them raises a large seashell horn to his lips and blows in it. The sound echoes in stones and fades into the sky, where evening closes around the last flame of the day. I see Janos has turned in a different direction than the rest of them. I follow his frozen stare and understand: the House of Webs blazes on the hill as a roaring, dancing forest of flames around which a scorching halo glows.

I must make it to him.

A dense row of City Guards has gathered at the foot of the auditorium, a dangerous range of rocks I have no way of crossing. They stand still with their gazes turned to the Tower, waiting for an order that has not yet been issued. Or perhaps the first blow that will give them a reason to attack. The points of their spears gleam in the light of the torches lining the auditorium. There is another ring of guards at the root of the Tower, two rings, a circle of spikes and metal and restless fires. There is an empty space made by fear around them. Apart from it, the square is filled by a sea of people, spilling, stirring, tearing apart and stitching itself together again.

I dive into it.

Valeria follows. Her hand squeezes mine. I see Dreamers pick up something in their hands that looks like sizeable rolls of fabric. They hold them by each end and raise them high. The fabrics fall open, and I recognize the large pictures painted on them.

The inkmaster leaves the island again, falls ill, does not return for the Ink-marking. He begins to dream again and study the composition of the tattoo ink. The Council approaches him, until its shadow covers him entirely, and drops the gondola in which he travels. The fabrics are unrolled one by one. The story has grown more complete: masked men attack the inkmaster's daughter, cut off her tongue and she flees into the House of Webs. There she begins to weave a tapestry, which tells the story of how the tattoos are stealing people's dreams on the island. The Council takes her away, and a weaver from the House of Webs goes after her, but ends up in the House of the Tainted, where the prisoners are forced to collect blood coral from the sea. Sediment leaks into the sea from the Ink Quarters and makes people sick. The island looks ever smaller in the sea. A great wave approaches on the horizon.

Valeria makes a sound next to me. When I turn to look,

tears are streaming down her face. One of the Dreamers raises the speaking trumpet made from a seashell to his mouth and speaks to the crowd, speaks of lies, speaks of the truth. Speaks of rescue. The seashell amplifies the volume of his voice. The words carry far beyond the limits of the square, the words scatter into the wind.

'Janos!' I cry, but I'm too far away. My voice does not reach him. Inside me strands chafe against each other, grow taut and loose again, cut marks in me. I cannot let them go, because they hold everything together.

Janos, I think.

He turns his head, studies the crowd with his gaze. Seeks.

The Dreamer continues to talk. The people listen. I see paper leaflets being passed from hand to hand, and I recognize the images of the codex in them, too. The square is a dream-square, the strands of the Web of Worlds still within my reach. I want Janos to see me. I want him to know what needs to be known, to heed the warning.

Janos, I think,

and then a bright and scorching pain flashes through me,

listen, I am still alive,

bare as the fire burning my skin,

I have something to tell you,

glowing as the stone walls being tormented at the heart of the blaze,

flee, flee now, because time is running out,

the thought surges into me like heat from beyond a breaking door,

demand that they show themselves,

and Janos's face snaps towards me. I see shock on it as he recognizes me from afar. The pain withers. I am on the square again and not amidst the raging flames. Only a narrow stripe of the day gone by is fading in the sky, and

I know somewhere the ships are waiting, ready to leave, although I cannot see them.

'You know the truth about the island now,' Askari says. 'Staying here offers no future for you.'

'Dreamer lies!' someone shouts in the crowd. He receives an approving murmur in response. 'They must be eviscerated from the island for good.'

Valeria wipes her eyes. I grasp her arm. In the auditorium Janos stares at me. Then he turns, strides to Askari and says something to him. Askari listens and glances at the crowd. Janos is still talking to him. I see Askari nod. He turns towards the square again.

'If this is all a lie,' he says into the speaking trumpet, 'if the Council wants the best for you, why are they not here? Why do they not show themselves and offer help when the island needs it most?'

The words float in the square. The crowd has quieted for a moment that lingers, until a low murmur begins to grow again at the bottom of a wavering silence. It grows and folds into a stir that turns the people towards the Tower. I turn to look.

The doors of the lower balcony of the Tower have opened. The tall fires of the torches burn on both sides of them and behind falls a curtain of darkness. From there, the black maw of the Tower, a law-reader steps into sight in his loose coat decorated with the sun emblem. He walks to the rail at the edge of the balcony and raises the speaking trumpet to his mouth. The reflections of the torches revolve on its mother-of-pearl surface.

'In the name of the Council,' he says.

'In the name of the Council,' the crowd says, but the response is more fragile than usual. I see several people around me whose lips do not move at all.

The law-reader clears his throat. He is too far away for me to discern the expression on his face clearly. Behind the Tower the sky is night-blue, and in the knots of the Web of Worlds the stars have begun to surface. The pressure in my innards is insufferable. My body is focused around it, ready to collapse.

'In its great wisdom the Council has asked you to wait,' the law-reader says from the balcony, his words amplified by the speaking trumpet. The people of the city are listening. 'They are right now discussing in the Tower how to best help the island, and they order you to come back tomorrow at noon.'

Stirring and rustling begins in the square. I hear Askari's voice from behind me, but I have no strength to turn to look.

'These people are here,' Askari says, 'because they need help now. How many of you have lost your homes?'

There are mumbles of agreement from the crowd. Next to me I see a man say something to a woman who nods.

The law-reader stares into the square. He wipes his brow and takes a short step backwards. He raises his speaking trumpet again.

'This gathering is illegal,' he says. 'The Council did not call it.'

'Maybe they should have,' Askari's voice carries from the auditorium.

A woman detaches herself from the crowd then. Alone she steps to the empty zone surrounding the guards arranged at the root of the Tower. She is not young or old, and she has wide hips and curly black hair gathered under a scarf; the light of the torches clings to its silvery stripes. She limps with one leg. Slowly, with difficulty she crosses the space separating the guards from the crowd.

She stops in front of one of them. Her voice is deep and far-carrying, like a song.

'If the Council has any interest in what is happening to our city,' she says, 'why would they not show themselves? Ask them to step forward.'

The guard's face is in shadow under his helmet. He does not lower his spear, does not turn his head.

'The Council takes no orders from the people,' the guard says.

The woman stares at the guard in silence for a moment. Then she speaks again.

'No,' she says. 'The Council claims to protect us: from the attacks of foreigners, from floods and disease.' She pauses. 'From dreaming.'

The crowd has grown quiet. The law-reader follows the events from the balcony. His hand raises the speaking trumpet, but lets it drop again. Air weighs on me, and my own blood weighs on me. My legs feel weak and hollow. I hold tight onto the tangle inside me. I hold onto Valeria's arm in order to remain standing.

The woman turns her dark face towards the crowd.

'Therefore I'd like to ask the Council,' the woman continues, 'why this flood has left my home in ruins.' She takes a deep breath. 'And why dreams have begun to bother my night-rest lately.'

Everyone knows Dreamers must be imprisoned so they cannot spread their disease. Yet no one takes a step. Even the City Guard is still waiting. My limbs pull me towards the ground. My skin is heavy, made of stone. The knot has tightened to a breaking point. Valeria is holding me upright.

A second woman moves through the crowd. No one stops her. She walks across the empty space and stops next to the first woman. She places her hand on the woman's arm.

'I have started dreaming too,' she says.

The crowd stirs. Several other women and a few men walk to the Tower, next to the first two. Each one of them places a hand on the arm of the person standing next to them, until they form a chain.

'Who wants to see the Council?' the woman who first left the crowd shouts.

'Show us the Council!' Askari shouts back.

'Show us the Council!' a sole cry sounds from the square.

A second voice joins the cry, a third, a whole cluster of voices. They find a common rhythm, like waves of the sea, and grow into a chorus repeating the same demand. The Dreamers are repeating it too.

'Show us the Council! Show us the Council!'

On the balcony the law-reader stares at the crowd below. He backs towards the door, stops. He strides back to the rail and raises the speaking trumpet to his mouth.

The words are drawn in my mind even before I hear them, and I think,

Janos.

His face turns towards me and his gaze meets mine,

Janos, run now and take everyone with you,

for the island around us will wither into ashes, I will wither into ashes and be gone soon,

board the ships, for they will seize their fires and blades and

'Guards!' the law-reader shouts. 'Kill all the Dreamers!'

the fires will be slow to die and

I have no strength to stop it, the order has been given, I can only look how

the screams of pain will last long and

the guards turn their spears to a lunge and take a step forward, towards the soft, unsheltered bodies of people, and their brief hours and brittle days and

your people have drowned the world over and over, and forgotten, and then done it again.

My legs give in and my knees crash painfully into the stones of the square. I feel the water absorb through the fabric of my trousers. A short distance away a City Guard thrusts his spear into a young man's back. Valeria's eyes darken and her breath runs ragged. The square around us has turned into a sizzling witch's cauldron, all movement and noise and blood.

I want the knot inside me to hold, but it pulls and tugs and slips, and my grip of the threads loosens, because each new wanting is without strength. The knot begins to unravel. Deep in the sea and ground and dust, the heart of the earth awakens.

'It has begun,' I say.

The ground shakes beneath us.

It is like stones being yanked in one direction with a swift drag. Valeria stumbles against me. I catch her and pull her down next to me. I wrap my arms around her. The ground continues to quake. A man and a woman next to us crouch to shelter three small children. I notice the gazes of people have turned towards the Tower and I look the same way. The law-reader has vanished from the balcony. The Tower begins to sway like a tree in wind. The stone sun at its pinnacle trembles and breaks off. It rolls out of place, hangs suspended in the air for a few moments before spinning down, and shatters onto the stones. The guards barely have time to move away.

Cracks appear on the trunk of the Tower, like in glass that gives in under too great a pressure. They rupture into black, hollow rifts, and the Tower spits stones onto the square like dead teeth. Boulders fall down and throw arcs of water into air as they hit the ground. People are running away from them, darting every which way. I hear a loud bang behind me. When I look, I see the arched gate has split in two. I glance towards the hill of the House of Webs. It glows as a smouldering ember at the core of the wrap of mist, and flame-threads run in all directions from it, seeking more to seize. Not many gusts of wind will be needed to carry the sparks to the straw of the roofs and wooden structures of houses, into the tanks of the Ink Quarters and to the House of Words, where paper waits, ready to burn with a tall flame.

I fumble for the Web of Worlds again, try to grasp what moves under the island, but the threads escape my reach and I am only able to catch a few that slip my hold.

The Tower swings, what remains of it. Large boulders sway above emptiness, peel open the hollow insides, and the black water of Halfway Canal bursts through, encloses the stones crumbling into it. The building collapses before our eyes, until only a hollow-carved stub remains, a piece of curved wall and a pile of structures. The crowd churns, is crushed into swirls and frays on the edges. I hear Dreamers shouting – *harbours! Go to the harbours* – but every thread-end I still hold cuts me inside like a thin and bright blade.

Someone comes running. I hear Janos's voice, but his words are swallowed by the surrounding rumble. Hands pull me up. I see City Guards scattered around the square. Some of them are trying to get orders through to the crowd, but others have dropped their spears and are withdrawing, looking for orders to follow. When they do not find them, they are caught in the flow looking for a way out.

We move, although I can barely see any more, and around us the island is coming to an end.

The ship creaks and tilts, although the sea below is not raging, not yet. The city is already half-ashes, the seam of sea and sky covered in darkness. An ember-coloured glow still shines from the island, a dimming eye. That which remains. Somewhere ahead, across a distance opens a shore, strange and difficult and necessary.

I look behind, and I finally let go. The silhouette of the island rips apart once more, collapses on itself. I feel the rifts in me as the last threads of the Web of Worlds come loose from my grip, the limits of my body give in and my spirit goes astray. Far away and yet within myself I sense the smouldering thoughts like the last spark of a long-burned fire:

she is stronger than I knew, for she still lives,

she is stronger than I knew, for she still lives,

and from her dreams all threads reach for reality, and above

the starry night sky pulls me up until I am wind and light, rips apart to reveal a universe where nothing withholds me, and

another landscape opens ahead, a world that is ready to crumble or change.

CHAPTER EIGHTEEN

I still wear scars on my knees from hitting the stones with the weight of the world. The mark on my forehead has faded on the edges, but it will never vanish.

I do not mind. Only the wounds of the dead do not scar.

For many years now, I have heard people speak of the island: seamen, merchants, those who seek stories. They tell of the crumbling outlines, turned unrecognizable long ago, and abandoned gondolas that drift half-sunken along the shores. But also of the odd fisherman drawing nets through the waters, or goats walking around small houses on the slopes, for when the ships left, some stayed. Someone always stays.

Some nights, when sleep is slow to come, I take myself for a stroll in the city, the way I imagine it now. No one walks in the Glass Grove. The sea has swallowed the Ink Quarters. A gull may land on the stained stones where wall-webs once ran, make a nest among the weather-worn pillars of stone and lost streets.

I like to think that in the House of Webs weeds and moss have taken root in the walls, and vines push through the broken windows. Maybe a tree grows there: behind the kitchen building, where hens used to peck grains from the ground and bean stalks climbed along poles. When the wind turns warmer after winter months, small, white flowers will blossom on the branches and butterflies will come, and bees. Or beetles, with shiny, green-black wings that whirr as they move. I will settle for beetles.

I know nothing more can remain of the Halls of Weaving than ashes. Yet in my mind's eye they are very much like they used to be. The ruins of time and seasons are scattered across the floor, but the wall-webs have stayed untouched in the looms throughout the years, forever unfinished, stalled before they had time to reach their full form. The glow-glass pipes along the corridor stand lifeless and hollow, like veins drained of blood. At the end a dark door opens into the Tapestry Room. It is empty now. If a tapestry was spared from the flames, wind, heat and humidity will have gnawed it down. Or perhaps someone stole away what was left, defying the ghost stories of mighty dream-magic which brought along the destruction of the house and the island.

I do not believe in ghosts. If the island is haunted, it is by my dreams and memories.

The Tower is still there, but it is nothing more than a broken fang now, any sharpness long worn away by wind and water. The roof of the hall has collapsed, and a deep rift has torn the floor. At the bottom of it ink-coloured water churns and flings pieces of broken wooden poles. Through the roof structures that have cracked into a loose net I can discern the brightness of the bare sky.

It is in these images that I see them clearly for the first time.

Four of them have been cast against the back wall, still

stuck to their seats. Stone slips on the humid, slanted floor, and half of the room has turned into a disjointed stage, the kind that has been tilted too far in one direction for a dramatic scene, but the machinery has got stuck and the show has been interrupted. They lie still, in strange postures, their eyes empty and without light. Their masks have fallen off and the flood has washed them away.

I do not approach them. Instead, I step towards the four still seated at the table. The table juts halfway in the air, over the sizzling current in the ravine. I stop next to the nearest seat.

The features are worn frail by the centuries. Under the traces of time I discern a high forehead and sharp cheekbones, a narrow-arching nose. The deep-hidden eyes do not look at me, do not know I am here. The gnarled fingers lie cold on the armrests. A growth of algae winds along the back of the cloak. A long and narrow crack runs across the stone neck. The other three statues stopped at the table are fully covered in spots of lichen, like a slow-moving illness has struck the dark-grey skin of stone.

Perhaps, when the sun reaches its highest peak, it will warm their skin for a moment, and a glow will rise to their faces that will resemble the glow on the faces of the living when they see something that makes them happy. But it is a mere echo of the light that is slowly burning the island and turning it into an islet of rock in the sea.

I leave the Council there, exposed under the touch of time and change.

Yet there is always another city I carry within, sealed in a crust of frozen past. For when sleep comes and turns me weightless, the island appears before me as it once was: in translucent brightness guarding it and distorting it.

In my dream, I approach the city through the air turned

water. The Tower stands tall again, with the sun of stone spreading its sharp ray-fingers. The lights in the windows fade and I sink ever lower, until the top of the Tower looms far above me. I descend under the houses and streets, deeper, towards the seabed. There, where the light is slanted and soft as smoke, blood-red coral forests reach higher than any Tower ever. They grow dense and distant, and the movement of the water makes them look like the branches are swaying in the wind. Yet I know that if I placed my hand on them, they would be hard to touch, unmoving and painful to break. I might as well try to break off my own finger.

Above the blood coral I see a figure floating in the water-space whose limbs are only moved by the sea. I swim closer, and the current turns the figure's head towards me. It is a young woman who wears my face. Her eyes are closed, like she is only sleeping. Seaweed has tangled around her body to protect and to bind. There may be a trace of life left in her, a last brief flicker that pierces her mind as it slides away. In that flicker she sees a future for herself and believes it to be true. Then there is but sea and silence, and an empty space where dreams lived.

Light unfolds, or darkness. The threads of reality are ready to move under my touch. I dream for those who cannot dream. I am awake for those who can never be awake again. I cannot do more, or anything less.

For our hours are brief and our days are brittle, and the marks our hands leave on the world belong to us and yet are beyond our own limits.

ACKNOWLEDGEMENTS

They say second novels are difficult, and *The City of Woven Streets* certainly lived up to that reputation. Throughout the writing process, I found myself thinking that there should be a support group for people working on their second book – and that I would start one myself if I wasn't so desperately busy trying to deliver mine.

In the hindsight, and at the risk of sounding slightly melodramatic, I can only describe the experience as feeling like I spent three years in a fictional dark cave of my own making, looking for a way out. Emerging back to daylight was greatly helped by some people offering kind guidance along the way. For this assistance, I would like to thank:

My lately-on-hiatus writing group in the UK – Howard Bowman, Sarah Davies, Patricia Debney, Denny Flowers, Nancy Wilson Fulton, Nancy Gaffield, Janet Montefiore, Jeremy Scott; my agent Elina Ahlbäck; my writing group in Finland – Päivi Haanpää and Marika Riikonen; everyone at my Finnish publishing house Teos, with a special gold star to Jussi Tiihonen; the editorial team at HarperVoyager – especially Natasha Bardon, Emma Coode, Emily Krump and Eleanor Ashfield; my family in Finland; Mari Paavola for the image of creatures enclosed in amber, among other things; and José Casal for teamwork, always.

The Shell Grotto in Margate, United Kingdom, served as an inspiration for the underground sanctuary Eliana discovers on the island, so I would also like to send my thanks back in time to the mystery artists who built its extraordinary seashell mosaics.